Drink The Water

Drink The Water

Alien Mysteries Book 3

Scott Michael Decker

Published 2015 by Creativia
Book design by Creativia (www.creativia.org)
Typed by Joey Strainer
U.S. Copyright application # 1-1654438881
Cover art by http://www.thecovercollection.com/

Titles by the Author

If you like this novel, please post a review on the website where you purchased it, and consider other novels from among these titles by Scott Michael Decker:

Science Fiction:
Cube Rube
Doorport
Drink the Water
Edifice Abandoned
Glad You're Born
Half-Breed
Inoculated
Legends of Lemuria
Organo-Topia
The Gael Gates
War Child

Fantasy:
Fall of the Swords (Series)
Gemstone Wyverns
Sword Scroll Stone

Look for these titles at your favorite book retailer.

Reader Comments on Drink the Water:
"... a wonderful imagination ..." – jeshi99

Chapter 1

"Don't drink the water."

Janine looked back, startled.

A man stood a few paces behind her, towering over her.

Kneeling at the end of the dock, nothing between her and the poisonous Nartressan sea, Janine felt a moment of vulnerability. A slight nudge would send her to her death. She couldn't see his face. The night fading, a blue glow to the east, only a few seaside cottage lights illuminated him from the side. "I know," she replied, standing, "I'm a biologist."

A dark prominent brow dominated the face, the eyes sunk too far into their sockets. The skin was white from too little sun, the hair black as though dyed. He was clean shaven, dressed in a spare formall that seemed too insubstantial to protect against the chill blowing off the bay, a small maritime insignia at the left breast. In the deeply sunken eyes was the hint of a smile. "You must be Doctor Meriwether," he said. "Carson, Thomas Carson, Chief Biologist at the Marine Institute." He jerked a thumb over his shoulder at the brightly-lit building on the hilltop.

"You look nothing like your vid," Janine said, wondering why she hadn't recognized him. She looked down to make sure she didn't trip over the equipment at her feet, and stepped—

Hands shoved her backward off the pier.

As she flailed her arms for balance, she looked at him, her body falling in slow motion toward the water.

His expression hadn't changed.

The water enveloped her, its chill cold fingers reaching every inch of skin. She didn't fight because she knew she was dead, the Nartressan water containing a prion that exuded a prothrombin antagonist. Her blood would stop clotting and would soon grow so thin as to seep between her epithelial cells. Within minutes, she'd be dead.

Janine felt tentacles wrap her ankles and yank her downward into the darker depths, vines grasping every limb, working their way up her trunk to her shoulders, to her neck, to her head. Seaweed wrapped her head, occluded her sight.

It'll suffocate me before I bleed to death, she thought, feeling curiously unafraid. Then her world went black.

* * *

Randall Simmons sat up and gasped for breath, sweat pouring off him, the remains of the nightmare dissipating from his mind.

"You all right?" his wife said, sitting up and rubbing his back.

He shook his head. "Another nightmare, same one."

"That's the fifth night in a row."

He wondered how long he could keep doing this. Last night, he'd stayed awake until past midnight, hoping to make himself so tired that he'd sleep through the night.

"You've got to see somebody."

He just grunted. She didn't understand, and he didn't expect her to.

"Take a day or two off, maybe a week."

He nodded in dull acknowledgement, both of them knowing he'd do no such thing, both knowing he was committed to his work.

Emergency Medical Technician, and now having nightmares about work. How many coworkers had burned out already, traumatized by the fruitless search-and-rescues, the weed snatchings having left the populace terrified and helpless?

He looked toward the window, a hint of morning light at the edges. Four hours sleep, restless, dreaming of weed strands, of one wrapping his ankle and yanking him off the beach and into the surf.

Randall stumbled into the bathroom, relieved himself, and looked at his reflection. Gaunt and pale, his black hair making his skin look paler than it already was.

His coke came to life, the electrical implant in his ear crackling, a red alert blazing on his retinal. "Alert, all responders. Report to base."

Randall was in his boots and out the door.

* * *

Brian Franks stepped off the yacht, and a seaweed tentacle wrapped his foot, the strand flattening to fit between the boat and dock. It yanked him off his feet, and he fell to the decking with a yelp, the slimy feel of seaweed on his leg matching the sick twist in the pit of his stomach.

"Help!" he yelled, but no one was near, and the weed dragged him to the edge. He grabbed for the gunwale and missed, flailed for anything to grab onto.

More strands grasped his leg, yanked him into the water, and pulled him deep, straight down, the sky receding as he sank into the murk, and he found himself wondering how the bay could be so deep.

And cold …

* * *

Her head clouded with weed smoke, Honeydew Diamond stumbled on the beach, thinking she'd put her high-heeled shoe into a hole.

The night dark, she had to look twice, disbelieving.

A seaweed strand wrapped her ankle. She pulled away, thinking it hallucination, and it pulled back, yanking her toward the water.

"Help!"

The friend she'd been with was nowhere around. She grabbed at the sand to stop her slide, the night on the beach with the high-paying customer turning into a nightmare on the beach.

The seaweed tightened and dragged her toward the water. She screamed, the sand scraping off her evening gown up to her waist, her breasts. A tentacle, then two, crept up her legs and around her hips. Again she screamed, a wave crashing over her, the roiling surf taking what remained of her gown over her head. I always knew I'd die in the nude, Honeydew thought inanely …

Chapter 2

"Don't drink the water."

Janine looked back, startled.

A man stood a few paces behind her, towering over her.

Kneeling at the end of the dock, nothing between her and the poisonous Nartressan sea, Janine felt a moment of vulnerability, as though a slight nudge might send her to her death. "I know," she replied, "I'm a biologist." Why do I have a sudden sense of déjà vu? she wondered.

The night fading, a blue penumbra to the east, only a few cottage lights illuminating him from the side, she couldn't see his face. She stood and looked at him fully, recognizing him finally from the numerous vid coms they'd exchanged. "You must be Doctor Thomas Carson. I'm Janine Meriwether, Assistant Xenobiologist at the Alien Microbiology Institute." She stepped nimbly over the equipment at her feet to greet him.

They shook.

"Pleased. You look just like your vid," he said, his dark prominent brow dominating his face above eyes sunk too far into their sockets. The hair was dark against skin too white.

"Aren't you cold in that formall? Seems too insubstantial in the breeze." She jerked a thumb over her shoulder at the brisk bay wind. She noted the maritime insignia at the left breast.

"Lived here all my life," he said. "It's invigorating. But come on, the panel's waiting for you. Dismayed them when they found you'd already left the spaceport, but I knew where you'd gone."

"And you came to find me." She grinned, having come to the dock to see for herself the poison seas she'd be studying for the next year or so, rather than wait for her escort. Janine decided she liked him.

"You grew up here, didn't you?"

She bent to snap her cases closed. "For a time, but I don't remember much except the cold and the wind." Snap-snap. "Father was in the diplomatic service, so we never stayed in one place too long. I spent more time in orbit than I did groundside."

Snap-snap, and ready to go. She handed him one and picked up the other two. Her mobile laboratory. She'd studied the prion remotely, but not up close. The vector resisted being taken off planet. The environment couldn't be duplicated, and the creature disintegrated in the face of all attempts to preserve it. She'd had just enough time before Doctor Carson's arrival to obtain a sample.

"This way," he said, gesturing toward a waiting hover.

She glanced back at the dock as she followed him, wondering what had happened back there. Just a dream, she thought, shaking it off.

The hover lifted and followed a path that wound its way up the hillside. She glanced down at the small collection of buildings that comprised the hamlet of Wainsport. Sparsely settled, Nartressa was ninety-five percent water, and its main export was seafood.

But not just seafood. The seas were so abundant that over twenty thousand robotrawlers plied its waters continuously with no noticeable drop in biodensity. Although the fish had been harvested for over three hundred years, only in the last forty years had it reached these proportions. The volume showed no sign of slowing despite multiple warnings from conservationists that the harvests were unsustainable.

From the hover window, Janine counted ten such robotrawlers off the coast, and above one hovered a suborbital resupply ship, lifting the trawler's hold right from its belly and dropping in an empty hold, the operation taking ten minutes.

The hover dash squawked. "Doctor Carson, distress call from Randwick. The weed's snatched another one."

"Pilot," Carson said. "Alert the panel we got a live snatching. They'll be happy to wait for Janine."

"Right away, Sir," the woman said, putting the hover into a tight bank, the engine screaming. She got on the squawk box.

5

Why didn't he use his trake? Janine wondered, the acceleration pushing her into the seat. She wondered what they would find. "How many people so far, Doctor?" The sector government had sent her to investigate not the forty plus seaweed grabs, but the seaweed itself.

"Forty-five confirmed snatchings. Another twenty people are missing without explanation. Keep in mind, Doctor Meriwether, the population here is small, just under a million, and about half of those people spend most of their time on orbital processing plants. And not a single body recovered."

"Janine, please. I hate to be called Doctor."

He grinned at her. "Certainly, Janine. Tom."

"Pleased." They shook and shared a laugh. "And prior disappearances? You were going to search the records."

"Found a few, but nothing that was definitely the work of the weed. Again, no bodies, and so it's difficult to tell whether the weed pulled them under." In their exchanges prior to her arrival, he'd explained the local term for the seaweed. "No one likes it," he'd told her, "It clogs the harbor, washes up on the shores, and gets tangled in the trawlers. Like the weeds in your garden, this stuff grows more rapidly than we can get rid of it. So we just call it the weed."

Previous biodiversity studies had yielded nothing remarkable about the seaweed, except that it was the most abundant flora on Nartressa. It was regarded as the primary food source for the prolific fish populations, more than two thousand species of which had been identified. Oddly, only the one species of seaweed existed, an anomaly that defied logic or explanation, since such genetic specialization tended to be an evolutionary dead-end.

Instead, the weed had thrived.

For three hundred years, humans had lived on Nartressa and had harvested its oceanic bounty without noticeable trouble. Until two years ago. A weed strand had snatched someone off a dock in full view of a crowd of bystanders, and since then, forty-five more people had been dragged into the depths and another twenty were suspected to have met the same fate. In the year since Janine had been contacted, thirty confirmed snatchings had occurred, the rate increasing.

And now they've snatched another person, she thought, the hover banking above a beach, houses clustered at the lagoon edge, a small crowd visible near the emergency vehicles.

Janine sighed as the hover settled.

* * *

EMT Randall Simmons quartered the lagoon surface with the drone, its images funneled to his corn through the subdural optimitter as he searched for any sign of the latest victim.

Of the fifteen times he'd been dispatched to snatch sites, he'd not found the slightest sign of the victims. No trace of any weed victim had thus far been found.

Or of the weed that had snatched them. No heat signatures, no chemical traces, no spectrometer signs. Worse, biometer traces left on land of the seaweed's passage bore not a single difference from that of the ocean water itself.

Randall felt the Chief's scrutiny. "Got anything, Simmons?"

He shook his head, the three lines on his corn flat, the surface of the water featureless, but for wind and surf.

"Uh, oh," the Chief said, "Here comes trouble."

Randall heard the approach of a hover, its engines whining under strain. In a hurry.

He guided the drone back across the lagoon, bewildered that even in the shallow water, no trace of the victim could be found.

Beyond the police tape, the wail of a woman rose. "Diagnosed with leukemia just last week, and now this!"

Twenty-four year old Benjamin Johnson, who'd gone for a jog around the lagoon, wasn't going to be found either, Randall knew. His mother, the woman watching from beyond the tape, had seen him being dragged into the water from her kitchen window and had commed EMS. Stationed on Randwick Island, Randall's unit covered an archipelago spread across six thousand square miles of ocean. They'd been on scene in minutes, the squad house on the hilltop commanding a view of the surrounding ocean. Despite their quick response, the trail had been cold already, the water an even temperature just ten feet from the shore.

Randall looked over the Chief's shoulder.

An oddly-dressed woman followed a tall, dark-haired man out of the hover, carrying three bulky valises between them. The woman's gotta be an offworlder, Randall thought. The Chief intercepted them, and a heated exchange followed, if the gestures were any indication.

Randall returned his attention to the drone, turning it back once again over the lagoon. The brisk breeze made it somewhat difficult to control even with its antigrav unit, its geopositioning only accurate to within a foot.

He brought up a grid of the lagoon, saw he'd quartered it all. On his trake, he opened a secure channel to the Chief. "Lagoon quartered. Start on the inlet?"

"No, bring in the drone. These critter-happy brain-heads want to talk to you," the Chief told him over the coke.

Randall brought in the drone, and the mother's wail grew louder.

While he packed it, the offworlder woman started unpacking her cases. Finishing, he loaded the drone onto his hover, and stepped over to watch her.

She pulled a bot out of one case. It looked like some of the planet's bottom feeders, multiple mechanical arms sprouting from a pendulous body the size of his head. It crawled along the police tape like some alien insect.

"Nothin' on the drone, eh?" she said to him, not looking his way.

He looked at her, startled. "Janine, right? What the black hole are you doin' back on this ball o' mud?"

"Randy? That you? Haven't seen you since the fifth grade. Wondered if I'd see anyone I used to know. How've you been?"

He extended his hand. "Could be better. The weed's got us all scared, and it's getting more aggressive."

"Any other witnesses?" Janine gestured vaguely toward the mother. "She's not in any shape to help. Won't be for awhile, either."

"Plenty other witnesses, unfortunately, and not a single body. Five in the last two months—"

The bot scouring the ground beeped frantically, sinking its pinchers into the sand two feet from the water. The soft soil erupted.

Randall leaped backward, pulling Janine with him.

A seaweed branch burst from the earth, wrapped the bot and hurled it ocean-ward, pieces flying different directions as the bot disintegrated.

The branch hovered in the air, as though taking stock, then slithered into the sea.

* * *

Brian Franks, CEO of Aquafoods Interstellar, snapped awake at the stern of his yacht and stood, his breathing rough. A shiver shook him. That's not the shiver of cold, he thought, wiping the sweat from his brow and trying to catch his breath. He looked toward the dock, and the steps built into the gunwale that he'd climbed … or thought he'd climbed …

I must have been dreaming, Brian thought, looking down at his leg, then back at the dock.

He glanced at the sun, then his watch. I must have sat down and nodded off, he thought, wondering where the time had gone. If I laid in the sun that whole time, I should be lobster red. He was amazed that he wasn't, the tropical planet of Bora Bora known for its bronzed people.

En route to a visit with the Chancellor, Brian Franks had landed half a world away, had chartered the yacht and sailed it singlehandedly to the Capitol island of Waki-Waki across serene seas of glassy clarity, and had pulled into the berth three hours ago. At seventy, Brian Franks was as fit as he'd ever been. His skin was nearly milk-white, and his hair jet-black. Brian wondered why he hadn't burned. Those melanin treatments must've worked.

He looked again at the steps.

His attaché, Steve, strode along the dock toward him.

Suddenly, Brian was nervous.

"How was the trip, Sir?"

Brian just stared at him.

"What is it? You look startled." The attaché stepped to the edge of the dock, stopping in the exact place where Brian had been standing when the weed had pulled him …

Brian started to warn him.

Steve stepped onto the yacht without incident. "Are you all right, Sir? You look pale."

"Help me off this boat," Brian said hoarsely, finding his voice.

His attaché was leading him into the marina clubhouse before he realized it, his hands cold and clammy, his heart beating rapidly. He couldn't seem to catch his breath, and his brow felt hot and moist.

"This way, Sir." The waiting hover-limo whined at a low hum.

"Sammy!" said a voice.

Brian ignored it, heading for the limo.

"Sammy Ericson! Hey, Sammy, ain't seen you in forty years!"

Brian whirled. "I don't know you, Sir!"

"Sammy? Come on, it's me, Alfred! Alfred Santos!" The man two feet away wouldn't be put off. "We were stationed together on Nartressa! Don't you remember?"

"You're mistaken, Sir. I've never been there. Pardon." Brian stepped into the waiting limo.

The man continued to watch him, looking bewildered.

Brian relaxed as the acceleration pushed him into the seat. Nartressa? he wondered. The marina dropped out of sight, the man dropping from his thoughts. Pull yourself together! Brian told himself, wondering what had happened at the dock.

His attaché began to brief him on the upcoming meeting, the hover heading into the city, the steep slopes of the volcanic mountain behind the city dominating the island. The hover-limo took him directly to the penthouse suite of the Bora Bora Hilton, the north tower overlooking the bay. And the blue, blue ocean.

Within minutes, servants had undressed him and were bathing him, another showing him a selection of tuxedos for the evening.

Dried and coiffed, Brian ate a light meal and donned the chosen tux.

"Any other arrangements for the night, Sir?" Steve asked.

Brian stepped to the door of the waiting hover-limo, wondering whether to order a delight for later. "Yes, Steve, but a somewhat older woman than before. Someone with experience." Better that than trying to forget in a cloud of weed smoke, he thought.

* * *

Honeydew Diamond woke sweating on the penthouse divan, the echo of her own scream in her ears, the second time in two days she'd had the same nightmare.

Steve, the nicely-dressed gentlemen who'd acquired her for his boss for the evening, rushed into the room.

"Sorry," she said, "just a nightmare." She looked around. No sign that her unnamed customer had returned from his evening engagement.

"He's not back, yet," Steve said. "Need anything to help you relax? He's got the finest Tilaxian wines, Sechuan powder, Nartressan weed—"

"No!" Honeydew said. Too quickly, she realized.

She'd had nightmares at least once a week for the last four years, since that night on the Nartressan beach, when the wealthy son of the shipping tycoon had taken her there to get the freshest weed right from the source. Instead, it'd gotten her. She didn't remember what'd happened. Didn't remember if she'd been dragged into the water or if someone had stopped the seaweed, or what. She'd found herself on an outbound shuttle, compensated at double her usual rate, a note in her pocket, without any awareness of what had happened in between.

"You look pale," the attaché said.

She found her reflection in a mirror. Her black hair made her white skin even whiter. "No more than usual. Tea."

"Huh?"

"Do you have tea? Hot tea?"

"Hot tea, please," he called to the air.

A bot brought it out.

"Fancy." She took a sip, felt its warmth spread through her, felt the cold dissipate from inside. The darkness still lurked, but was held at bay. She vowed she would never give in to the darkness. "How soon?"

He hesitated a moment. "The Limo is still at the reception. You have other obligations?"

She shook her head. "I just hate to wait."

"The immerser is over there. Fantasies, games, adventures. Bystanders or interactives. He'll let you know when he arrives. Just call my name if you need anything."

She nodded and watched him leave the way he had come. She might offer herself to him if she had the opportunity, confident his boss would double her usual pay. But what she wanted was companionship now. She hated being alone.

The darkness encroached when she was alone.

She pulled her knees to her chest and watched the hoverport for her patron's arrival.

Chapter 3

Triangular blue tubes coursed through bedrock, sparkling with energy, pulsating at each juncture, like neural signals in some vast underground brain.

Janine sat up, startled, her coke beeping insistently, her dream fading.

The spider-bot was alerting her it had obtained the samples she'd requested.

She was out of bed in a moment and only the icy floor reminded her she needed to dress. Pants, shoes, shirt and jacket, and Janine was out the door, valise in hand.

The compound, although fenced, had only a cursory gate which always stood open. She headed for the nearest hover and cursed it to life, its liftoff slow, comming Doctor Carson.

Her geopositioner showed the spider-bot a mile down the hill, at the marina. Engines screaming, the hover banked and shot that way, the bay-side cluster of houses looking like a quaint seaside village of old New England, manicured hedges separating stone-faced cottages.

She landed the hover beside the boathouse, noticing a knot of people at the dockhead. A few looked her direction as she leaped from the vehicle.

The cluster parted for her. On the dock sat the bot.

Intact.

She knelt beside it, not quite believing. "Who put it together?"

An old salt with peppered hair and a half-mechanized face gestured vaguely out to sea. "Found it on the dock like this when I got here."

She looked it over.

Undamaged, not a screw missing.

Did I imagine its coming apart? she wondered, opening her valise beside the bot. "All right, monkey, in your nest."

"Yes, monkey mama," it replied, and climbed into its setting. The bioanalyzer beeped and lit up, its cover closing automatically to prevent contamination.

The approaching whine of a hover alerted Janine. That'll be Carson, she thought. She looked at the old sailor. "I'm Janine Meriwether, Xenobiologist at the Alien Microbiology Institute on Sydney." She stuck out her hand.

"Cap'n Baha, Abraham Baha. Pleased."

They shook. "Likewise. Ever seen this happen before?"

Cap'n Baha shook his head. "Every sea eventually gives up its drowned, but not this one." He gestured vaguely again out to sea.

"What happened?" She pointed to her own face to indicate his half-mechanized one.

"Harvester got tangled in the weed. We were chopping ourselves loose when it yanked the whole rig under. Net-shank whipped past my face and took half off, exposed all the way to the brain. I was the lucky one."

Janine frowned. "How's that lucky?"

Cap'n Baha shrugged. "I lived. No one else did."

Doctor Carson ran over, his hover powering down behind him. He stopped, puzzled.

She gestured at her valise. "Intact, not a screw missing."

"But ... " His brow wrinkled with bewilderment.

Janine shook her head at him. "I've never seen anything like it." She looked out to sea, wondering what they were dealing with.

* * *

"You've been on eight, ten drowning search-n-rescues, right? Worked with teams half across Nartressa, and you know this Xeno, too, eh?"

Randall nodded at the Chief, fidgeting uncomfortably. He stood in front of the Chief's desk, and he'd just been asked to accompany the Xenobiologist Janine Meriwether to multiple snatch sites for the next two weeks.

"Look, Randall, I've got a crew to run, rescues to attend to, medical emergencies to respond to. I need someone to keep this offworlder out of my office long enough for me to do my job. And you're looking haggard, Randall. Needing a break, I can tell. Not sleeping well, nightmares, panic attacks. How about something different for awhile?"

Randall left the office, blinking away tears in the stiff breeze, looking across the saddleback between the EMT compound and the research station.

The island's twin peaks were connected by a road, and off the road were twenty or so cottages, one of them Randall's. The best he'd been able to wrangle from the Chief had been, "I'll have to discuss it with my wife." Dejected, he walked along the road, wondering what he'd tell her.

The late summer grasses lining the road waved in the wind, just a tree or two between him and a view of the ocean. The planet was virtually devoid of larger vegetation, these few trees having been brought from off-planet.

Unless you counted the weed, he thought.

The water was a dull metal gray, the surface calm with occasional patches of weed visible just above the waterline. From a distance, it just looked like seaweed. The detritus lining every shore, washed up by the tide and the waves, looked like the seaweed that Randall had seen in stills from Old Earth, the leaves rubbery, dark green-brown, the connecting branches looking like the tentacles of some menacing alien creature and, on the ends, some bulbous nodules that served as floats.

The washed-up seaweed was poisonous, and no matter how it was processed, it couldn't be used as food. How the indigenous fish population managed to eat it was a mystery, as well as how the fish ended up being edible. Someone had explained it once to Randall, but he'd been unable to follow the logic. How the weed could be smoked was another mystery, but he'd been told that the smoke induced euphoria and visions.

He walked up the path toward his home, the disarray of the front yard reminding him it needed tending. Little else grew except the native grasses, the imported trees requiring nutrients that didn't occur naturally in the rocky soil.

The house was empty, his wife not yet home from her job at the hospital, three hundred miles and two hours away.

He fixed himself some tea and sat in the living room, still not sure what to tell her. He knew if he didn't take the offer, the Chief would put him on disability. Too many of his coworkers had gone out on stress-leave for the Chief not to see the signs in Randall's face. But going with the Xenobiologist seemed like admitting to failure.

He yawned, knowing he needed to cry, knowing he needed to sleep, the steam from the tea warm against his face.

The triangular blue tunnel led slightly downward, its ribs pulsating evenly, the sound of rushing fluid all around him. The apex of the tunnel was high enough above his head that he didn't need to bend over, but the walls leaning in from the sides caused him to feel claustrophobic. He put his hand to one of the blue, rubbery ribs. Warm to the touch, and reactive, pulling away slightly as though unaccustomed to touch.

The ridged floor also gave slightly as he walked along the tunnel.

He came to a six-way intersection, wondering which way to go. Each tunnel curved away slightly, and he realized as he looked among them that he didn't know which way he'd come. Panicked ...

He woke, chilly, sweating, his breathing rough.

Randall wiped his brow, looked around his living room. Beside him on the table, the tea was cold. The windows were darker.

From outside, he heard the whine of an approaching hover, its engine high-pitched.

His wife's shuttle.

What will I tell her? he wondered.

* * *

Brian Franks slipped a ten-galacti chit to the valet as his hoverlimo purred to a stop in front of him. He slid into the back seat and the door was closed behind him, shutting out the revelry still pouring from the Chancellor's palace.

The array of electronics lit up as the hover lifted off. Usually, he welcomed the soft voice over his coke, the arrays of symbols across his corn, the soft hum of machinery under his hand.

"Remote office off," he said, stiffing a yawn.

Coke and corn shut off.

The reception with the Chancellor had gone well. He'd received Brian with all the pomp and circumstance of a visiting dignitary.

Although no contracts were signed, no agreements made, no details discussed, the Chancellor's greeting alone had assured Brian that his company had already been chosen for exclusive rights to trawl Bora Bora's waters.

Aquafoods Interstellar was the largest operator of seagoing fish trawlers in the galaxy, and Brian had made it that way. He'd taken a small company with just four worlds under contract and had extended its reach to the breadth of the galaxy. Now, nearly two thousand watery worlds depended on the distribution that his company provided.

Premier among its products were the Nartressan lines, the crown jewel of Aquafoods Interstellar, making up fully a quarter of its volume by weight. But because the catch from the Nartressan waters was such premium quality, the product cost half-again more than comparable seafood and was fifty percent of AI's profit margin.

The Chancellor's favor in AI's contract would sway the watery world's legislature to grant the company exclusive rights to the rich fisheries of its tropical seas, Bora Bora being eighty-five percent water.

Brian yawned again, realizing he'd been awake more than twenty hours since landing his yacht that afternoon.

The hover entered a triangular blue tunnel, which narrowed, seeming too small for the ship. The clear plasma ball enclosing Brian hurtled through the tunnel, ribs passing so fast they appeared to go the other direction. The ball shot into pool of pulsating liquid, a clear green fluid with fingertip-size bubbles suspended in it, the pulses compressing the plasma ball with each beat, beat, beat.

Brian started awake, gasping as though he'd been drowning. The city lights rushed past below, the hum changing as the hover slowed.

What was that? he wondered, wiping sweat away and trying to still the rapid beating of his heart, heart, heart.

He pulled himself from the hover, stepping onto the penthouse hover pad as though expecting it to fall way from under him.

The curtains were drawn across the floor-to-ceiling windows of his suite, just one lamp visible though the curtains.

He scanned himself in, the door sliding aside.

In the dim glowglobe light, a woman stirred restlessly on the divan.

Wanting to put his terror and disorientation behind him, he sat beside her.

* * *

Honeydew Diamond screamed as she plunged into the warm pulsating liquid, a clear green fluid with fingertip-sized bubbles suspended in it. The breath she drew of that same liquid went in without the sensation of drowning, but she screamed again anyway. The pulsating became pushing, and the liquid hurtled her toward an aperture, which opened, opened, opened, in time with the pulsating liquid.

She fought for something to grab, being pushed toward the aperture, the gigantic valve flapping opened and closed.

She flailed—

"Hey, come on, you're all right," the man said, catching each of her arms by the wrist.

The echo of her own scream remained a memory in her ears. "I'm sorry I—"

"Shhh!" he said.

She shushed, a distant memory of gentle voices calming her. How many years had it been since she'd heard a calming voice or felt a calming touch?

The hands that held her wrists were gentle, the eyes that beheld her face were older but kind.

"Not very seductive, huh?"

The man snorted. "You've had difficulties."

Honeydew shook her head. "Compared to some, I've been lucky." She remembered the liquid. "Drowning in green water," she said, shaking her head.

"Green—?"

She saw his eyes narrow, his gaze becoming vacant. "Sorry to bother you with that. It was nothing." She put her hand to his face. "You're so kind. And handsome." She pitched her voice just so and gave him a soft smile.

She saw his eyes drop to her breastline. She drew him close.

* * *

"Tell me about the green water."

Laying on her back, his moistures trickling from her, Honeydew glanced at his darkened face, was surprised to find him fully attentive. Most men just wanted to drift off to sleep afterward.

Because he'd been so kind and gentle, she'd pleasured him deeply in the experienced ways available to her, and he'd reciprocated without her asking, and the culmination had brought her an uncommon pleasure and deep satisfaction. From his breathing, she'd thought he'd surely fallen asleep.

"I'm here for you," she said, "not you for me."

"I'll double your fee."

"No, thank you. It's time for me to go." She rose and reached for the gown.

"I had a similar dream."

Something in his voice stopped her, some quality of tone. "What was it about?" She slipped into her gown anyway.

"A tube, triangular and blue. I was shooting through it in some kind of orb, and then I burst into this thick green liquid, pulsating and squeezing the orb, compressing it." His gaze looked hollow in the dim light, the curtains beginning to brighten with dawn.

"I was drowning in the liquid, but I could breathe it, but the pulsing—"

They looked at each other.

"Like a heartbeat," they both said.

Honeydew shuddered.

"The thick green liquid," he asked, "what do you remember about it?"

"Clear," she replied, "I could see shapes. Bubbles suspended in the liquid, small, none of them larger than my fingertip."

He nodded his gaze vacant. "No blue tube?"

She shook her head. "What does it mean, to dream something so similar?"

He shrugged. "Some connection, somehow. Listen—"

"Steve's awake," she said.

His eyebrows went up.

A soft knock at the door. "Mr. Franks?"

"Breakfast, please," he said toward the door. "For two, please."

A moment of hesitation. "Breakfast for two, Sir. The usual." The sound of retreating steps.

She looked at him. "I should be going."

"You knew he was there before I did."

She shrugged. "A survival skill."

"What's my name?"

"Brian Franks, CEO of Aquafoods Interstellar."

"Who did I meet with, tonight?"

"Chancellor of Bora Bora."

"And how'd that go?"

She found herself knowing without knowing how she knew. "It went well, you're sure you'll get the contract for ..." She wasn't able to say and shook her head.

"What did I do before meeting with the Chancellor?"

"Sailed halfway across Bora Bora in a rental yacht. Alone." She shook her head, again not knowing how she knew. "I'm not supposed to know that, am I?"

"No one but Steve knows it. What happened when I docked?"

Honeydew shook her head and turned to find her clothes. "I don't know. Look, all this is interesting—"

"I dreamt I was pulled into the water."

She froze. "How'd you know?"

"That you dreamt the same?"

"Except mine wasn't a dream. How did you know?"

"I don't know how I know. You don't either, do you?" It was almost an accusation.

Honeydew couldn't hide the fact. "Look, Mr. Franks, I need to go. Whatever wild idea you've got in your head needs to stay in your head. You're a nice man, and you've been more kind to me than anyone has been in a long time, and for that I'm really grateful."

He propped himself on his elbows. "But you need to go."

"Yeah, I do."

He sighed and nodded. "All right. Call on Steve if there's anything you need, ever. I'm probably a fool to make that offer, but there it is."

Honeydew Diamond walked out of the Hilton with a greater sense of loss than she'd experienced in a long time.

Each time she sold herself, she experienced regret about the encounter, doing what she did, that she had to do what she had to do, but it was a loss dulled by the many times she'd experienced it. This time, she had the unmistakable feeling she'd missed an opportunity, a feeling compounded by the fact that she'd had far too few opportunities in her life to begin with.

She sent a curse back over her shoulder, knowing that tomorrow night's customer would be far more difficult to handle because tonight's customer would still be on her mind.

Chapter 4

Janine inspected the spiderbot en route to Shoalhaven, a quarter way around Nartressa. The island was isolated amidst a large patch of seaweed, situated in a gyre, the nearest ocean currents a hundred miles out to sea. Randall piloted the craft with sure hands.

The first sample procured by the bot that morning was en route to the Institute, the initial genetic analysis so bizarre that it was already making waves in the scientific community. The protein structure appeared to be a triple helix composed of three pairings of six nucleotides—adenine, thymine, guanine, and cytosine—plus two new proteins never before seen in carbon life-form evolution. Both these proteins were already notable for their volatility, appearing to destabilize upon contact with air.

What bewildered Janine, and would surely stump any biologist, is how the Nartressan biosphere isolated naturally-occurring oxygen radicals from the seaweed.

The hover under full power, Janine inspected the monkeybot. It had come apart when flung into the ocean by the seaweed strand, but had been completely intact when found the next morning on the Wainsport dock.

Joint by joint, seam by seam, Janine looked it over closely, in particular inspecting the wearpoints, those pieces needing periodic replacement due to simple erosion. On her last two assignments, worlds of moderate temperature, weather, and low-toxicity atmospheres, Janine had not been concerned about wear, and her inspection of the spiderbot had been cursory.

"How's it look?" Randall asked over the hover's whine.

Janine shrugged, glanced at him briefly. He'd not been talkative as they'd loaded her gear and taken off, seeming to be preoccupied with something. He'd probably rather be out rescuing somebody than shepherding me around, she thought, sensing resentment.

She sighed, knowing she hadn't come to Nartressa without her own baggage. A year ago, she'd been diagnosed with uterine cancer, and when she'd gone back for more testing a month ago, they'd told her it had metastasized to her ovaries. I can't think about that right now. When she'd volunteered for the Nartressan assignment, she'd told herself she'd have to think about what she wanted to do about the cancer eating its way through her uterus.

"Looks ... perfect," she said finally, shaking her head at the spiderbot. She pulled out a handheld scanner, picked magnify, and examined the wearpoints with increasing magnification until the image was so jittery she couldn't tell what she was looking at. What she couldn't see was any evidence of wear. None. "Too perfect," she added.

"Makes you think the weed's got a brain."

"Sentient," she corrected.

"Yeah, that."

Definitely irritable, Janine thought. Finding no indication of the slightest imperfection, she set the bot back in the case and turned it on. "Good morning, Monkey."

"Good morning, Monkey mama."

"Self diagnostics, please."

"Self diagnosis in process." Lights blinked and motors whined.

"Why 'Monkey?' " Randall asked.

She shrugged, watching it. "I think it looks more like a monkey than a spider." Then she snorted. "And 'spider mama' doesn't sound as good."

They shared a chuckle.

"Diagnostics complete," the spiderbot said, "All systems normal post outage. Hardware one hundred percent, software one hundred percent, sensors one hundred percent."

"Outage? What outage?"

"Outage occurred from sixteen twenty-one local time yesterday until oh five thirty-five today."

Over thirteen hours.

On her handheld, she checked the time of the alert that morning, when Monkey had told her it had acquired the sample.

Oh five thirty-five.

"Am I seeing what I think I'm seeing?"

She turned the display toward him, nodding.

"I'm no rocket scientist, but that means the sample was inside the bot when it was turned back on."

"That's exactly what it means," Janine said, looking out the window at the weed-choked waters below them.

* * *

Randall turned his attention to the controls, terrified at the thought that the weed might actually think. All those disappearances, all the snatchings, not just a product of an instinctive impulse, but of some intentional, sinister purpose. A drop of sweat trickled down his back between his shoulder blades.

Ahead, the gray-blue sea was mottled with darker patches, and just visible on the horizon, the island of Shoalhaven was a small gray bump on a larger gray tableau.

"Is that it?" Janine asked.

Randall's wife hadn't been happy when he'd told her he'd been assigned to nursemaid the Xeno, adding more unpleasantness to an already unpleasant predicament. The sparse population on the oversized watery world almost guaranteed he'd be frequently gone overnight and two or three nights at least once per month. He saw his wife little enough as it was, her twelve-hour shifts and two-hour commute times leaving her with little sleep and even less time, all of it exacerbated by his departures at any hour.

"That's Shoalhaven," Randall replied. "Sits in the middle of a gyre, surrounded by weed."

"How do they come and go?"

"Same way we are. I doubt they use any kind of seagoing craft." Randall brought the hover lower, until the vehicle nearly skimmed the ocean surface.

Clumps of seaweed were buoyed by bulbous knobs, holding up structures that might reach hundreds of feet to the ocean floor. Within these seaweed forests flourished the legendary Nartressan fish, billions of them, over two thousand species thus far indentified, with a dozen more discovered each year. The fish seemed limitless, and the prices they fetched on the open market exceeded nearly all other marine products. Their taste unmatched, the species ranged from buttery sole to piquant crab.

Starboard was a trawler, churning away at the edge of the seaweed, a trail of bubbles betraying its path on the outskirts of the forest. At least thrice a year, a trawler would get caught in the seaweed, and it was Randall's and his fellow EMT's jobs to retrieve the crews when the vessels foundered.

"How many trawler personnel die each year?" Janine asked.

Randall smirked at her. "I don't have the stats, but more than half of all deaths I'd say are trawler crew." He glanced at her hands. "Bizarre how none of the bodies have been recovered."

Janine dug her fingers deep into the console arms. Her knuckles were white, her jaw clenched, her forehead glistening, her eyes wide and unblinking, her breathing rapid and shallow.

"You all right?"

She swallowed heavily. "Can we fly a little higher?"

He heard the strain in her voice. "Certainly," he said, and brought the hover up to a hundred feet. "It has an override, by the way."

She shuddered visibly, looking terrified. "Just … being that close …"

"To the weed?" Randall frowned, wondering if she'd be able to do her job. "Uh, why so frightened?"

"I'm not frightened." She looked at him sharply. "Well, maybe a bit spooked. I've had these dreams …"

"About the weed? Odd …" A sense of unreality touched him, as though he perceived something more than the information his senses provided him. He recalled an instance at flight school where a corneal feed had malfunctioned and had projected multiple overlays to his visual cortex. For a moment, he'd seen multiple scenes, including auditory and tactile sensations, and olfactory and gustatory senses as well.

"The blue tube," he said.

She gasped.

"Ribbed, triangular, rubbery."

"How …?"

"I dreamt I was inside one."

"Stop the world, I'm getting off. I think I need to leave this planet. I wish I'd never come back. This is too frightening."

"Did you have a dream that the weed pulled you under?" Randall looked at her when she didn't reply. He knew already that she had. He hadn't needed to ask, and he wasn't sure how he'd known. "So have I."

"Somehow I knew that."

"And you don't know how you knew." He met her gaze, saw his own terror reflected there, realized he was sweating. His chest was hurting, and his heart was pounding. "There has to be some explanation," he said, as much for his own benefit as hers. He took a deep breath, trying to calm himself.

They were nearing Shoalhaven, an island less than a hundred yards across. Two buildings and a dock were the only structures, a hover parked near one building, a boat at the dock.

As he banked around the island, he realized that the boat at the dock was capsized, weed strands draped across its hull. Randall brought the hover around, selected a spot near the smaller structure.

A woman emerged from the house as they landed, wiping her hands on her apron.

Randall and Janine got out and introduced themselves. Ropes strung between the house and the smaller outbuilding swayed in the wind.

"Ruth McKutcheon," the woman said, her gray-streaked black hair in a bun, her skin as pale as a cloudy sky.

"Do you mind if I record our conversation, Mrs. McKutcheon?"

"No, not at all, Doctor. Been told my story to so many people, not sure of the need. Came some way to hear a pitiful tale, you have. Hope it's worth the trouble."

"Thank you for having us," Janine said, "apologies for the bother."

Randall was surprised how quickly she'd picked up the lingo, then remembered she'd lived on Nartressa for a few years as a kid.

"No bother. Come in for some tea, and be shut of the chill."

A gust buffeting them, Randall followed into the modest abode, a three-room flat-roof shack. The other building was even smaller. "What's over there?"

"That?" Ruth didn't glance, stepped into the house. "Lavatory, and my son's room." She turned to the kitchen. "He barely comes out anymore since the weed snatched his father. Sits in there and smokes himself silly, just like his daddy used to do. One day I dare say the weed will snatch him too." She busied herself with the stove.

Randall glanced at Janine, who raised her eyebrows.

"Before you get to thinkin' I ain't missing him none, think again. A good man but hurtin', couldn't never get over our first boy drownin'. Can't say I have either. It was horrible." Her voice didn't reflect the feeling, and she might have said "elevator." She turned from the stove to look at them. "Take yourself a seat now."

Randall promptly sat. A couch and two wide chairs faced the window. Outside, the dock and the capsized boat were easily visible, the scrubs grasses rippling in the wind, the weed-clotted ocean beyond rising and falling, the seas rough today.

Ruth joined them. "Had a stroke, Angus did. About forgot everything he learnt. Seven months ago, and that I know because it were one month to the day before the weed snatched him. Had to tell the poor soul his name, so bad was his memory after that. Doctors told me it was an aneurysm, hemi … hemi something is all I could tell you. Pariah something or other lobe."

"Hemiplegic parietal lobe?" Janine asked.

"Sounds close to me. Cancer, aneurysm—he wouldn't have lasted much longer, anyway. Hard to watch him suffer like that. Never recovered, Angus just suffered in silence all the ten years between our eldest son's drownin' and his own demise. About ate him up, it did. Got diagnosed with pancreatic cancer just six weeks before the weed snatched him, already metastasized. Had the stroke two weeks after that. That, and smoking that weed. I didn't allow it in the house, so he built a smoke shack beside the lavatory, upwind of it, spent most of his time there."

"What did he do for a living?"

"Sold the weed. He'd drag it up from the beach, or winch some in from the dock, throw it over those ropes to dry it, then bale it up. Sometimes his buyers would beg him to bale up more of it, but he just didn't have no spark anymore." Ruth shook her head.

The teapot whistled and she rose to get them each a cup.

"What happened?"

Randall took a cup from her. Steam shrouded his face. The tea smelled … odd, but fruity, like apples.

"About six months ago, the seas high like they are today, he stepped onto the dock with a winch and some hooks to bring in some fresh weed." Ruth stood and stepped to the window. "I was standing right here, watching. I'd told the damn fool the sea was too high, but do you think he'd listen?"

Randall could almost see it happening. The tea was slightly sweet—warm and comforting as it coursed through him, essences of apple tingling his nose.

"Of course not," Ruth said. "He hurled each hook out as far as he could throw it, and started winching in a bundle. I could see from here he'd snagged a clump too large for a single person to handle, had one of those big bulbs you sometimes see where the water's deep and the weed so heavy it's got to have a huge buoy to keep the strand afloat.

"Thought it odd at the time it was so close to shore, but not Angus. Just kept reeling it in.

"He'd just about got it to the dock when the strands whipped around him and dragged him into the water, capsizing the boat. Happened so fast he didn't have time to scream. Then the bulb dragged itself back out to the sea, taking Angus with it."

Randall realized Ruth was crying softly. Janine stood to comfort her. He looked out past the dock, saw in the distance one of those gargantuan bulbs. Although small from this far away, Randall knew they grew sometimes to as large as fifty feet in diameter, the tops smooth, but hundreds of strands attached to their sides, and below, a trunk twenty feet thick reaching to the ocean bottom. It resembled a gigantic underwater tree a hundred feet around, its branches waving gently in the ocean currents.

The vividness of the image caused him to start. He'd never thought about the marine underworld. He'd always been indifferent to what it looked like under the oceans of Nartressa.

Randall frowned at the tea in his cup, wondering if Ruth had added something to it …

* * *

As his attaché drove him through the crowds at the Bora Bora spaceport, Brian Franks checked the Commodity-Futures Board on his corn. Fish futures had spiked sharply, he saw.

On the far side of the tarmac sat his yacht, and on this tourist-thick, resource-poor backwater, no one had given thought to the design and layout of the spaceport. Customs, security, baggage, ticketing, and quartermaster were all located in randomly-placed buildings around the large lot. In between them all, the dark-skinned natives were festooned with wares hawked them vociferously.

He felt sorry for the economy traveler trying to navigate the Bora Bora spaceport. Even for him, despite the waivers and VIP clearances, the process was still disconcerting.

A pale boy with dark hair waved a news pad over his head, tabloids screaming similar headlines: "Nartressan terror strikes again."

The stories available through his corn-coke, Brian wouldn't normally have noticed, but the boy caught his eye and held it.

"One galacti, Mister," the boy said, stepping nimbly onto the running board.

Steve reached back to swat him off.

Brian stopped him. "Here you go," and they traded.

The boy grinned and stepped off the cart.

"Sorry, Mr. Franks, didn't see him."

Brian waved it away and activated the device. The two-inch touch screen came alight and dumped its contents into his subdural over the short-range optimitter.

The lead story described the thirtieth snatching by the Nartressan seaweed this year, the vid caption showing the young Xenobiologist sent to analyze the indigenous plant. The story noted that the price of fish, and particularly the coveted Nartressan catch, was likely to rise as a result of the terror instilled by the seaweed.

Fish futures were likely to rise even higher, Brian knew, in spite of analysis predicting an uninterrupted harvest.

The cart surged clear of the crowds and found a tarmac lane, picking up speed. The wind in his hair and the sun on his face, Brian smiled, each uptick in fish futures putting millions in his pocket.

A flash on his corn alerted him to an incoming com. He activated his coke, wanting only the audio link, disliking the video. "Franks here," he said on his trake.

"Sandusky, Mr. Franks." Chief of operations for the Sydney sector. "Trouble on Nartressa. We lost a—"

"I'll com you back on a secure line," Brian interrupted.

"Uh, sorry, Sir, but uh—"

"In five minutes."

"Uh, uh, yes, sir," and Sandusky disconnected.

They know better than that! he thought. Company business was always conducted over secured neuranet links, and never over open coms. Too much corporate espionage. Brian had a staff of five hundred devoted to similar activities. The "Market Analysis" division spied on his competitors, even to the point of monitoring the personal lives of their corporate officers. Decrypting internal company messaging and cracking their neuranets was standard operating procedure.

Steve pulled the cart to a stop beside the yacht, "The Seaweed."

It had been dubbed thus in partial jest for the nuisance that the plant was to the thousands of trawlers plying the Nartressan waters. The yacht itself was a fancy model, complete with a luxury stateroom, an elaborate communications center, and enough acceleration to get him halfway across the galaxy in less than a day.

At the threshold, he balked, not knowing why stepping aboard the space yacht disturbed him. The memory of the tentacle around his ankle set him sweating.

"What is it, Mr. Franks?"

Brian waved it aside and forced himself to board.

What the hell was that about? he wondered.

* * *

Honeydew plugged the tabloid into the socket on the seatback in front of her, the eyes of the boy who'd sold it to her in the crowded, chaotic spaceport staying with her. She didn't usually buy such extravagances, especially not from native vendors hawking suspicious items, but the boy's eyes had mesmerized her.

Something about his dark hair and white face.

"Nartressan Terror Strikes Again," the voice blared and she quickly turned it down, the vid showed the young Xenobiologist sent to study the seaweed.

Honeydew didn't have a coke, trake, corn, or subdural to view such things with. The surgery, usually performed between fifteen and eighteen years old, was moderately expensive, and typically done when most adolescents were completing their basic educations and looking at which university to attend. Between fifteen and eighteen, Honeydew had been looking at which name to use and which customer to attend to.

Orphaned before she could remember, Honeydew had been taken in by a madam on Sydney who'd put her to work helping the older girls get ready for customers. Part of her duties was to keep watch for liaisons turning sour, when the customers sometimes got violent. The madam wanted to know instantly, telling Honeydew, "It's important to know the difference between an enthusiastic slap and an angry slap. And you must always call me when blood is drawn. Always."

Her early years had been spent observing the liaisons closely, and she never questioned that she would eventually do what she observed the older girls doing.

At fourteen, she'd asked the madam when she could start. Her menses had begun some months before, and already the customers leered at the breasts that seem to burst overnight from her slim, boyish chest.

"I have something else in mind for you, Honeydew," the madam had said, and soon after she had begun attending to some of the girls who left the house to meet their customers elsewhere, something reserved only for the privileged girls.

Nowhere had there been room for a "normal" life. Honeydew had known nothing else, didn't want anything else, and wasn't inclined to pursue anything else. Especially not having some fancy electronic gear surgically implanted under her skull, a process that would interfere with her work for at least two months. Honeydew had never gone a week between customers.

So she eased herself back in her seat aboard the starliner, the only passenger in her row to use the seatback player. While the starliner prepared for liftoff, the tabloid fed her headlines and vid through the shiplink, and at the end of the Nartressan seaweed story was a link to a related story: Trawler dragged under.

"Aquafoods Interstellar, producer of exotic seafood delicacies, announced today the loss of a trawler on Nartressa, along with its suborbital resupply ship. The company extends its condolences to the families of crew members. In a side note, futures spiked again for the third straight day in seafood delicacies, despite company assurances that production would continue uninterrupted..."

Honeydew shuddered, remembering her dreams. She abruptly brought up another story simply to be shut of that one. While the tabloid droned on about celebrity news, she checked her appearance in a handheld mirror. Her jet-black coif was perfect against her clear-white skin.

"And in other news, the government of Bora Bora has announced the awarding of an exclusive contract to Aquafoods Interstellar for its rich fisheries. CEO

Brian Franks stated that the Bora Bora contract would be mutually beneficial, bringing badly needed jobs to the populace." A picture appeared.

Honeydew recognized his face instantly, the black brows on the white forehead below a crown of dark hair. Frowning, she thumbed back to the lead story, the snatching death of a 24-year-old male from the island of Randwick, and the vid of the Xenobiologist sent to Nartressa to investigate the seaweed.

Dark-haired and light-skinned, the scientist looked to Honeydew to be the epitome of the book-smart, people-dumb, lab-coat wearing brainiac.

Doctor Janine Meriwether, eh? she thought. Even has a brainiac name.

"Freeze," Honeydew said.

The frame froze, the scene taking in the rescue crew, reporters, bystanders, police officers, and other apparatchiks of officialdom, all standing around and commiserating morosely. She began to count. When she got to twenty, she stopped counting. Mirror out, she looked closely at her hair and skin.

Dark as midnight, white as cream.

Wasn't my hair a different color? She distinctly remembered the madam's commenting on her strawberry tresses. Somewhere in the mist of time, her hair had changed color.

And freckles! I used to have freckles! she thought. Now, her skin was so white and fine she needed only a touch of blush at the edge of cheekbone for highlight.

She looked at the frozen vid. Only two out of over twenty people had something other than black hair and white skin. Maybe that's because of the local weather, she told herself, knowing on a level she couldn't articulate that something else was at work.

She flipped back to the Aquafoods announcement, the still of her erstwhile customer in front of the company logo.

Dark hair.

White skin.

Dreams of viscous green fluid.

"Are you all right, miss?" A steward asked her. "You look pale."

"I'm fine," she managed to say, her voice faint.

"Liftoff in one minute. Please buckle your restraints."

"Certainly," Honeydew said, absently buckling her five-point. The flight was a blur.

Chapter 5

Janine buckled her five-point as the hover hummed to life, excited and terrified at the same time.

All through her youth, moving from planet to planet about once a year, Janine had made friends each place, but never lasting friendships, knowing that in another year, she'd have to move to another planet.

So instead of friends, she'd acquired specimens.

Alien specimens.

Large, small, flora, fauna, viral, microbial, marine, terran, orthopteran. Cryogenic tubes by the thousands painstakingly sealed, labeled, categorized, and organized. And always in the back of her mind, the hope that one day she would stumble across the alien life form that would remake human civilization and launch humanity toward its next evolutionary phase.

On more than one occasion, her diplomat father would grimace at the sheer size of her luggage or the exorbitant freight bills they'd incurred from shipping her ponderous collection, as well as the bureaucratic red tape they'd have to navigate to import all the alien biological matter. Never once did he discourage her passion.

The avocation kept her focused on the possibilities on the next planet they'd be moving to, instead of missing the place that they'd moved from.

Her college years had been the most difficult, because that meant staying in one place for more than a year. How she'd managed three years at Auckland University, she didn't know. Partly, she'd been on such an accelerated course of study that she hadn't given herself time to notice she was bored with the planet, getting in three years an education that would typically take six.

The hover acceleration pressing her into the seat, Janine looked over her notes, wondering if she'd found on Nartressa exactly what she'd always wished for.

And feeling terrified.

"That boy didn't look so good," Randall said.

Janine frowned. The woman's son had come out of the shack just as they were about to depart Shoalhaven. He'd stared at them wordlessly from under a disheveled head of thick black hair, his skin terribly pale, his eyes sunk deeply, his shoulders drawn forward.

Then Janine had noticed his lips moving, and when the wind changed direction, she'd heard him say distinctly, "The triple helix is exponentially more complex, the protein pairings more numerous to the power of six, the heretofore ionic imbalances offset by the two nucleotides endogenous to the Nartressan evolution."

"What?" Janine had said, not believe what she was hearing.

"The galactic secret service is monitoring our conversations through the subdurals they planted into our brains at birth. They've been necrophiliating our bone marrow ever since, boiling our blood to make their soporific for the sleepy masses. They don't want you to think. I'm a neologistic Freudian; who cares if I have a subdural?" And the young man had thrown a scowl at them both and staggered back into the shed.

"He's just high off that weed," Ruth McKutcheon had said. "Pay him no mind."

Janine glanced at Randall in the hovercraft beside her, the craft flying low over the ocean. "Ever seen someone who's addicted to something?" she asked, disturbed that the boy had made sense for a time.

"In Rockdale, I stumbled across a group of weedheads in an alley," Randall replied. "Looked just like him. Pale, drawn, disheveled. I got out of there pretty fast when I realized they were about to attack me."

She shook her head and gestured vaguely behind them. "For all his intoxication, he sounded pretty coherent at first." She wondered why they were flying so low and saw the top of a seaweed bulb ahead, a large one, easily twenty feet in diameter, probably with a main stalk reaching hundreds of feet to the ocean floor.

"I've heard one hit can make you delusional. Not sure why anyone would want to mess up their brains like that."

"Humans aren't the only ones. Most creatures will act the same if you give them an unlimited supply of something that makes them feel good."

"You'd think humans would know better."

Janine snorted, nodding. "Hey, what are you doing?"

He slowed the hover as they approached the seaweed bulb.

It looked larger than she'd thought, fully thirty feet across, water lapping at its edges, its top nearly flat.

Janine did some quick calculations. An immersed bladder with a consistently thick membrane would bulge out of the water, the pressure greater on the sides than on top. But the surface of this bulb was slightly rounded, its top nearly flat. She wondered what evolutionary factors might have brought that about.

A gust of wind shoved the hover to the right, and Randall corrected for it.

Janine wondered what the winds were like during a storm. "Looks pretty unremarkable."

Just visible under the water surface, sprouting from the bulb edges, were hundreds of strands, their leafy tentacles moving slowly with the currents. The tentacles suddenly stiffened and whipped out of the water.

"Get us out of here!" Janine yelled.

Randall wrenched the stick on one side and forward, and Janine watched in horror as the tentacles reached for the slowly-responding craft, the turbines slamming into high thrust, but the whine of its rotor just increasing.

The hover lurched forward, the smooth front slapping away a large tentacle, and the hover dipped, careened off the water and lifted with a lurch.

Janine looked back as Randall banked.

Hundreds of tentacles flailed at the air in their direction.

Grinding at the rear shuddered through the hover, and the ship slewed wildly. "Sounds like ice in a blender!" The shudder ceased and the hover righted, but an alarm began to sound and lights blinked frantically on the dash.

"We're going down!" Randal shouted, wrestling with the controls.

"Look!" She pointed at an island to starboard.

"Where'd that come from?" Randall goosed the controller and the hover banked that direction.

The hover was losing speed fast, slewing from side to side, its one engine whining under the strain while its second engine fluttered and wowed.

"Our angle's too steep!" Janine shouted.

At what seemed liked feet above the island, Randall yanked back on the rudder and the hover flipped up and dropped, and all Janine could hear as the back end disintegrated against rock was her own scream—

* * *

Randall first became aware of shouting, then shaking.

Someone was trying to help him.

Bearded, graying, wrinkled, and one-eyed, the head was half-covered with electronics.

"Janine!" he tried to say. A gargle came out.

The world righted but threatened to fall on its side. One step, two steps, the heat and smoke, the cold and wind. He coughed repeatedly, then fell to a knee. "Janine," he said again, and this time he heard the word.

The horizon went vertical, the sand slapping into the side of his face, and he saw the old man step gingerly into the burning wreckage and pull on something.

When Randall saw him extract her from the debris, he allowed the pain to pull his eyes closed, feeling deep inside that something was horribly broken, like a ruptured spleen or perforated bowel or punctured femoral. EMT response to a place as remote as this was hours away at best, and Randall thought, I am going to die here …

* * *

Randall started awake and wondered why he wasn't dead.

The hover remains smoldered nearby.

Janine! he remembered.

Two feet away, just beginning to stir, was the Xenobiologist, her face covered in blood, but old, caked blood.

The pain in his legs slammed into his brain like two-foot metal spikes, and he gasped.

"Randy?"

He could barely see, the pain was so bad, but he didn't feel the awful abdominal distress that he'd felt before. Hands on his belly, he felt for tenderness.

Intact. Bruised maybe but untraumatized.

"Are you all right?"

"Yeah, yeah, I think so." His voice was barely a whisper. He squinted past her, trying to find ... "Did you see him?"

"Who?" She looked puzzled.

"Help me sit up. I think both my legs are broken."

She poked his legs in three places. "They're not broken, just badly bruised."

He frowned, tried to ease himself to a sitting position. The pain seemed to dissipate with motion. Bewildered, he looked around.

"See who?" Janine repeated.

"Old guy, his head ..." Randall gestured, puzzled and wondering if he had dreamt.

"Half-covered with electronics?" Janine asked.

"You did see him."

She was shaking her head. "There's no one else on this island. I saw him at the docks at Wainsport, where my spider-bot turned up." She looked forlornly at the wreckage.

Randall doubted her bot was intact inside the pile.

"Surprised we survived the crash," she said.

"I'd swear the old man helped me out of it." Randall shook his head and tried to stand, his coveralls blackened from the chest downward.

Sore, but otherwise intact.

Janine gasped.

His abdomen was cold in the wind, the cloth falling away in burnt layers, the skin under it without mar or blemish, as healthy as before the crash.

"Aren't those formalls supposed to be ...?"

Randall nodded. "Fireproof. Standard EMT equipment." The badges at left breast and both shoulders were intact. He had to hold up the formalls at the hip to keep from exposing his undergarments. He looked around for something to hold them up.

The island wasn't more than fifty feet across. Nothing except wreckage and short, wind-whipped grasses. He walked around the remains of the hover. A deep gouge in the sand began at the edge of the island, and then the trail of debris began, strewn clear across it and into the water at the other edge.

Lucky not to have been thrown into the sea, Randall thought, looking quizzically at his burnt formalls.

"What now?" Janine asked, poking in the rubble.

"A beacon went off the instant we started having engine trouble. As remote as we are, EMT response will be hours away, at best." Didn't I just think that? Randall wondered, a touch of déjà vu upon him.

He saw she'd extracted the remains of her spider-bot.

Crushed beyond repair.

Randall sighed and wondered how long they'd be stranded.

* * *

"Nartressa," Brian said.

"Yes, Sir." Steve turned back to the controls after a moment of hesitation.

He looked as if he were about to question my decision, Brian thought, unaccustomed to being questioned. He had just gotten off the secured comlink with headquarters. Forty-two crew aboard the trawler had died, and fifteen more aboard the suborbital resupply. His com center overlay on his corn nearly obscuring his view of the cabin, Brian Franks reviewed the damage-loss estimates from the sinking of the trawler and resupply suborbital ship on the watery planet.

How had the seaweed claimed a suborbital? Brian wondered.

Like most fish-harvest operations, production on Nartressa included a three-vessel processing link: The trawlers, which plied the waters of the planet and harvested fish from its rich marine beds, the suborbital resupply ships, which brought empty container vessels to the trawlers and lifted away the hundred-ton containers, and the five orbital processing plants that rendered the catch into a variety of final products, which were then shipped across the galaxy.

The suborbital resupply ships should have had more than enough thrust to tear away from the seaweed, no matter how many tentacles had latched on.

Fifteen years ago, a trawler had been lost in similar circumstances, and only one crew member had survived with horrible injuries. After that, Brian had run analyses of hypothetical scenarios involving the seaweed, the trawlers, and the suborbital resupply ships. In every possible variation except one, the suborbital ship had been able to generate enough thrust to escape the seaweed. The one exception had been when the resupply ship had tried to liftoff with the trawler itself and a container full of fish, the suborbitals sometimes dispatched to carry a trawler from one fishery to another. The suborbitals had brought the trawlers planetside to start with, the ships having the capacity to lift a trawler and a full container into orbit, together.

Real-time video of this attack indicated that the seaweed had struck at the most vulnerable moment for both ships. After the full container was harnessed to the idling suborbital and before the container was unharnessed from the trawler, the crew below set about unclamping the container. At that moment, the seaweed had struck, quickly pulling the trawler and the idling suborbital into the ocean with what appeared to be startling ease. Only minutes passed between the first sign of trouble and the complete submersion of the suborbital.

The loss of a trawler, one of twenty thousand plying the waters of the giant mudball, was inconsequential, but the loss of the suborbital, which resupplied forty to fifty trawlers, was a significant setback. The remaining trawlers might be redistributed among the other four hundred suborbitals, but it would severely impinge the maintenance schedules, work rotations and flight intervals needed to keep up production quotas.

Replacement was weeks away if a backup suborbital could not be brought out of the repair pool. Attrition due to break downs, auxiliary equipment malfunction, or personnel shortage was already running higher on Nartressa than Brian wanted to see.

Scenarios to prevent the loss of another suborbital had been run by his risk-analysis team. They predicted that if the suborbital ran its engines at high idle instead of low idle, the delay in achieving liftoff could be shortened to less than a minute. The cost-benefit ratio in expended fuel versus the price of replacing a suborbital and its crew was far greater than Brian would have thought.

The trawlers themselves had been redesigned for Nartressan waters to minimize their vulnerability to the seaweed, their hulls smoothed, their superstructures simplified and nearly all protrusions eliminated to make the vessel difficult for the seaweed to grasp. All except the trawling mechanism itself, which of course had to extend into the water to harvest fish. Even that had been designed for quick detachment, and the prow where it extruded redesigned to seal quickly after the disposable trawling extrusion had been discarded.

But no one had thought that the seaweed might be able to pull down a suborbital resupply ship.

"Com," Brian said, looking over a rendering of the suborbital. "Sandusky, Northern Ops," Brian said. "Secure." Odd, he thought, how no bodies had been recovered.

"Secure com channel open," the ship replied.

"Sandusky here, Mr. Franks."

"I'm en route, ETA eight hours. When I get there, I want secure com channels to all Nartressan Personnel. Before I arrive, I want you to assemble a design team of your best suborbital maintenance and fabricator people. Remember the retrofits we did on the trawlers to make them weed-resistant?"

"Yes, Sir. Doin' the same for the suborbitals, I take it."

"Exactly. Now, it's a bit of a rough road ahead as we try to do that and fill in for the downed suborbital, but we have enough reserve capacity to have ten suborbitals off line at a time. By my estimates, that's still not fast enough, Sandusky. Find a way to accelerate the retrofit."

"Yes, Sir."

"Any thoughts on how else to prevent the loss of another suborbital?"

"Well, Sir, I was watching the vids, and noticed how thick the weed was around the trawler. If we can track weed activity around every trawler, maybe we can spot when it gets thicker."

Brian liked the idea. "What kind of satellite system does Nartressa have?"

"The usual weather monitoring. Uh, Sir, we've also got our own marine life trackers. We know where the largest schools of fish are."

He'd forgotten. "Try out a test recalibration. See if we can track the seaweed density."

"Just what I was thinkin', Sir."

"Excellent idea. You'll have some preliminary results when I get there?"

"Yes, Sir."

"Thanks, Sandusky. Out."

The com link died.

Then Brian requested an analysis of what weapon would work best against the weed.

Not his first choice, as the Xenophiles and Envirophiles would denounce Aquafoods Interstellar and advocate for a boycott, but Brian Franks wasn't about to let a pesky weed disrupt the fish harvest.

* * *

Honeydew Diamond opened the door of her apartment on Sydney and stood at the threshold. Her instincts told her instantly something was wrong, that her apartment wasn't the same as she'd left it.

She counted to ten, listening with her entire being, the way the madam had taught her. "You have to be still, even in your own mind," she'd said. "And in that stillness you will come to know what you face."

Honeydew knew someone was in her apartment.

But the person wasn't there to hurt her.

"You didn't have to break into my apartment," she told the silence. Then she stepped inside and closed the door.

The man on her couch was so pale he almost glowed. His black hair fell down his forehead, nearly into his face.

"What do you want?" She pitched her voice full with disdain.

"Your help. You'll be paid well—far in excess of your usual rates."

He had a stillness and certainty that she found disconcerting. She kept silent, keeping herself still, as though she might battle him with it.

"Well?"

She didn't respond.

He glanced at the apartment around them. "Humble, simple. Not what I expected from someone who fetches the prices you do. But you're focused on other things. Not as though you entertain here. No friends, no family, just a few former colleagues and the madam who trained you. Very little to move you." His eyes found her again. "Aren't you for hire? You'll be paid well."

For what? she wanted to ask, but refrained.

"For a little corporate espionage of your last liaison, the Aquafoods President and CEO." The man held up a handcom.

Audio began to play. "Tell me about the green water." His voice. Brian's.

Honeydew looked away. "You mean spying."

"Spying, yes."

"How long?"

"One year, with an option to extend that."

"Do you know how much I make in a year?" She hadn't put her hand on her hip, but she might have.

"Yes."

She was startled that he'd answered so simply. Her mind racing, she calculated what he knew, realized he could have the madam hurt, her sorority sisters maimed, her secret accounts drained. He hadn't threatened those things, but he implied he might. The threat of a threat.

"Plus expenses," she added.

"Of course."

"How much?" She was more concerned than surprised at the ease of the terms. The task wouldn't be easy.

"Thrice your earnings last year, half now, half at completion."

"Five times," she said immediately.

He chuckled softy. "Four."

"Four, but define completion."

He tilted his head to the side.

Honeydew recognized the preoccupation of someone conversing on a trake-coke.

"The end of the contract between Nartressa and Aquafoods Interstellar."

She sensed obfuscation. Calling him a liar wouldn't avail her any advantage. "Seems you could bribe a few officials to achieve similar ends. Why me, why this route?"

The man smiled. "Other routes haven't worked. Oh, uh, you'll need the usual implants—coke, trake, corn, subdural—and they'll be linked to our monitoring center. Of course."

"Of course." She'd expected as much, along with a geogalactic positioning sensor. "What happens if he discovers the surveillance?"

"Contract ends. You're on your own. If you last an entire year or we achieve our goal, you get the second installment. If neither happens, you keep what you've got, and not a galacti more. Are you in?"

Honeydew knew she was in for something.

Chapter 6

Five hours after the crash, Janine and Randall had been airlifted to safety by the nearest rescue unit, the Gosford-based crew, had been strapped into cryo-gurneys for examination, and had been flown directly to Botany Bay, half-way around the planet, neither of them in any acute distress—Janine's blood-covered scalp and Randall's burnt formalls notwithstanding. She had slept the entire way, the deep dreamless sleep of healing. After their arrival, they'd been subjected to every medical test available on the relatively remote planet, shuffled from one room to the next, one machine to the next, and the only odd finding was the high level of nitrogen in their blood.

"As though you've been underwater for several hours," the first doctor had said.

Janine sighed and suffered through yet another examination. Nurse tech, Nurse, Doctor, supervising ER physician, and now the Medical Director of the Botany Bay Hospital.

From her room on the third floor, she could see the Capitol of Nartressa laid before her. Despite the view, she chafed at the delay in getting out.

Botany Bay sat on the eastern edge of the only continent on Nartressa. It was the first settlement on the planet, founded some four hundred years before, and it had thrived instantly, the fish so thick they had jumped into the settler's boats, or so the legends described it.

"Remarkable," the Medical Director said.

Just what everyone else had said. "Can I go now, please?"

"We'd like you to remain for another twenty-four hours of observation."

"But you can't force me to stay."

"No, we can't. If something happens, some unforeseen complication, we—"

"Can't be held liable. Yes, I know. I'm a doctor, remember?" She had always disliked asserting that, but right now, she felt she had to get out of the hospital. She'd been poked and prodded for most of the last twelve hours, since arriving by hover.

"So, no, we can't force you to stay," the Medical Director said, "but I must say, in all my years, I've never seen anyone survive such a crash with nearly no trauma. And that little laceration on your forehead appears completely healed, despite only twenty-four hours since the actual crash. You and Randall are phenomenally fortunate."

She nodded, feeling fortunate.

The docupads signed, her clothes back on—the collar still stained, as the blood had not come out completely—Janine asked to be shown to Randall's room.

En route, Dr. Thomas Carson intercepted her. "You're all right! I felt so guilty sending you with that skyjockey. I knew I should have hired a private pilot, a professional ..."

Janine waved it off. "It was the weed."

Dr. Carson looked dumbstruck. "How could that be?"

She described what happened.

"He shouldn't have flown so low. We'll get you a real pilot."

By now, they stood outside Randall's room. In addition to his having surely overheard, Janine objected for other reasons. "Ultimately, the choice is mine, and I'm sticking with Randall."

The professor sighed. "Very well. When you're ready, I have the claim forms at my office for the spiderbot that you lost in the crash." He marched away, shaking his head.

Bemused, she shook hers and entered Randall's room.

The EMT watched her as she entered. "He was right, you know. I shouldn't have flown that low."

"You didn't cause the weed to grab the hover, all right? Not another word. It's not your fault!" Janine wondered why she felt so exasperated. "What are you still doing in that bed?"

"What are you doing out of bed?"

"If your tests are like mine, you've just got some elevated nitrogen in your blood. Otherwise, you're as healthy as can be, and I'll bet you feel younger than you ever have."

He nodded. "You knew that without my saying it."

She met his gaze. "Just as you knew the same about me from across the hospital."

"What do you suppose is happening?" He gestured at his abdomen.

Janine frowned, knowing on some level more was going on than she liked.

Randall looked up at her. "The boys back at the station think it was the rear planar assembly that gave out. They sent me the stern vid feeds right before we encountered trouble, just as the weed was reaching for us."

"Oh?"

"Never touched us, except for the strand across the prow. But the vids do show pieces falling off the tail section, and those planar assemblies have been known to give out."

Janine felt the blood leave her face. "And he had the gall to accuse you of flying too low!"

"Hey, cool off. You stuck up for me, right? No harm, no foul. Let's get back on the horse that threw us off, eh?"

Janine smiled, liking him.

* * *

"How's that rear planar assembly, Charlie?" Randall asked, doing a walk-around of the new hover.

"Replaced it this morning, Randy, just like the chief told me." Charlie shook his head, his grease-spotted formals rippling in the breeze.

The chill off the water was particularly sharp today, carrying a smell of cold apple cider. The wind was funneled up from the sea toward the island apex by two ridges, and here where the two men stood, it blew against them like a giant hand.

Charlie leaned close. "You keep your wits about you out there. And this outlander Xeno whatever she is, keep your distance, all right? Half the squad knows things are tense for you and your wife."

Randall nodded. He and Kathy had argued again the moment he got home from the hospital. She'd practically begged him to delay a day before re-embarking on this trip with the Xenobiologist. Working for the same company that ran the Botany Bay hospital, Kathy had surely accessed his records from South Derth, where she worked. And she knew better than he did what all those tests meant. "Thanks, Charlie," Randall said. "I'll be careful." They shook, and he opened the cabin door, looking around for Janine.

She was walking toward the hover, leaning into the wind, gestured to the passenger door and went around, not even trying to talk in the sharp, cold wind.

The door "thunked" shut as he pulled it closed, then hers did the same. Only a distant whistle could now be heard.

"Wind's pretty strong today," she said.

He nodded, got the thumbs up from Charlie, scanned through the checklist. On her side of the dash, he saw the optimitter come to life.

"Who do you want to visit today?" he asked.

A face popped up on his corn, behind it a map with coordinates.

"The new spiderbot won't arrive for another day," she said. "I'll miss Monkey."

He saw her blinking. "How long had you had the bot?"

"For years, bought it in postgraduate school, used it in my doctoral thesis."

Randall put his hand to her upper arm. "Hard to lose a friend like that." He blinked away moisture in his own eyes, thinking about two of his unit out on stress leave and a third on permanent disability as a result of the seaweed terror. He felt close to going out himself.

The nightmares had abated since his rescue from the crash site. Only recently had he slept without dreaming of slimy tentacles, ribbed blue tubes, and viscous green liquids.

He turned his attention to the controls, the hover humming under him. He radioed for clearance on his trake.

"Clear," came across his coke.

Even in the stiff headwind, Randal lifted smoothly and brought her around over the dock, the small town of Wainsport and its equally small marina looking like the quaint backwater coastal village that it was.

He plotted a course for their destination, rising to two hundred feet, and set the autopilot. Their nose was pointed forty degrees starboard of their destination just to compensate for the crosswind.

"Hey, Randall, look at these."

The hover control consol shrank to one corner of his corn. Randall peered at the images Janine was showing him, banks of faces like a high-school yearbook. The faces of the forty-five people who'd disappeared in the past two years from the shores of Nartressa.

"What am I looking at?"

"Black-haired, all of them."

"And white skinned. So? Nine-tenths of the people on Nartressa look like that."

"Even at seventy years old?"

Randall shrugged. "My great-grandfather never sprouted a single gray hair, nor my grandfather, who's now retired in Botany Bay."

"Look at this."

A face occupied the left side of his corn, demographic information spilling down the right. In red, flashing, was the word "Cancer" and a date of diagnosis. The next face appeared, and flashing in red "Dementia," and the next face, flashing red "Liver failure," and the next, "Kidney failure."

"Do you remember what Ruth said about her husband?"

"Pancreatic cancer," Randall said. "That woman at the beach said her son had leukemia." He looked at her. "You're the Xenobiologist. Ever hear of an alien plant or animal that senses people's health problems?"

She shook her head. "Dogs sometimes."

"But those are pets, right?"

"Exactly, long proximity and close affiliation. Let me sort these profiles. Not everyone who was snatched was diagnosed with something."

On his corn, watching what she watched, he saw her sort through the forty-five profiles, forty-six including the twenty-three year old from the Randwick beach.

On his corn, Randall shrank her display to bring up the hover controls. Their destination was Rockdale, a fair-sized city on the west coast of the second largest continent, home to the only land-based Aquafoods Interstellar facility, where trawlers were brought for routine maintenance and retrofitting.

Randall had seen the trawler-repair plant, a sprawling complex that dominated half the bay. Beside that was a trawler graveyard, behemoths cast aside to rust away in the wind, rain, and sun. These were vultured for their spare parts for a quick fix when a winch drum had to be ordered from off planet or a conveyor assembly had to be replaced. These parts were kept there rather than on one of the five orbiting processor stations where the suborbital re-supply ships took the full trawler containers. The trawler graveyard seemed a sad place to him, where the skeletons of once-productive machines lay rotting, their insides picked apart, their outsides rusting, their protruding cranes and superstructures creaking forlornly in the constant wind.

Fifteen of their thirty-six profiled victims had been based in Rockdale, their coworkers having watched helplessly as the seaweed had snatched them over the trawler side.

"That trawler and suborbital that went under. How many people aboard?"

Randall hadn't expected the question. He saw she had finished with her sorting, and requested the information from his subdural. "Fifty-seven," he said. "Forty-two on the trawler, fifteen on the suborbital. What are you thinking?"

Janine held her chin between her thumb and forefinger.

She looks deep in thought, Randall thought, I'd better not disturb her. He remembered that over the last two years, there had been an additional fifteen disappearances, people who had inexplicably vanished. All or nearly all had either been aboard a trawler or had last been seen in close proximity to the shore. Nartressa being ninety-percent ocean, it was somewhat difficult not to be near the sea.

His corn still carrying a view of her corn, he saw new sets of numbers spilling down her screen. Enlarging it, he saw what appeared to be statistics on the fish harvest.

Then she brought up a planetary analysis program.

He couldn't resist. "What are you doing?"

"An ecological modeling program. Calculates the long-term sustainability of ecosystems. Given how little we know about Nartressa, it won't provide an accurate picture, but if I can get a generalized idea of the impact of the fish harvest, I'll be able to confirm a small hypothesis I've got going.

"One of the unknown variables is this triple-helix genetic structure. You're familiar with the basics of the human genome? Double helix, four base pairs of proteins, mitosis of the helix into single strands, which then joins with the mitosized strand from the egg or sperm, creating the new, unique being?

"So how does a plant with a triple helix reproduce, presuming mitosis produces three strands, which in this biological soup includes not four base pairs, but nine? And a plant which appears to be the predominant flora—so predominant that ninety-nine percent of all plant life on Nartressa consists of the seaweed?

"A dominance, oddly enough, that isn't replicated in its animal marine life. The diversity of fish species here is enormous. Two thousand five hundred and counting. And even when a particular seabed has been thoroughly explored and all its species categorized, a year later entirely new species appear without apparent evolutionary precursors. An animal marine diversity alongside a floral homogeneity. An evolutionary oxymoron."

Janine sighed.

Randall laughed and shook his head, following most of her arguments, but not the implications. All he understood was that the two shouldn't exist alongside each other.

"Such specificity and dominance is contrary to evolutionary dynamics. A single plant simply can't have developed like this."

"Could it be at the peak of its—"

"That's it!" she shouted. "Of course!" She lurched across the console and planted a wet kiss on his cheek. "That must be it! Evolutionary imbalances are always corrected. Always!"

Bemused, Randall chuckled, feeling a warmth that had seemed missing from his life for quite some time. And feeling embarrassed by it.

Then she froze. "One small assumption," she said, her voice quiet.

Randall saw Rockdale on the horizon. "What assumption?"

"That animal and plant don't mix. What if animals and plants interbreed in this biosphere?"

"That's a crazy thought."

"Yeah, you're right, it is. I don't know where I got that." She shook her head and looked at him. "Sorry, didn't mean to embarrass you."

"Not embarrassed at all," he said, his face aflame.

* * *

"The blue points are schools of fish," Sandusky said, "The red points are our trawlers, and the green points, which we were able to add through refractory chemical analysis, are seaweed stalks."

From his seat in the division manager's office, Brian browsed the fifty- by one hundred-mile expanse of ocean. Three trawlers plied the waters off the west coast of Rockdale, the Aquafoods trawler repair facility at the very right edge of the screen. The image was also being relayed to their corns, the vidscreen a fast-fading anachronism. The office sported viewports floor-to-ceiling, the pale blue planet below half in shadow, evening encroaching from the east. From here in orbit, it wasn't possible to see the spectacular underwater light display that trawler crews frequently reported.

Brian noted a rough match between the number of schools and the number of stalks.

Another red point emerged from the edge, moving far too fast to be a sea-based trawler.

"What's that?"

Sandusky checked his handheld. "EMT vessel, en route to Rockdale. If I'm not mistaken, Sir, that's the Xenobiologist I told you about, investigating these snatchings; she's accompanied by a veteran EMT, a Randall ... " He checked his handheld again "... Simmons."

"Who's the Xenobiologist?"

"Doctor Janine Meriwether, from the Sydney Alien Microbiology Institute."

"Start a profile on both. I want to know every bit of information she sends off planet. Better yet, Sandusky, get me live audio."

"Sir?"

"Put a mike in the hover cabin if you have to. I want to know what they know about the seaweed."

"Sir, I don't know if that's—"

"I know damn well it isn't, and I don't care. Just make it happen, Sandusky."

"Yes, Sir."

Brian had not averted his gaze from the map. All he could see was that the fish and the seaweed were far more numerous than he could have possibly foreseen, outnumbering the trawlers by a thousand to one.

"Why the blinking every second or so?"

"The sensors for finding the fish are the same for the seaweed. They have to be recalibrated between scans, which takes just under a half-a-second, so the scans aren't quite real-time."

"How long to install real-time scanners?"

"A week, perhaps."

"You've got two days. Another weed attack like that last one, and our volume is likely to drop. What's that?"

Another red light had entered the area, this one moving far faster than the hover.

"Suborbital resupply ship, Sir."

"Following the new protocol?"

"Yes, Sir."

The suborbitals had been ordered to keep their engines at high power while they attached and detached the containers from the trawlers. Although this shortened the time needed for a suborbital to escape, it was still vulnerable.

Brian watched the suborbital slow as it approached the trawler, red converging on red.

Several green points converged on the two red points.

"Abort the transfer!" Brian yelled, hurling a finger at the screen.

"Abort! Abort! Abort!" Sandusky yelled, his voice echoing on Brian's coke.

"Suborbital vid feeds!" Brian said.

The view shifted, four views now displayed, and already the trawler was wrapped in tentacles. Another twenty seaweed strands reached directly for the suborbital, its engines blazing. A tentacle spun up each of the guy wires connecting trawler and suborbital, the sea frothing as though in anger. The suborbital engines were screaming, some tentacles letting go when scorched under their heat.

The trawler stern went under, the prow poking into the air.

The suborbital half spun and slewed to one side, then over corrected and flipped, crashing top first into the trawler stern, the vid twisting wildly, and then the cameras went underwater, a brief view of green quickly replaced by black.

The com channels squawking on his coke, Brian stared at the black screen, his head pounding. Two in two days, was all he could think.

No blasted weed was going to disrupt his catch!

* * *

Honeydew Diamond looked skeptically at the blue gel that that the man had given her, looked in the mirror at the livid welts bisecting the top of her head, and sighed.

The sutures from her surgery had just been removed earlier that day, and the doctor had told her that it would take two months before the incisions were completely healed and the hair had grown back.

He—the "company liaison" who'd insisted she call "Shannon"—had then said, "Here, use this. In one week, no one will know you just had your sensor extensions installed."

Honeydew was still mastering them, the trake being the most difficult of the four devices. Every time she went to speak to someone on it, she vocalized the words as well, and everyone around her thought she was talking to them.

The other three components she had mastered quickly, although she was still learning the features of the subdural. The coke was a parallel auditory receiver wired into her auditory receptors. The corn was a parallel visual receiver which sent images to her visual cortex. The subdural was a microcomputer planted just under the skull near the midline ventricle and linked the other three implanted devices to the neuranet.

Eager to get to Nartressa, Honeydew looked between the nasty-looking incision and the suspicious, unlabeled container of blue gel.

A faint aroma of apples wafted up from the jar.

She couldn't figure out why that alarmed her.

Quickly, before she could change her mind, she dipped two fingers into the gel and applied it to the fresh, pink scar.

Her scalp tingled and an odd feeling of peace settled upon her, reminded her somewhat how she felt when she smoked the weed.

She found herself sitting on her divan, the jeweled box where she kept her implements on the table in front of her, the box open, the weed rolled and ready to smoke. Realizing that she didn't remember the last few minutes, she lit the weed and drew deeply, the faint aroma of baking apples somehow familiar.

Standing in front of the chillbox in her kitchen, Honeydew looked through the items to find the frozen fish, "Aquafoods Interstellar," in small letters on the box corner. Cod fillets, her favorite. She turned the package over, looking for the small print. "Harvested from the seas of Nartressa in compliance with galactic ecological preservation laws."

Why the sudden desire for the most expensive thing in her chillbox, she didn't know. She opened the package, a faint odor of fruit under the stronger smell of fish.

The pound of fish disappeared in moments. She hadn't realized she was famished. The hundred galacti worth of fish was delicious, divine, scrumptious!

She stood amidst a forest of her sisters, her bouy bobbing gently on the waves above her, holding her main stalk erect, her thousands of tentacles waving in the slow ocean current.

Schools of beta offspring fed off her alpha tentacles. The sensation of their suckling left her with both a pleasant satisfaction and a slight titillation. Pods of premature alpha offspring sprouted at various points from her stalk, two or three bulging with anticipated parturition, the glowing neural membranes just visible through the uterine sacs. A school of gamma tuna bred with one of her mating pods, the muscles of multiple vaginas throbbing with ecstasy.

Honeydew felt one of her own pods respond in kind, and a school of bass launched from midway down her stalk, the fish turning to feed from a nearby gamma sister stalk. Life in vigorous proliferation around her, Honeydew felt profoundly fulfilled. Sisters elsewhere weren't faring so well, she knew, their offspring netted by the floating machines and their branches withering uneaten, their pods unbred. The balance that Honeydew and her sister stalks had achieved was being slowly undone by these alien interlopers and their constantly patrolling vehicles.

Signals flashed to her by the new blue-tendril network from nearby sisters told of recent retaliation, several sisters acting in unison to pull the floating machines and their flying cousins underwater, and splitting apart their containers to free the offspring trapped inside.

A recent effort had been met with spitting fire, and the sisters had suffered badly, losing many upper tentacles. One buoy had been punctured, the sister having then slithered to the ocean floor, unable to hold herself erect, where she now lay dying, her sisters around her unable to help.

Honeydew had long been alarmed by the decreasing number of fish, but in her remote location, not a single island within hundreds of miles, safely embedded in a forest of stalks over one million strong, her alarm had been manageable.

But the spitting fire added to her alarm, for in her ancient memory was a time of similar fire, when the earth below had torn asunder and had launched a great spitting fire that had filled the skies with ash and had heated the water until it boiled.

Underneath her alarm was certainty, her age itself a testament to the durability of her race. The alien interlopers knew not the resilience and resourcefulness of Honeydew and her sister stalks.

Honeydew sat up abruptly and drew a deep breath, as though she'd lain submerged for a long time. In front of her was the open jar of gel, the open box of weed, and the empty package of fish. Honeydew blinked rapidly and caught her own reflection in the mirror across the room.

She stood to inspect the incision—or rather, tried to.

The site where just last week a surgeon had implanted subdural, coke, trake, and corn could not be found, despite the sutures having been removed that morning.

Even the hair had grown back.

Honeydew parted her hair every which way to try to find the scar.

Nothing.

Somewhere, a certainty emerged that this was meant to be. And behind that certainty was direction, a purpose she had not heretofore known in her drift from planet to planet, bed to bed.

She raised "Shannon" on her coke. "I'm ready," Honeydew told him.

Chapter 7

Standing on the dock, looking out over the bay at Rockdale, Janine swore softly. For days, she had been trying to obtain clearance from an Aquafoods supervisor to accompany a crew on a trawler run. I have to see the seaweed! she thought, her interviews of witnesses yielding no new information.

In the week she had been here, two more trawlers had been attacked. After witnessing the horrifying attack on trawler and suborbital on their way in to Rockdale, Janine and Randall had heard rumors from crewmembers they'd interviewed that trawlers were quietly being issued flame throwers.

Two days after their arrival on Rockdale, a trawler off the coast of Gosford had been attacked by the seaweed as its container was being lifted by a suborbital, and the trawler crew had fought off the seaweed with their flamethrowers, burning off the tentacles.

Janine had been livid, and she had stormed into the local Aquafood administrative office and demanded to speak with a supervisor. Her behavior had gotten her arrested.

Now, fuming on a dock overlooking the Rockdale bay, Janine wondered how to get aboard a trawler. Making a scene at the Aquafoods office and getting headlines on the local newsfeeds had endeared her to the small cadre of environmental protestors on Nartressa but had alienated Aquafoods, making it unlikely she would obtain their permission to accompany a crew on a trawler run.

The Institute of Alien Microbiology had filed a complaint with the Galactic Commission on Indigenous Species, but it might be years before the commission concluded its investigation or issued a cease and desist injunction against Aquafoods Interstellar, an injunction certain to be appealed, a process certain to take years.

Unwilling to wait while Aquafoods crew roasted the seaweed indiscriminately, Janine wondered how she was going to get close enough to the weed to study it, and perhaps understand why it was attacking the trawlers, why it was snatching people from docks and shores.

The just-rising sun was warm on her back; she leaned forward against the railing. Her shadow was long on the water in front of her, the sun behind her giving her head a halo.

Some savior, she thought, snorting contemptuously.

A shadow on the water approached hers.

She turned.

"Good morning," Dr. Carson said, casual in his manner, as though he'd seen her yesterday.

"Good morning," she replied, remembering the dock she'd stood upon the day of her arrival. "If you're here, it's not good news."

He chuckled, his white skin nearly translucent in the morning sun. "Oh, I suppose I could have commed. My concern is that I think your coms are being monitored."

"What?" She was livid again. She already knew who and why. "That bastard Franks, right? How can he get away with that?"

"The question, really, is 'Who's going to stop him?'" Carson said. "I don't suppose you'd consider expanding your activities to include non-scientific pursuits?"

"What?" she said again, her intonation quite different. The soft morning breeze blew her hair from her face.

He turned toward the bay and leaned against the railing. "You live in a world of pure information, Janine. Nearly devoid of alternate purpose, of political consideration, of corporate greed, of governmental corruption." Doctor Thomas Carson looked at her. "I've been trying to study the seaweed for fifteen years now, and Aquafoods has exerted its considerable corporate power to stymie my efforts at every turn."

She frowned. "What are they afraid of?"

Carson grinned. "Exactly my question."

In the silence, Janine considered the implications. "Their profits must be enormous."

"Somewhere in the neighborhood of fifty percent of company profits derive from the sale of Nartressan fish, as best I can gather. Despite its stock being traded publicly and their books purported to be 'open,' I'm skeptical they're as honest as that. Any threat to kill the golden goose must be stopped at all costs. You'll never get aboard a trawler, I'm afraid. Not legitimately."

She shot a look at him.

"A cross-complaint has been filed by Aquafoods Interstellar with the Galactic commission on Indigenous Species."

"In other words," Janine replied, "The Institute's complaint will go nowhere."

"Precisely. You've made quite an impression on the local protest community. You've inspired them to stage an occupation of planetside offices. You should consider some of their methods, too. By the way, I brought you your new spiderbot. It was delivered to our offices at Randwick, and I didn't want it to go astray, so I personally delivered it to your hotel room."

"And when you didn't find me there, you came to find me here?"

"I knew where you'd gone."

Janine grinned, decided she liked him. "Thanks for bringing it."

"You're welcome. Any thoughts about this triple-helix genetic structure?"

"I'm halfway through a paper, keeps me up half the night writing it." She had never felt so excited, not even when she'd been working on her doctorate. "The implications of three strands are astounding. And having nine base pairs of proteins—we'll blow the top off existing theories of life."

Doctor Carson grinned. "Precisely the kind of information that Aquafoods wants suppressed. Be careful, Janine."

She frowned as she watched him leave, the bright morning sun in her eyes, the cold ocean breeze at her back.

Why did he really travel halfway around the planet? Janine wondered.

* * *

Randall stopped on the cold dark street, hearing clinking glass and alcohol-loosened laughter. He debated going in, knowing he couldn't convince himself otherwise. Earlier, he'd awakened in a cold sweat again, the hideous nightmare leaving his mind. Seeing that it wasn't even midnight, and knowing he'd toss and turn until dawn, Randall had decided instead to go for a walk through Rockdale, hoping for a brief reprieve from the horror that his nights had become.

Days too. He'd left earlier in the week to spend a day or two at home while Janine concluded her interviews with trawler crewmembers who'd seen their fellow crew dragged off the boats by seaweed tentacles. Although he'd hoped for a few days peace at home with his wife, they'd spent the time arguing bitterly over his being gone. They'd had one night of passionate lovemaking, but the next night they'd lain awake next to each other, both of them furious with the other, Randall that his wife felt jealous of his traveling around with the exotic Xenobiologist, his wife that he appeared to have enjoyed his time away from her.

His nights miserable, his days filled with strife, Randall walked into the bar, hoping to forget. A neighborhood bar, a faint scent of apple coming from somewhere in the shadows, the clink of ice in a glass, the low murmur of conversation that halted upon his entrance.

He found the long wooden counter and slid onto a stool.

Conversation resumed slowly.

"What'll you have?" asked the beef slab with the tattooed arms behind the bar.

"Just a brew, a local, if you've got it."

"A gnarly Nartressa? Or something a bit more tame?"

"Yeah, something tame."

"Three galacti."

Randall put a chit on the wood.

The brewkeep popped a bottle and put it beside the chit. "You, uh, from around here?"

"Randwick."

"Welcome. Prefer the locals. Like it that way. Not many offworlders find this place."

"Been getting a few with the weed acting up?"

The brewkeep nodded. "She'll settle down, though. Always does."

"Let's hope. Too many calls for my liking."

"What do you do?"

"EMT."

The brewkeep whistled tonelessly. "You see it firsthand."

Randall nodded, and drank deep. The cold brew of thick green liquid went down smooth, soothing the rougher places inside, the hint of apple stronger. Yeah, he thought, just what I needed. A knot of anxiety deep inside him loosened.

He looked around, his eyes adjusted now to the dim interior. Five, six other patrons, a couple in the corner with a glowing ember between them. Two others at the bar, a third person in a booth alone, the eyes peering furtively from under a dark brim, eyes that missed nothing.

Randall drank and ignored those eyes, though they raked him between his shoulder blades. He'd lived on Nartressa long enough and had worked enough dangerous missions to know when something was amiss. Half a world away from the person he loved and unable to keep a civil tongue in his mouth for her, his nightmare nights wrecked upon rocky shores in stormy nightmare seas, Randall ignored the annoying stare and drank the thick, green nectar.

Suds puddling in the bottle bottom, he frowned.

"Buy you another?"

Randall about leapt off the stool.

"Hey, there, just a bit jumpy, eh?" The old codger pushed back the brim. His eyes were kind and knowing. "Best not to have another if you're that nervy."

"What's it to you?" Randall hadn't meant to snarl.

"Easy, friend. Startled you and didn't mean to. My apologies." The old guy wore the formals of a sailor, his pantlegs bunched tightly at the bottom, his sleeves tight at wrists, the waist cinched and slim, the suit otherwise loose and flowing.

"Sorry. Having a bad night."

"We all do. To be forgiven. From Randwick, eh? You know anything about that Xenobiologist? The one who got arrested?"

Randall snorted. He'd bailed her out. She had looked so pathetic amidst the rabble in the jail cell, the usual flotsam and jetsam common to most port towns clogging the bunks. Janine had been cowering in one corner, looking ready to bite anyone who got near.

"This is an Aquafoods planet, run by Aquafoods money and Aquafoods rules. Only Aquafoods justice is available in these courts. I hope she doesn't intend to fight."

Randall smiled, having heard similar from friends and relatives who'd gone to work on the trawlers. The orbital factories were the cushy jobs, though. Far easier to work in weightlessness. Frequent furloughs planetside were needed to keep muscle tone and bone density, giving them regular breaks from orbital work.

"What's she hope to find out, anyway?" the old man asked.

Randall shrugged. "Why the seaweed is attacking."

The man grunted. "Won't get any help from Aquafoods. Don't know why she's asking them."

Somewhere within his mild intoxication and heavy misery, Randall felt a touch of alarm. "Who should she ask?"

The old man grinned. "Shannon." He took off his cap and stuck out his hand.

The hand felt as scarred and calloused as it looked. "Randall."

Shannon's jet-black hair was cropped close to his skull, so close the veins under his scalp were visible. "Used to work for AI until I got hurt. Had to sue the bastards to get my claim paid. Now they won't give me a job anywhere on the planet. Punish anyone who dares ask for his due. Come with me, boy. Too many ears in here."

Randall followed him out into the cold dark night, the chill slapping his cheeks, the breeze off the bay biting at his ears. They walked in the direction of the giant drydock cranes, tall enough to lift a trawler from the bay for repairs, guy lights blinking slowly in the night. "Where we goin'?"

"You'll see. AI wasn't always the sole arbiter here. Used to be a research station on Nartressa."

"Like the institute on Randwick?"

Shannon snorted. "Five times larger. Abandoned some years back, no one's saying why. AI took over the above-ground portion and turned it into a trawler repair base, mothballed the underground because they didn't have a use for it. And it suited the company to have as little information about the indigenous life go public as possible."

Randall frowned. "Surprised they'd even let Doctor Meriwether come, then?"

Shannon smiled at him, gestured toward an alley. "This way. AI couldn't suppress the snatchings forever. Thirty-five in the past two years, right? More like two or three hundred."

Randall grimaced, wondering how the company had managed to keep that information from going public. The alley was dark, little more than a gravel walkway between two fences. Fifty feet in, and Randall just about couldn't see Shannon.

"Here," Shannon said, his voice a whisper.

Hinges creaked, but Randall couldn't see a thing.

"Down," Shannon whispered.

Randall felt his way down a ladder. The floor rose to meet him more swiftly than he expected. He made room for Shannon to descend, and again hinges creaked.

Shannon flicked on his lamp. "This is where your Doctor Xeno should start."

A pair of four-wheeled quadcarts stood at the top of a ramp. Randall peered downward, able in the dim light to make out several tunnel entrances. "Where do they go?"

"Down to the bay, down under the bay." Shannon grinned.

"Janine should see this." Randall said, reading the signs above each tunnel below.

"Bring her to the bar tomorrow night, and don't tell her a thing. Let's go back up topside."

* * *

Brian Franks frowned at the screen.

"Bravo-Echo-five-nine," dispatch yelled, "Converging seaweed, alert, alert! Bravo-Echo-five-nine, alert!"

The third attack in a week, the fifth in two weeks, the last two effectively thwarted by flamethrowers.

Brian thought, Come on, weed, we'll burn you out of the water! "Vid feeds," he yelled, and two views popped onto his screen, one from the suborbital and one from the trawler.

Two thick tentacles reached for the trawler, and two for the suborbital.

Brian watched, incredulous, as the slow-moving tentacles whipped back and hurtled toward the trawler, and he realized belatedly why they moved so slow.

Each tentacle crashed across the trawler amidships, and the vessel cracked in half, the vid skewing wildly and going dark, the screams of crew audible under the great crunching sounds. The trawler foundered, the rear half dropping underwater like a stone, the front half bobbing helplessly, figures like dolls falling from the superstructure into the roiling waters, until the prow took on too much water and sank beneath the waves.

Amidst the flotsam and jetsam floated the tree-truck tentacles, their girth exceeding any known tree, their sides sprouting nubs where smaller tentacles had been.

59

Brian stared at the scene, realizing by their girth that these seaweed lengths that had smashed apart a trawler weren't just tentacles, they were main stalks, the shaft of seaweed that reached from the ocean floor to the surface, where giant buoys held their lengths erect.

Two of them.

Smashed apart a trawler.

Stunned, Brian blinked blankly at the screen.

"Sir?" Sandusky said.

"What? What is it?" He realized that all the com channels were quiet, shocked to silence.

Just as he was.

"Sir, what now?"

His mind felt empty. The beast they fought was far deadlier than they'd imagined, capable of a brute force that had been heretofore unknown.

"For now, a buffer of one-quarter mile. Every trawler is to maintain a buffer of a quarter mile from the nearest seaweed until we develop a strategy. I want an all-supervisors meeting in four hours aboard Orbital Processor Prime. When they're here, you'll find me in my quarters, Sandusky."

Brian didn't hear the reply, his ears ringing. A hiss like an over-pressurized tank blotted out all sound.

He made his way to Sandusky's cabin, which he'd commandeered as his own. I should think about bringing my yacht, Brian thought, realizing the battle for control of the Nartressan seas was going to be a long one.

She stood outlined in the viewport by the bright surface of the Nartressan waters below them, her formalls tight and translucent. He saw she wore nothing underneath.

"How'd you get here?"

"By your invitation, remember? But don't worry about me. You have far greater problems." Honeydew smiled without mirth. "Which I can help you with."

Brian snorted and stepped to the bar. The thick, green local brew seemed particularly inviting. He slammed down a small glass. "I seem to remember something about that. I also remember your being adamant about not coming."

"I changed my mind. The news hasn't been good. The company stock is sliding, and this'll send it farther down. There's a rumor that Bora Bora's considering someone—"

"No!" He snarled, and hurled the glass past her.

It shattered against the facia stone mantel.

"Where'd you hear that?"

She shrugged, looking unperturbed. "Friends."

He realized he wasn't the only high-flying CEO with a taste for expensive prostitutes. "What the black hole do you know about this?!" He realized he was yelling, and it felt good to yell. "How by the barnacles on a sunken derelict could you possibly help me?!" He realized how furious he was, that somehow he'd crossed the room and was yelling, his face inches from hers. "How, bitch?!"

And her face spun away, his backhand taking her head around.

When her face spun back, a trickle of blood dripped from her cheek and a flood of pity poured out of her eyes.

He grabbed a fistful of her formalls in each hand and ripped them off of her.

* * *

Exhausted, Honeydew crawled from beneath his limp form and winced, trying to find out if any of her bones were broken.

He had pulverized her, and then he had raped her.

At one point, she remembered watching in detached curiosity as one of her teeth had shot from her mouth and bounced daintily off the plasma viewport, the blow catching the base of her jaw on the left side.

She crawled toward the bathroom, sure she was leaving a trail of blood. His rape had been as brutal as his beating, and she could barely crawl, her hips, thighs and back so bruised that the muscles didn't work right.

It had been worse than any customer she'd ever had.

For all that, she hadn't lifted a finger to defend herself, hadn't put up the slightest resistance. She was sure her face was so badly disfigured that she'd never work again. The strain of just getting to the bathroom was so exhausting that she passed out on the cold tile floor.

Several strands of seaweed pummeled a trawler with their buoys, each blow shaking the ship violently, dislodging crew and pieces of superstructures and cranes and skyhooks, until the trawler looked like it might sink out of despair, and then a stalk thrust into the ship from the stern and impaled it to the bow, the trawler splitting lengthwise and each half falling into the sea.

Honeydew woke with a start, the cold tile floor against her cheek, and she grabbed onto the vanity to pull herself to her feet, noting a remarkable absence of—

She gasped at her reflection.

Not a mark.

She felt with her tongue.

Teeth intact.

Fingers to her face, she pushed to try to find the least bit of hurt.

Nothing.

She ran her hands over her body, searching for the bruises and broken ribs and lacerations she was sure he'd inflicted.

Not a mark, not even the yellowing of an old bruise.

A pounding at the door. "Sir, the supervisors have assembled." The pounding again, insistent. "Sir, they're ready for you. Four hours on the mark."

Honeydew hid herself in the bathroom while Brian roused himself. While he stumbled around in the cabin, she cowered in the bath.

After he'd gone, she stood again before the full-length mirror and inspected her figure under the bright lights.

Not one blemish on her body. No evidence of the brutal beating and rape she'd endured.

Disbelieving, grateful, stunned, Honeydew showered in the luxurious stall, the purifying, steaming water hitting her on all sides.

She found the shreds of the formalls that he'd torn from her body, and she found bloodstains and broken lamps and busted end tables, but no matter how hard she looked, she couldn't find the tooth that had come flying out of her mouth.

With the patience of a saint, she cleaned up the cabin, repairing what she could, scrubbing the bloodstains from the carpet and the furniture, disposing of those items that couldn't be repaired.

And then she sat to await his return.

Chapter 8

"It's just like the research facility on Sydney," Janine said, looking around in wonder.

Outside dusty glasma panes swam a school of bass—or what looked morphologically as close to bass as an alien ecobiology might produce. Beyond the school stood a forest of seaweed stalks, their leafy tentacles fluttering slowly in the gentle ocean currents. A school of smelt appeared to be feeding upon one beleaguered stalk, and beside that another stalk appeared to be under frantic siege by a school of minnow, the turbulence they created obscuring what they were doing.

Delighted, Janine glanced at Randall. "This place has everything we need to find out about the seaweed."

He smiled and shone his handheld light around. "Except for power."

The only natural light was what filtered down through the water beyond the thick glasma panes.

"If this place is anything like the research station on Sydney," Janine said, "there's a microfusion core somewhere underneath us."

"If we bring the station up to full power," Shannon said, "someone's sure to notice."

Janine and Randall had met him at the bar just as the first images of the seaweed assault on the trawler had come across the vid. The twenty-foot thick stalks smashing apart the ship had been horrifying, but what had really sickened Janine was seeing the dead stalks floating afterward on the ocean waves, their tentacles limp and lifeless.

The two stalks had sacrificed themselves to sink the trawler.

Sick with disgust, she had insisted on coming down to the research station immediately.

Seeing a patina of dust on everything and cobwebs everywhere, she wondered what had happened—how a fully functioning research station had been mothballed.

"They didn't even take their current work with them," Randall said, shaking the dust off a stack of flims.

"In a hurry," Janine said, now seeing other signs of a hasty departure. A half-open drawer, a cup, a half-filled wastebasket. Not even mothballed, Janine thought, a process of deliberate decommissioning. No, this research station had been abandoned in a hurry. She looked at Shannon. "What happened to this place?"

The man shrugged. Like many of the natives, his hair was jet-black and his skin milky white. "There's old tales, but I never paid them no mind."

"What tales?"

Randall smirked. "Experiments. Monsters being decanted from Petri dishes. Genetic monstrosities oozing from beneath laboratory doors. You know, the standard campfire horror stories."

"Yeah, those tales." Shannon looked mildly mystified.

Janine glanced between the two men. "Didn't you grow up on the other side of the planet?"

Randall shrugged. "Native of Randwick. How about you, Shannon?"

"Rockdale, born and raised, why?"

They both looked at her. "Half a world apart," she said, "and you don't find it odd you know the same stories?"

Randall glanced at Shannon. "My father worked the Botany Bay Orbital Cannery for twelve years." The five geosynchronous orbiting canneries were named after the nearest large cities, the processing platforms visible in the skies at night.

"Me Madre worked them all—repaired the robotics," Shannon said, then shrugged. "We've all got tales about the weed, but those tales have come to life in the past couple years, scares us all, it does."

Janine nodded, wondering what the research station itself would tell her—if she could bring it to life. "Let's find the microfusion core."

* * *

Randall peered at the panel with his quickly-dimming handheld lamp. "Hey, Shannon, you gotta charge pack?"

"Sure do. Last one." Shannon brought it over.

Randall shut off their only light to change the pack. Fumbling in the dark, he hoped it worked, realizing they'd have to find their way up through nearly a mile of maintenance access tubes in complete blackness if the charge pack didn't work.

Light flooded the room, and Randall sighed, a drop of sweat running into his eye. "Let's get this thing operational."

Neither he nor Shannon had wanted to try, but Janine had insisted.

"Look!" she'd said, nearly yelling, her face inches from his. "People are dying up there. The seaweed is sacrificing itself to stop the trawlers. This can't wait! We have to find out why!"

Randall suspected she cared more about the seaweed than the trawlers or their crew. He checked over the switches on the panel once again, assuring himself they were all off.

"Ready?" Janine said from across the room.

He could see she was ready to pull down the large mechanical lever, whose linkage would lower the microfusion core into the generator housing. They had spent an hour running battery-powered diagnostics on the core, which had been burning at a simmer since the research station had been shut down. At a simmer, such power cores might last thousands of years. When run at full capacity, they needed replacement about every half a millennium. The power core had passed all the integrity tests and even at a simmer would easily power most of the lights.

The panel where Randall stood stretched twenty feet side to side, and was five feet tall, from his knees to a foot and a half above his head, each bank two inches wide. Two tiers tall, each bank of breakers was controlled by a central breaker. He and Shannon had gone through them to make sure they were all thrown.

"Ready," Randall replied after one last scan.

Janine pulled down on the lever, putting her weight on it.

For a moment, nothing happened.

Somewhere a motor whined.

First one, then two lights came on. A thump, then the bank lit up, and light flooded the room. The central breakers all remained dark. Good! Randall thought, glad the power was contained. Now, from this room, they would be able to control which parts of the facility received power.

"Which one for the main processing core?" Janine asked, stepping up beside him.

"Processing? You mean computer? That one I think."

Janine threw the breaker before he could stop her.

"I hope no one's listening," Randall said, shaking his head at her.

"Hasn't been used in a hundred years," she replied, smirking. "No record on Sydney of this research station. If there had been, I'd have seen some mention."

Randall saw a display pop up on his corn. "Still works."

"Initializing," a voice said on his coke.

"That's bizarre," he told her. "One research station not knowing about a sister facility less than a parsec away?"

"I've thought about that since you told me this was here," she said, looking over the power panels. "Either it was a military intelligence black operation or it was closed under such a cloud that all mention was eliminated from published material."

Randall and Shannon looked at each other. "Or both," Shannon said.

"I wonder what they were doing down here," Randall said, shuddering involuntarily.

* * *

Brian frowned at his attaché. "What do you mean, she's fine?"

"Perfectly healthy, Sir. Were you expecting her to be ill?"

He'd expected her to be injured and maimed. He shook his head, mystified. Did I imagine beating her raw? And raping her?

Brian wasn't sure what had possessed him. All during the video address to Aquafoods installations around Nartressa, Brian had felt the distraction of the horrific beating and rape he'd inflicted on the woman.

As though something had snapped inside, as though the person who'd pulverized the whore were someone else, a different person, as though Brian had watched the incident from over his own shoulder.

Now, four hours later, he stood outside the door to Sandusky's cabin, and Steve, whom Brian had sent into the cabin to survey the damage and assess the woman's condition, was reporting that she looked perfectly healthy.

"Sir?"

"Step aside, please. Return in one hour." Brian's voice was wooden, his face without expression. Her gasps four hours ago were all he heard. Why hadn't she screamed? Why hadn't she resisted?

His attaché left.

Brian waited until the corridor cleared, then he stepped inside the quarters.

She was sitting placidly on the divan. Her stare was the only obvious indication that he had beaten her horribly. An end table was missing, as was a picture from the wall. A trinket or two from the mantel. But no bloodstains, no broken glass, no busted furniture. And her face held no indication of the nose he remembered breaking, or the fountain of blood that had sprayed from the cut on her scalp where he'd broken the end table upon her head.

She stood and walked toward him.

Evincing no pain.

He'd heard her bones grinding against each other as he'd spread her knees wider than the human anatomy allowed for, and the dull sickening pop as either her hip had come out of place or her femur had broken.

And then he'd raped her.

She stopped in front of him, her eyes clouded with the indignities he'd inflicted upon her.

"Well?"

He frowned. "Well, what?" He couldn't understand why she was still here. He wasn't really sure how she'd managed to find her way aboard. Equally disturbing was the fact that he had no desire for her to leave.

"Going to beat me more?"

"Why are you still here?"

"Do you want me gone?"

"No," he said too quickly. "But … I don't understand."

"Why I'm still here?"

"Why you're not a bloody pulp. I busted your skull open. I broke your nose. I dislocated your hip."

"And you raped me. I've never let anyone rape me."

"And I raped you." Brian shook his head, dropped his gaze. "I've never raped anyone before, or beat someone so mercilessly. I didn't know I was capable of that."

"You can rape a planet without a care. Why not me?"

Now he was furious. But something about her manner, her stare. He felt as though thousands of sentient beings were looking at him through her eyes.

"Listen to me babble inanely," she said, throwing up a hand as though to dismiss herself. "How about something to drink?"

He stepped further into the room, watching her approach the bar. "A small one, please. I've still got work to do, shareholders to assuage."

"Split a local brew?"

He nodded, glancing at the gray blue planet out the viewport behind her. "Three trawlers and two orbitals in two weeks. At least seventy crew members missing and presumed drowned. The seaweed is fighting back. The crews are demoralized, afraid to bring the trawlers within a mile of a stalk, much less a quarter mile. Volume is down by fifteen percent since the first trawler was pulled under."

Brian stood in the middle of the room. He took the glass half-full of dark green brew and drank deeply. The almost-fruity liquid slid down his throat with surprising ease, and he drank the rest in his second gulp.

She sipped on hers and giggled at him, the eyes wary.

He didn't blame her. He was wary of himself, not sure what had possessed him. He sensed it was something he would eventually reconcile himself to, perhaps even forgive, but he knew she never would.

"Why? Why are you here? Why did you stay?"

* * *

Fortunately, Honeydew was prepared for this question.

Following the surgery en route to Nartressa, she had looked into his background.

"You're more than you appear," she told him, a half-shaded truth. "You and that planet," she glanced out the viewport. "You couldn't have risen through the Aquafoods hierarchy without influence. You're seventy-five years old, don't look a day older than forty, and you worked your way up from trawler foreman, which you started at age forty-two on Sydney.

"I came here because you're fated somehow, some way, for unusual things. I stayed because we both know that that's not you." She looked at him closely. "You won't be doing that again." She saw his eyes narrow. "Perhaps you're not sure that that's true, but I am. Next time, I fight back."

She sauntered over to the floor-to-ceiling viewport, knowing her form was silhouetted through the diaphanous dress. She half-turned to show him her profile. "Your fate is down there." Below, the darkened planet was brightening in the east, the lights of Rockdale visible on the black slate.

Beads of sweat stood out on his forehead.

He'll require no more pushing, as he's always done that for himself. It's the direction he pushes that will need my adjustment, she thought, reading his face.

"There's a reason we've both dreamt of Nartressa."

A sharp intake of breath.

"You didn't know …?" She saw him shake his head. "An alien ecology like this should have been more thoroughly studied."

"You're wondering why more isn't known about the seaweed."

"And the fish," she said. Seeing his brows narrow, she smiled. "Never thought to have the fish analyzed. Nearly a hundred product lines are sold across the galaxy, and five hundred other product lines carry additives made from the byproducts. The bulk fish emulsion itself is considered de rigueur among horticulturists. And you've never considered the why of it."

She sipped her brew. "And this! A beer made from the seaweed. No one drinks anything else within a parsec. Don't like to drink? Then just try smoking a little." She didn't mention the blue salve given to her by "Shannon."

"No one seems to have assembled those pieces and considered that a single agent may be driving our indulgence of all these Nartressan products."

"You're wondering why more isn't known about Nartressa."

"Exactly!" she said, nearly shouting. "There's an imperial research station on nearly every planet with a viable alien biosphere. Nartressa has a biodiversity whose complexity exceeds ninety-nine percent of the planets known to the Empire. Where's the research station?" She sipped her brew and stepped away from the viewport. His gaze had stayed upon it, and upon the planet beyond it.

"What do you think?"

He'd said it in such a monotone that Honeydew wasn't sure he really wanted an answer. Perhaps it was just his way of acknowledging how many questions there were for which they had no answers.

"Well?"

"Well, what?"

"What do you think?"

"I think the seaweed is trying to get your attention."

Chapter 9

"I think the seaweed is trying to get our attention."

Janine climbed out of the access tunnel, shivering at the cold night air. It had been warmer below, where the wind off the ocean could not penetrate.

Directly above them blinked one of the orbital cannery stations, the burner of a suborbital approaching it, the ring of lights around the orbital cannery defining its shape.

On her corn, Janine had the subterranean biocomputer provide her with an analysis of a typical cannery.

Numbers spilled down her corn.

She and Randall had set up secured links between their subdurals and the research station biomainframe. Knowing they would be missed if they weren't back at the hotel by dawn, they'd decided against exploring the facility further, but instead had asked the newly reactivated biomainframe why it had been shut down.

"Information not currently available. Data missing, and appears to have been deliberately destroyed. Reconstruct from parity files?"

As any effort to destroy such sensitive information would surely include all forms of archiving, Janine doubted it would be successful, but had ordered the computer to proceed anyway.

On the climb up, so as not to alert anyone to their having reactivated the microfusion core, they'd foregone using the lift. The descent having taken an hour, the ascent had taken two, the motion sensors along the way lighting the stairwell, which previously had been lit only by their handheld.

"What a way to get our attention," Randall replied, turning to help Shannon up the ladder. Older and now wheezing from the long climb, Shannon sounded exhausted.

"You going to be all right?" Janine asked, not able to see his face in the dark. The only light was a hint of dawn in the east.

"Yeah," Shannon said. "Takes me a little longer to recover."

"Next time we'll take the lift." Janine glanced upward again, the orbital cannery eerily clear.

"Best time of night to see it," Shannon said.

"Ever been up there?"

"They tried to relocate me there after the accident. Had trouble standing at the conveyors for long periods."

"Nartressa looks beautiful from orbit." Janine had seen it from orbit on the incoming shuttle.

"Like a pearl," Shannon said, nodding. "Meet again tonight?"

"Sure, same time?" she asked.

They said their goodbyes, Janine and Randall heading toward the main part of town, where their hotel was.

"It might take us days to find out why the research station was shut down."

Janine just grunted, wondering how much to convey to the Director of the Institute on Sydney. Accustomed to having a fair degree of latitude in how she conducted her research, Janine still knew that the unearthing of a heretofore unknown research station was vital information and "eyes only" for the director.

She reminded herself it was heretofore unknown to her.

Not so deep in the bowels of the imperial bureaucracy. Which was why she felt reluctant to disclose its existence before she found out why it had been shuttered.

The small city known as Rockdale was mostly grid-like in layout, only its outer areas proving less orderly. They strode along a dark and quiet street, shops interspersed with homes, all of them having the rocky facades common to the planet, as Nartressa was nearly devoid of trees. If the seaweed might be dried and used for building, she thought idly, then there might be some relief from the drab-colored rock.

The buildings grew taller, the sky behind them lighter, and Janine's eyes more watery.

"Breakfast before bed?" Randall asked, gesturing at a corner diner, its seats filled, the lights bright inside.

Janine shook her head. "I'd fall asleep on the pancakes."

Occasional passers-by nodded as they reached the main part of the city, and the sun lit the top of their hotel.

Janine looked toward the hotel entrance. "Uh, Randall, I don't like the look of those people."

* * *

He didn't either.

He liked it less when the small knot of people saw them, and hurried their way.

"Come on," he said, and pulled her into an alley. "Fast!" he said, hissing through his teeth and breaking into a run, keeping her arm tucked under his. Among them, he'd recognized a few trawler crew members whom Janine had interviewed earlier in the week.

A light on his corn flashed red, drawing a map. They had a hundred yard lead. Randall led her down the alley to the next street, up half a block, and then he pulled her into a building entrance and glanced back to the alley twenty-five feet away.

No pursuers yet.

His corn indicated they should enter.

The door opened to his touch. An apartment, multi-story.

Ascend stairs one floor.

Once there, his corn told him, take the only elevator to the fifth floor, the top. The lack of a view made him nervous, but he couldn't have said why. Fifth floor corridor down to the end, and stairwell down one floor.

The elevator lights indicated that the elevator was already descending. A second elevator opened, as though beckoning. His corn told him to take it.

He stepped inside, pulling Janine with him.

"Do you know what you're doing?" She sounded scared.

He shook his head. "I have no idea." But something or someone was guiding him.

On the panel beside the door, the light indicating the basement lit up without his pushing it.

Janine gasped, and Randall began to sweat. "I wonder who's controlling this thing."

The doors trundled open to a dank, dark basement, and a long corridor lit up before them. Randall saw no other way to go but forward.

Janine pushed the elevator buttons to no avail.

"Push the emergency button."

Dead silence. No response.

"We won't be getting back on," she said.

Somehow he'd known that. "We won't need to," he replied, knowing that too, but not knowing how he knew.

The corridor was plain, the walls without break or feature, the ceiling with a bare light every six feet.

Ending in a door. He pulled on the handle.

It opened to his touch.

Beyond it, a cage. And a lift.

Colder air crept up his legs. Cold air from deep in the earth.

Metal grid beneath his feet, he glanced at Janine.

Her eyes wide, she stood rooted to the corridor floor, shaking her head.

"There's nowhere else to go," he said, certain of that as of the sunrise. "I don't remember seeing two elevators in the lobby, do you?"

She shook her head, little fast shakes like those of a nervous puppy.

Randall swallowed hard. "I don't like it either. Come on." He was surprised when she stepped aboard the lift without further prompting. Machinery deep below began to whine, and the cage dropped, sheer rock wall on one face, the surface smooth but scarred, as though chiseled hurriedly.

A hundred, two hundred, perhaps three hundred feet.

Randall soon lost all sense of proportion. The chill deepened, and they clutched each other for warmth, their breath frosty with steam. The single bulb above them seemed the only source of warmth besides the other person.

Ice streaks appeared on the rock.

Then the cage jerked to a halt and the cage door slid aside, where a rock ledge opened onto a narrow corridor.

They took it, a chillier breeze blowing steadily between the rough-hewn walls. The floor was mostly even.

A glowglobe approached, floating inexplicably just above head-height. It stopped a few feet away, blinked off twice, then retreated from them, stopping twenty feet down the corridor.

Randall realized they should follow it. "Come on." He led her slowly along the cold passageway, his feet stirring up dust on the uneven floor. Except it wasn't dust.

It was snow.

The glowglobe retreated, a slight hum indicating an antigrav unit. The globe stopped when they stopped, resumed when they followed, and Randall soon saw why. Passageways branched off the one they followed, at odd angles and odd times, without any apparent logic or order. Some sloped downward and some up. Some were warmer and he longed to follow them, especially when he realized he was shivering.

The passage curved gently around, staying mostly level but descending for short periods, the glowglobe staying consistently twenty feet ahead.

Then the passage way opened into a cavern.

Several doorways of converging passages opened off the cavern. Across from them were two closed doors beside each other.

In the center of the cavern was what appeared to be a lift, above it a shaft. A stiff breeze sang a low hum between the lattices of the metal-grid flooring.

The glowglobe led them around the lift to the pairs of doors, then settled against the wall above and between the two doors, where it winked out.

"Journey's over," Janine said, smirking.

Randall saw light seeping from under both doors. "I think it's just beginning."

When he stepped in front of the left-hand door it slid aside. Beyond, modestly-appointed quarters awaited an occupant. He felt the warmth from inside, and yearned to enter. He felt so tired.

He stepped in front of the other door, but it remained closed. Janine joined him and the door slid aside. "Odd," she said. "Here, I'll try that one." She stood in front of the door that had opened for him.

Didn't budge. They exchanged a glance. "That one's mine, apparently, and this one's yours."

They traded places, and both their doors opened.

"I don't know about you, but I'm desperate for a warm place to sleep."

He looked at her and nodded, then stepped across the threshold. The door slid shut behind him.

Inside, another door connected the two rooms.

A small bed against one wall, a kitchenette just inside the door, a third door to a ...

He realized he'd needed to relieve himself for a long time.

"Excuse me," she said, and disappeared.

He did the same.

Shower stall, clothes cleanser, hair helm, sink and of course ...

He sighed, grateful.

The mirror told him he'd been up all night. So did his eyes, which threatened to close as he watched.

When he'd finished, he looked at the open door between the two suites and wondered whether she wanted it closed.

He found himself on the bed and never got a chance to ask.

* * *

The protein soup in the giant glasma cauldron bubbled ominously as he gave the order to add the electrolytes.

Injection nozzles at equidistant points around the cauldron injected a blue liquid into the greenish fluid surrounding the protein, its surface smooth. Internal pumps turned the chorionic fluids a deep aqua, and the protein ball twitched, twitched, and twitched.

The encephalometers lit up.

"I think it's waking, Sir," said his young lab assistant, his voice clipped and precise.

Brian sat up in a cold sweat, waking at a knock.

"You asked me to wake you, Sir," said his young attaché, his voice clipped and precise.

Same voice.

Brian shuddered, shaking off the dream. "Thank you, Steve," he said quietly, not wanting to wake the slumbering woman beside him. Somehow, their joining had been more exhilarating and passionate than their first time on Bora Bora, in spite of his having brutalized her just yesterday.

She reminded him of someone he'd once loved, and loved deeply.

But I've never been in love with anyone, Brian thought—not that I remember.

He still didn't understand what had come over him.

His attaché waited in the kitchen, fixing what looked like eggs Julienne. "Sir, as it appears your stay here will be longer than anticipated, I've arranged for accommodations ground-side at the Rockdale Hilton."

"Why there?" Brian couldn't remember why he'd heard the name before. Hiltons were on nearly every planet.

Steve shrugged. "The largest Aquafoods installation on Nartressa is in Rockdale, Sir, no other reason. I can change it if you have concerns."

"No, no," Brian said waving it away. He looked out the floor-to-ceiling viewport. From the look of the planet surface, the sea awash with light, it appeared to be noontime planet-side.

"I tried to find something with a comparable view, Sir."

Brian snorted. "Room there for her?"

"Yes, Sir." The attaché seemed pleased his humor had been appreciated.

He'd listened for but hadn't heard any hint of disapprobation. *Why would I need his approval?*

Brian ate without tasting, showered without feeling, dressed without looking, the whole time reviewing catch-volume reports on his corn. Since the implementation of the quarter-mile rule yesterday, volume was down fifty percent, and assembly lines at the orbital canneries were sending workers home early. Fish futures had doubled, and the Galactic Board of Trade had opened an investigation into possible market manipulation. Further, the Occupational Health Board had launched an inquiry into the sinking of the four trawlers and two suborbitals, and had done so in addition to requiring that Aquafoods review its safety procedures.

Blasted bureaucracies! he thought, aggravated at their meddling. *The next thing you know, they'll send an intelligence agency in here to tell me they've been spying on the seaweed!*

He'd just put the finishing touches on his couture when Honeydew emerged, yawning.

"I missed breakfast, didn't I?"

"Steve left something in the oven, I think."

When she slipped her arms around him, he considered reprimanding her, unaccustomed to displays of affection from anyone. She let go and retreated to the kitchen, where she found breakfast.

"I'll be meeting with the planetary executive team and then we'll be moving planet side. Steve's arranged for the penthouse suite at the Rockdale Hilton."

Sounds of eating ceased.

"What is it?" He could see from the living room that she looked pale, more so than usual.

"Nothing. I'm sure it'll be all right."

"You won't be anywhere near the beach."

"I realize. Scares me even so, but I'll manage."

He nodded, turned his attention back to the mirror, adjusted the handkerchief in his left breast pocket.

A knock at the door.

Odd, Brian thought, knowing almost no one had access to the corridors in this part of the orbital cannery. He waved to Honeydew to retreat to the bedroom, indicating quiet.

Then he went to the door.

"Brian Franks?" a dark-suited bureaucrat asked. Then she flipped out a badge. "Galactic Bureau of Investigation."

* * *

"What did they want?" Honeydew asked, trying to divert her attention from their destination. She had been clutching the armrests so tightly, she could barely pull her fingers off of them. They were halfway to their destination, and even before they'd left the orbital cannery, Honeydew had been panicking.

Return to Nartressa?

Set foot on that horrifying planet?

Where the seaweed had dragged her ...

She had to remind herself that she didn't remember what happened, that for a long time she had thought that the entire experience was a drug-induced dream. Until three years ago, when she'd started to have nightmares about the incident. Something had happened on Nartressa, and even if she wasn't sure exactly what, the thought of returning to the planet cramped her gut, set her heart aflutter, caused her scalp to crawl, and put beads of sweat on her forehead.

"Said they needed access to our surveillance cams in Rockdale," Brian told her, "suspected some kind of nefarious activity there. They were pretty close-mouthed about what they were looking for. Smelled bad to me, so I told 'em to stick their request into their backsides."

Honeydew laughed. "You didn't!"

"Of course I did."

She was so amused, her trepidation faded somewhat.

The land mass below them looked puny, set upon a nearly endless sea. The Nartressan surface being ninety percent water, Honeydew realized just how little land surface there actually was. The sea surrounding the tiny continent, one of two continents on the entire planet, was patched with discoloration, the patches covering nearly half the open water.

"What are those darker patches?" she asked.

"Seaweed forests," Brian replied, bringing the yacht into a turn.

The momentum pushed her into the seat. "Seaweed?" Honeydew tried to wrap her mind around just how much that was. The best she could come up with was millions of plants. She said so.

"At least a half-a-billion, by our best estimates," Brian told her. "In other words, we don't know."

Honeydew was mystified. "This is the hundredth page of our novel, and we don't even know how many seaweed plants there are?"

"Look, I'm not here to research the native life forms. I'm here to make profit. It happens that this is the most profitable fishing lease in the Aquafoods portfolio, and the most prolific by volume in the history of such operations, and both of these facts are high motivation to keep this operation running smoothly. I'll rip out the seaweed stalk by stalk if I have to. I'm not about to let a pesky plant get in the way of my harvest."

She heard the resolve, thought about the number of plants, and shook her head.

The yacht leveled out over the ocean west of the island, its tallest feature—the Hilton—plain in their viewport. Her anxiety was not assuaged by their having the penthouse suite. Any place on Nartressa was too close to the seaweed.

The yacht landed smoothly, and Honeydew rushed into the penthouse just to avoid looking toward the sea, visible on three sides.

Inside, the penthouse was palatial, but its uncovered windows provided her no surcease from the sea, so she sought the nearest bathroom.

"Are you hiding?" Brian asked.

Honeydew realized she'd been cowering between the shower and the sauna for nearly an hour, curled up on the floor, the only place where she couldn't see a speck of ocean.

He closed the bathroom window blinds. "I've closed the blinds all around the lower floor. Sorry, I didn't realize this would be so difficult."

When she emerged, her trepidation was substantially lower, but she still felt panicky, as though some impending doom lurked from below, like a giant watchful eye, or the tongue of a gargantuan lizard.

She picked her way through a meal, too anxious to eat or even appreciate how good the food was.

The suite was lavish, with high ceilings, windows on three walls, and swimming pool taking up half the lounge area, the loft area accessed by an all-glass staircase spiraling around a glittering column of crushed crystal, the gurgle of the small waterfall soothing.

"I'm heading to the bay. They've recovered a trawler that was dragged under last week. I need you to come with me."

Honeydew was so anxious that she didn't really hear his explanation, just something about an "assistant." The wardrobe of precisely-cut business suits was fascinating, as much for the distraction they provided her as the wonderment they induced. She'd always looked on from afar with an odd mixture of envy, disgust, and disdain as smart-looking women in such dress had hammered out contract details and logistical analyses.

She looked at herself in the mirror with similar feelings.

"Just don't smile," he told her.

He needn't have said. She couldn't have smiled if she'd wanted, she was so nervous.

In the hotel foyer, booted-and-bearded trawler crew tracked their progress to the door. Several lined the sidewalk as well. She heard one mutter something about an offworlder.

Brian stopped to interrogate the older woman with shoulders wider than his.

"Doin' here? Waitin' to ask that Xeno-somethin'-or-other to ask what's she doin' about the weed attacks. Why ain't she stopping them?"

The other pedestrians on their way to the docks looked equally afraid, peering furtively from under low brims, their collars turned up against the sea-blown chill.

"Not a friendly folk," Honeydew said.

"Nearly all have lost friends or family."

"Probably wondering if they're next," she added walking briskly at his side downhill toward the trawler repair facility.

Just out to sea, a ferry skimmed rough waters toward an inlet. Cranes towered over the bay, one winching out a large barge, its container bay empty.

"That's a trawler, isn't it?" She saw him nod and reach into his pocket.

He showed an ID to the guard at the gate.

"Mr. Franks!" The guard snapped to attention. "An honor! No idea you'd be here today. I'll—"

"Keep it to yourself and earn a bonus. Surprise inspection. One word to anyone and I won't be happy."

"Yes, Sir!"

She followed Brian down to the dry dock, where the still-dripping trawler rested on trusses, looking forlorn. Stands of seaweed lay across both bow and stern, and everything was coated with a layer of silt, as though she'd lain on the seabed for months, not days. "Why so dirty already?"

"That silt is actually bacteria—Oxyphilic bacteria. The Nartressan seas are anaerobic—no air to speak of in the water, and this bacteria is what removes that air."

Ferry passengers strolled past the dry dock, many of them looking morosely toward the drydocked trawler, some of them stopping to contemplate the recovered vessel with looks of awe.

"She was a fine ship, she was," one sailor said, turning toward Honeydew, "Did a tour on her just last year, rode rough seas like a champ, seemed to steer clear of the weed like she knew it'd be her doom." The man turned and sniffled, blinking rapidly.

From the other direction, other trawler crew were heading toward the ferry, exchanging banter with the incoming crew.

"How long do they stay out there?"

Brian frowned. "Two weeks, twelve hour shifts. The days here are closer to thirty hours, so their shifts are probably fifteen. Two weeks out to sea, one week back on land."

She saw that the disembarking crew looked significantly more disheveled and bedraggled, their step dragging, their shoulders slumped, while the sailors going the other direction looked fresh, bright and trim.

Brian pulled her with him into the stream of embarking crew. "Where you going this tour?" he asked a thick-chested sailor with tattoos to his wrists.

"South toward Hurstville aboard the Norma Jean. We'll be lucky with the distance restrictions to have half our usual twenty-five to thirty containers.

Don't know what idiot ordered that. Me, I'd rather risk the weed than leave the hold empty. The fish follow the weed. Everyone knows that. Say, you look like a suit from corporate. Hope I didn't offend anyone."

Honeydew tried not to laugh, couldn't help but smile.

They followed the sailor aboard. "How long 'til we shove off?"

"Give it a couple hours. They're still loading provisions." The thick-chested sailor went below while Honeydew followed Brian aft.

"The bay is so quiet," she said, the activity behind them seeming muted.

A jetty extended halfway across the inlet, waves breaking against its far side. Half the bay was occupied by Aquafoods trawlers and ferries, the other half looking like the sleepy port that it should have looked like.

Honeydew stood at the aft railing, drinking in the sights, sounds and swells, a slight apple scent upon the wind.

Below, iridescent hydrocarbon effluent common to such harbors reflected the cloudy sky at her.

She gasped at motion.

"What is it?"

"I thought I saw a tentacle." She clutched the gunwale tightly.

"Ridiculous. The seaweed never comes in this far."

The ship shifted under them, and just off the stern, three tentacles thick as tree trunks leapt from the water.

Honeydew screamed.

Chapter 10

"Janine?"

She heard Randall's voice though the thick metal door. "In here," she called, not looking up from her work.

"What are you doing?" He stopped just inside the door. "Is that a mobile med-surge extensible?" he asked behind her.

She turned to look, saw he was admiring a machine against the wall behind her. Just like an EMT, she thought, smiling. "Ever use one?"

"Yeah, but only briefly. Wish we had a mobile unit here on Nartressa. You know how many patients have died en route, when all they needed was an on-the-spot appendectomy? Fifteen minute procedure with one of these med-surges. I should take it with me."

"Yeah? That's nothing. This lab extensible is really a fine piece of equipment." Janine had each hand sheathed in an extensible, the wall display lit up with diagrams, a red-green-and-blue triple helix snaking from one side, numbers spilling down the other. "Watch what happens when I expose this Nartressan DNA to a little oxygen." She moved a sleeved hand forward and to the right.

On screen, a yellow O2 moved to a protein pair, held by its covalent bond in a pair of atomic-sized pincers, and the moment the oxygen touched, one of every three proteins—the ones marked zeta and epsi—collapsed, and the pair reorganized themselves with the remaining proteins into a double helix, the collapse releasing a vapor.

"That looks familiar, like regular DNA."

"It is regular DNA," Janine said. "The introduction of oxygen causes a break-down in the zeta and epsi proteins, triggers a reorganization, and makes the result look like the usual building blocks of life. No one has ever seen a genetic structure like this."

Randall looked doubtful. "Why not?"

"Because the six-protein triple helix devolves into the four-protein double helix that we're all accustomed to looking at." She renewed the display to bring back the triple helix. "These two proteins, zeta and espi, are unstable in contact with oxygen. Hence the poison Nartressan seas—since the only bacteria able to grow in the water is anaerobic, able to thrive only in the absence of air."

"So where does the seaweed get its air? Doesn't it at least need carbon dioxide, like all plants?"

"Absorbs carbon dioxide, gives off oxygen, or so our conventional organic carbonaceous cycle would lead us to believe. On Nartressa, something takes the air out of the water without killing the fish, and does so quite effectively—or the seaweed would die. I suspect we have an unknown agent in the water that binds with air—carbon dioxide, specifically—and takes it to the seaweed, where the carbon is integrated into the plant," she said.

"But what happens to the oxygen?"

"That's the mystery." Janine saw he was shaking his head. "There are mysteries within mysteries in this ecosystem. One detail that's not a mystery is that life here is far more fragile—" she gestured at the triple helix—"than we know, and I'm willing to bet Aquafoods Interstellar would pay billions of galacti to learn about this!" She gestured with an extensible, the screen image holding up an O2 molecule.

"Janine?"

His tone of voice sounds way too serious, she thought.

"Haven't you wondered why we were brought here? Why a laboratory equipped with all your favorite toys happens to be across from quarters that appear to have been designed to cater directly to your tastes?"

Janine heard a note of panic in his voice. Waking after a restful sleep and finding the laboratory had delighted her, and she had not wondered for a moment at the inconceivability of it. She knew that Nartressa should have a research laboratory similar to the one on Sydney. Of course she would find it.

"Doesn't it seem strange to you?" he asked.

She shook her head. "Not for a moment." She didn't understand his snort of disgust. "What are you saying?"

"Don't you see? We're being lured down here."

She snorted back. "Ridiculous."

Out in the corridor, a metal gate crashed against stone.

Janine followed him out.

The lift had stopped at their level, its arrow pointing downward.

Behind her, the laboratory door slammed shut.

She tried to get back in, but it was locked. She raised her eyebrows at Randall. He smirked. "Believe me now?"

She put her hands on her hips. "If this place wants me to do anything, it'll have to bring me my spiderbot!" She looked around and waited for something to happen. When nothing did, she looked at him. "What now, pilot?"

"Doesn't look like we have a choice, does it?" He gestured at the lift.

* * *

Randall was surprised she got on as fast as she did. Not afraid of much, he thought, appreciating that in her. He joined her on the lift, and they dropped into darkness.

The descent slowed, stopped, and the lift began to accelerate to the side.

"What the weed?" he said, startled by the motion.

"Sideways elevator," she said, "standard equipment."

The wind rushed past them through the metal grate, the tunnel nearly pitch black.

When the lift slowed, he was ready, leaning back against the deceleration. And then the lift went up and stopped, jerking to a halt. Lights went on. The rotunda looked nearly identical to the one they'd left. Unlike it, this was heated and lighted. Three passageways entered what was clearly some kind of control room. Opposite them were three more passageways labeled "submersible."

Randall stepped toward the control room, Janine toward the submersibles. Displays on the walls were duplicated on his corn. Three monitoring stations with multiple camera views showed all systems in standby. He looked for signs of neglect, decades having passed since its last use. He found no neglect, but neither did he find any indication of recent occupation.

A sanibot emerged from a wall and began to clean all surfaces thoroughly.

Frowning, he went to find Janine.

She was just emerging from a "submersible" tunnel. "They're in perfect condition—just what I need to study the seaweed up close!"

He spent the next ten minutes trying to discourage her, but couldn't, no matter what he said. Had his wife tried to dissuade him from a particularly dangerous mission, she'd have been just as unsuccessful.

"Look, at least wear one of these enviroshells."

Three suits lined each corridor.

Grudgingly, she donned one.

So did he.

"Uh, you should stay here," she said.

"I'm going with you," he insisted, and he wouldn't let her dissuade him.

The submersible cabin was large enough of three people, its hull made of six-inch thick glasma, the depth here too great for any light but the faintest to penetrate from the ocean surface. Randall saw his corn link in, and his subdural connected with the submersible computer, coke beeping. Arrayed in a circle around the cabin were various extensibles in all shapes and sizes, some of them shaped so bizarrely that their purpose eluded him.

"Power up," Janine said, her voice echoed immediately on his coke.

The ship hummed to life, and external lights flared. They both gasped. Hundreds of plants in a variety of shapes, sizes, and colors filled their displays. The thick jungle looked impenetrable.

"Must have grown around the pod while it lay berthed."

"We should be able to cut our way through," Randall said.

At that moment, his corn flashed.

"Delivery in the rotunda?" Janine said. "Down here?"

They exchanged a glance.

"I'll go see." Randall made his way out of the hatch and into the corridor without too much resistance from the bulky enviroshell.

In the rotunda, in front of the lift was a valise. Identical to the one Janine had lost in the hover crash.

The spiderbot.

He took it to Janine.

The blood left her face when she saw it. Wordlessly, she took the valise and headed for the exit.

The submersible came to life, snapped its doors closed, half pinching her in its grasp.

Randall leapt to her aid, trying to force the doors to loosen their grip.

Janine gasped, "I can barely breathe."

Randall put two hands on the nearest edge, a foot on the farthest edge, and tried to pry them apart, grunting with strain.

Janine pushed as well, one hip and part of a shoulder firmly wedged between the doors.

Red lights flashed and bells rang, warnings of imminent launch.

"Push!"

And Randall redoubled his effort. The submersible bucked, and water spilled over his leg.

Janine slipped out, and he let the doors slide shut, the pod shuddering as it slid from its berth.

Water sloshing across the floor, Randall dragged himself to a chair and strapped himself in, the submersible navigating itself through the thick underwater forest, unresponsive to his commands.

He wondered where it was taking him.

* * *

Brian pulled his blaster from his underarm holster and fired at the middle tentacle.

The branch recoiled but stayed erect, and three more tentacles leapt from the water on either side, lashing themselves across the ferry aft. The three tentacles hovering over the stern dropped onto the deck, the middle one between Brian and Honeydew.

There was no place to run, he saw.

The middle tentacle that Brian had fired upon lay at Honeydew's feet. The burn marks just a foot away. The two-foot thick tentacle glistened with seawater, its surface looking rubbery, leaves the color and texture of spinach lining its length.

We're surely dead, he thought, the ferry lurching under him. He looked at Honeydew, the deck beginning to tilt, the ship groaning under the strain.

She looked calm, despite her initial scream, her gaze on the burnt tentacle at her feet.

She knelt.

"What're you doing?"

And put her hands on either side of the burn. Her hands turned blue, and the charred flesh was slowly replaced by healthy-looking seaweed.

The seaweed stopped pulling on the ferry, water lapping over the gunwale, the stern only inches from going under.

As though it were a piece of clothing and just as light, she lifted the tentacle and wrapped herself in it.

The ferry righted itself as two tentacles slid off into the bay, and Honeydew wrapped herself from neck to toe in the third.

"No, don't!" he pleaded. Somehow, he knew what she was doing.

She stopped and looked at him. "It's the only way." And the tentacle yanked her off the ferry deck and into the bay.

The splash and bubbles were all that remained.

Standing at the gunwale, Brian stared at the water, wondering how she had known what to do. Others began to crowd around.

"Sacrificed herself, she did," said the thick-chested sailor with tattoos all the way to his wrists. "Sacrificed herself for us all."

* * *

Blue turtles swam around her in the thick green liquid, playfully nudging her.

Honeydew wondered what happened to her clothes, then decided she didn't care. She breathed the viscous gel as she might breathe air, and other than the tickle of a gag reflex, the gel went in and out easily, and she never felt out of breath.

The herd of blue turtles was guiding her somewhere. She swam along among them, enjoying their caresses, hanging onto the shell of one, then another, the animals seeming to enjoy her touch.

She vaguely remembered the ferry and her initial terror, but that terror had quickly fled when Brian had fired upon the tentacle. She had known desperation, seeing the tentacles wrapping the ferry, but it was the desperation of the seaweed itself, which seemed to communicate itself through the tentacle at her feet.

She had knelt and placed her hands on either side of the blaster wound and the whole world opened to her, an awareness of billions of plants and their bewilderment at their offspring being harvested relentlessly.

The wound had healed under her hands, a tingling surging through her palms and into the rubbery tentacle skin, and the seaweed plant had stopped its assault on the ferry.

Honeydew sensed desperation but also curiosity from the seaweed, so she had bade it to wrap itself around her.

As it coiled around her, she had known what she needed to do. And all fear had left her.

Now, hours later, the ferry a distant memory, Honeydew spied a bulbous capsule ahead, floating in the viscous green fluid, tubes as big around as she was tall attached to the capsule.

She swam toward it, the herd of blue turtles dispersing.

The outer membrane was rubbery and semi-translucent, and she wondered how to get inside.

A series of ridges formed, each one about a foot apart, one under her hands, and she pulled herself along them, ladder like, toward the underside, which appeared to be flattened.

There she found an aperture, and she pulled herself into the capsule, and into air. The viscous green liquid spilled down her front as she exhaled it, and she coughed the last of it from her lungs.

Breathing air again, she felt her nudity. Nothing to be done about it now, she thought, and looked around.

Triangular passages as tall as she was converged on the bulbous capsule, a total of six, she counted. They angled away, some up, some down, but all of them at a gentle enough incline that she could take any wherever they led.

And where did they go? she wondered. One that went downward, she saw through the semi-translucent capsule wall, immediately plunged into the sea floor. Some of them were completely straight, so she couldn't look along them. Her sense was that they were conduits, but what did they conduct? And where? And for what purpose? She was thinking that the xeno-whatever woman would probably know, but Honeydew had no experience with such things.

Then why was I chosen? she wondered.

In a state of wonder and awe, she went to each of the six passageways, seeing their blue ribbing and rounded triangular shapes. She went in one a few feet, felt the warm rubbery texture of the ribs, and how they recoiled slightly at her touch. Her feet also sank slightly into the floor in a similar way.

She looked up at the capsule ceiling, realizing then that the reason she could see was because everything gave off its own luminescence.

Even her own hand.

Staring, fascinated, she didn't see where the pod came from.

She turned when she heard the thump.

A globular submersible rested between two tubes where they attached to the capsule. Inside the submersible, whose outer shell was completely transparent, lay a figure, a human being.

He looks unconscious, she thought, I wonder if he's hurt. She stepped back to the aperture and dived into the viscous green liquid, swam around to the submersible and tried the hatch.

Stuck.

She realized that the man's face and eyes had followed her. Not unconscious, but certainly in some distress, as he appeared not to be moving otherwise.

She swam around to the front, where she could see him the most clearly. She gestured to the hatch, motioned that he open it.

His hand flopped toward a switch panel, and machinery whirred. Thick green liquid surged into the submersible, and Honeydew swam around, unstrapped him, and pulled him from the vehicle. She hung onto him and maneuvered him down the side of the capsule toward the aperture.

Now, how to get him inside?

Having nothing to hold onto, Honeydew tried to shove him up into the capsule through the aperture. Failing that, she draped one of his arms over the rim, went around, draped the other arm over the rim, checked to see that he wouldn't slide away, then climbed into the capsule and pulled him in.

She realized he wasn't breathing.

A pulse, but weak, his toes beginning to turn blue.

She leaned on his chest, pushing out the water. Air went in, but still he didn't breathe. Ripping open the chest seam of his enviroshell, she put her palms to his chest.

Her vision narrowed, and she entered a tube filled with bluish platelets, an occasional white globule visible. She swam through them into a small chamber, seeing that the larger chamber beside it fluttered rapidly. She put her hands on the chamber walls and shocked it. A regular rhythm resumed, and she heard the sucking of air as a bellows somewhere inflated. The fluid surged around and propelled her out as she lifted her hands from his rising chest.

He coughed, sputtered and rolled over, wheezing and coughing to clear his lungs.

Honeydew sighed, knowing he would be all right.

He shook his head and looked around, coughed again. "Who're you?" His eyes traveled up and down her body.

"I'm..." She looked at him blankly, unable to come up with her own name. Odd, she thought, I know what I want to say. "My name is..." Again, words failed her.

His brows drew together.

"I try to say my name, and the words won't come out my mouth. My name is—" She gasped in disbelief. "You must think I'm crazy! I know my name!"

"It's clear you do, but can't say it. Don't you have any clothes to wear?" His eyes traveled the length of her body again.

She knew that look, but now it felt different. That man look, the one they got when they wanted to fornicate. Whether they were paying for it or not, what felt different was how it felt to her. Now she felt ... anxious.

Somehow, she'd changed.

When did that happen? she wondered.

"Any other enviroshells in the, uh ..." She looked toward the vessel he'd arrived in.

"Submersible? No enviroshells, but I'll bet there's formalls."

"I'll go see." She stood.

"How can you hold your breath that long?"

Looking down at him, she saw how hard he tried not to look at her body, and how quickly he failed. "Hold my ...? You can't breathe it?"

His eyes went wide.

She dove in as easily as a fish, swam around to look at him through the semi-transparent membrane. Shrugging at him, she paddled to the hatch of the submersible. Inside, she opened compartments until she found what she wanted. Sealing the hatch, she swam back underneath.

Being formalls, they formed themselves to her body and didn't conceal much, but at least he looked more comfortable.

"How'd you get down here?" he asked.

She made a swimming motion, vaguely remembering the tentacle that she'd wrapped herself in. "What's your name?"

"Randall Simmons, EMT," he said. The patch at his left breast said, "Nartressan Dispatch & Rescue."

"Where'd you get the submersible?"

"It got me," he retorted and began telling her what happened.

She listened with increasing concern, asking questions to put together what he'd been through. "Research station? Under Rockdale? You and this Xeno-whatever from Sydney they sent to tell us why the seaweed is killing people?"

"Yeah, Janine Meriwether, Doctor of Xenobiology, or something like that. What's your name?"

Honeydew smiled. "My name is—" Her mouth opened and no sound came out.

"Been through something yourself, it sounds like."

"Brian and I were on the stern of a ferry when the seaweed attacked. It was getting ready to pull the ferry under when I stopped it."

"You?" He threw his head back and laughed, and then the laugh faltered.

"I coiled a tentacle around myself, and ..." Honeydew couldn't quite describe what she'd done. "It dragged me into the water and left the ferry alone. I was guided down here by a herd of blue turtles." She smiled at the memory. "They were so playful."

He shook his head. "How do we get out of here?"

The question hadn't occurred to her. "There's a reason to leave?"

He looked at her oddly. "These blue passageways, have you explored any of them?"

She shook her head.

"Just like my dream."

She recalled hers, and remembered what Brian had told her of his. "You dreamt too?"

He nodded. "So did Janine."

"Triangular blue tubes, ribbed and rubbery, green viscous liquid with bubbles suspended in it, and a pulsating pump like some type of heart." She looked past him at one passageway, one that led upward. "Let's try it."

The floor was soft and gave as they walked on it. The almost-gummy walls converged overhead, the gentle undulations about six inches apart, the whole structure emitting a soft blue glow.

The tunnel curved up and to the right, taking it above the one beside it, which curved down and to the left. The gentle ascent brought them to an intersection with a similar blue, triangular tube about eight feet tall, ten feet wide at the base.

"We have to keep track of where we came from," he said. "In my dream I got lost."

She felt his anxiety, wondered at it, and wondered that she felt none. Even her not being able to say her own name seemed a simple inconvenience, not something to worry about.

A pulse of light rippled along the crossways corridor toward them. Randall pulled back but Honeydew held her position, sensing no menace.

The light reached the junction, flickered between the four different arches, then went the direction they'd been heading. Another pulse approached and without hesitation followed the first, then another.

"It's telling us we should follow."

"The last time I did what it said, it trapped me in the submersible. Come on," and he took a step into the right-hand passage.

A red field lit the ribbing and a "zzzt" of electricity sent Randall to his knees.

"Uh, I think we're supposed to go this way."

He stood, looking a little disoriented, his gaze on the now-red passageway. "I think so, too."

Honeydew led the way, the half-spiral straightening. Ahead was rock, the tunnel penetrating seamlessly.

It abruptly turned and ended at what looked like a normal, human-manufacture pressure door.

They looked at each other. "Do you think someone built the tubes?" Randall asked.

"I think someone grew them." Shaking her head, Honeydew turned the wheel.

Chapter 11

Shaking her head, Janine turned the wheel.

The research station had not obstructed her ascent, nor had it aided. After she'd squeezed out of the submersible, she'd returned to the lower rotunda, frightened and expecting the machinery to pursue her.

It had been as still as before.

Getting oriented had been baffling, until she remembered to use her encrypted optimitter. Guided by the map on her corn, she'd made her way upward, finding what looked like an exit to the surface, a pressure door with a wheel in the middle.

The seal stuck.

Probably hasn't been used in a long time, she thought, trying to remain positive, not wanting to acknowledge the other possibilities.

She tugged on the wheel.

Nothing.

The wheel seemed to be working properly. She turned it to its limits a couple of times, and then pulled, hard.

Nothing.

She examined the seam. If I could just pry it open. The passageway empty, only the spiderbot in hand, she had nothing to pry it open with.

Making sure it was in the open position, she put her foot on the jamb and pulled on the wheel.

Nothing.

Guess I'm not supposed to leave. "Computer," she said on her trake.

"Yes, Doctor Meriwether?" The voice was a soft contralto.

"Open this door."

"I have been instructed not to at this time, Doctor Meriwether."

"So I'm supposed to starve?"

"Adequate sustenance is available near command central."

The map on her corn highlighted the location, six levels below where she was. "You can't hold me prisoner."

"At this time your attention is required at command central."

"Why?"

"I don't have that information."

Janine sighed, spun the wheel to lock the pressure door, and headed for central, valise in hand, murder in mind.

Central was shaped like a theater, semi-circular tiers of workstations facing a holo that stretched nearly forty feet from floor to ceiling.

She chose a station in the middle, on the third of five tiers, and sat. Opening her valise, she activated the spiderbot. "Good morning, Monkey."

"Good morning, Doctor."

"Call me 'Mama.'"

"Yes, Mama."

"Monkey, record holo screen and all my inputs."

"Recording subdural and holo screen. Interface directly with computer?"

"No. Remain in optimitter communication, but do not interface directly."

"Yes, Mama."

Janine stared at the black holo screens and wondered what she was supposed to do. She remembered her command the first time she and Randall had entered the research station. "Computer, result of earlier instruction to attempt parity reconstruction."

"Parity reconstruction partially complete, projected completion unknown. Full reconstruction unlikely, as parity appears corrupted. Display catalog on parity reconstruction?"

"Display."

The holo came to life, columns of information dropping down the screen, each entry of a vid containing surveillance of events at a critical location inside the research station, at the top the most recent, at the bottom the most remote.

She shortened the timeframe to the ten minutes prior to shut down, chose the room where she now sat.

A tall man with black hair stood right behind the chair she now occupied, his attention on the holo, a vein pulsing at his temple, a runnel of sweat down each cheek, lights flickering in the background.

"See? What did I say?" A woman in military uniform screamed at him. "We have to shut down!"

The man's expression didn't change, but the vein pulsed faster. "You're right. We've failed." He looked to the left, then the right. "Everyone, your attention please. Begin emergency disconnection protocol, all stations, then evacuate immediately. Archive control team, please remove modules containing the last two years and secure them in hover bay twelve aboard shuttle gamma."

Lights flickered across his face as acknowledgments were received.

The holo twisted and collapsed. "Reconstruction incomplete."

Janine backed up the recording. "Profile, please."

The right side of the holo displayed demographic information: "Doctor Samuel Ericson, Chief Civilian Research Director, Nartressa Research Station, 2435 to 2443, born 2401, educated at Brisbane University, Doctorate in Alien Microbiology at age twenty-five, residency completed at Sydney institute of Xenobiology, recruited by Naval Intelligence in 2430. Now missing and presumed dead, having disappeared status-post Research Station shutdown in 2443."

Janine calculated. Forty-four years ago. Not as long as she might have thought. She had seen his work at Sydney, his focus primarily on evolutionary models meant to predict what life forms might appear on habitable worlds, derived from ecological conditions congruent with evolving meteorological factors. As her focus had remained mostly on prion protein development, the basic building blocks of life, his work had borne little relation to hers.

She widened the view, then selected a sequence from a laboratory one month before shutdown.

The same woman in uniform was talking in a low voice with Doctor Ericson. "I agree that the potential capacity of a protein processor with these six nucleotides is exponentially more sophisticated than anything we're currently able to build, but this other experiment … I don't know."

Doctor Ericson raised an eyebrow. "Having ethical concerns? Look, it's clear that the triple helix integrates into the human double helix with an ease whose potential reaches beyond anything we can imagine. I'm not trying to do anything here that anyone else wouldn't want to do. It's essential that we incorporate epsidine and zetasine into our experiments, despite their molecular instability. Our understanding of the Nartressan genome depends on it."

"But why this?" She gestured to a part of the laboratory not captured by the camera. "How does this lead to a greater understanding?"

The image flickered, striations distorting the picture, the sound dropping three octaves and a hiss replacing the upper registers. The corrupted parity disupted the quality of the archive reconstruction.

Janine stopped the vid, searched for the forms "epsidine" and "zetasine."

"Epsidine is the name given to the first of two nucleotides discovered within the triple helix structure of the Nartressan genome, and zetasine is the name given to the second. These names are variations of the fifth and sixth letters of the Ancient Greek alphabet, the first four letters assigned arbitrarily to the four nucleotides of the human genome."

Janine brought up a profile of the woman, whose carrot-red hair was striking for its contrast to the Doctor's jet-black hair.

"Colonel Karen Delaney, Chief Military Commander, Nartressa Research Station, 2439 to 2443, born 2395, graduated first in her class at Brisbane Naval Academy, 2419, graduate Naval Research Academy, 2422, awarded Medal of Valor in non-combat operations on Sydney, 2430, and transferred soon after to Nartressa Research Station."

Janine saw that the list of accreditations went on and on, a highly distinguished career that ended abruptly with "missing and presumed dead, having disappeared status-post research station shutdown in 2443."

Janine requested a list of personnel with similar citations.

Over three hundred.

Twenty three hundred people operated a similar research station on Sydney.

"Computer, known survivors, please."

None.

How does a military and civilian crew of a research station numbering over three hundred turn up missing without a trace? she wondered.

* * *

Randall looked out over the cavern and tried to understand what he was seeing.

The pressure door had opened into some type of control room overlooking a subterranean cavern. Three-tiered and semi-circular, the control room was configured to allow as many as fifteen people to work alongside each other.

Machinery hung from the ceiling cavern, multiple arms whose purpose eluded Randall, like those on the submersible. On the cavern floor were about five hundred pillars, bundles of blue tendrils dropping from the ceiling to each, their tops visible from his vantage point, about half of them alight with a deep blue glow, which was the only source of light. Inside the closest ones were vague humanoid shapes.

"Are those people in there?"

The unnamed woman shook her head. "I don't know."

Randall's scalp tingled as a shiver crawled up his back. He remembered the encrypted optimitter connection he and Janine had set up with the main bio-computer on their first trip underground. "Subdural optimitter link on," he said on his trake.

"Attempting to link. Link verified, identity recognized. Welcome, Randall Simmons."

He looked at the woman. "Can you link in?"

"With what?" She looked at him blankly.

"With the underground biomainframe."

"There's a computer down here?"

Obviously not. "Look, I hate to keep saying, 'Hey, you.' What do I call you?"

"I'm—" Again that blank look. She giggled. "Clearly I'm not going to remember my name. You can call me Shannon."

"Shannon?" Bizarre choice, Randall thought. That resident of Rockdale, wasn't his name...?

She smiled. "Yes, it seems to fit."

"All right, Shannon. Can't you link in?"

Again she looked at him blankly.

"With your subdural," he clarified.

"Oh, uh, it didn't occur to me that I could." Shannon looked almost embarrassed. "Until two weeks ago, I didn't have any of that equipment."

You're lacking a lot more than electrical implants, he thought. She's either daft or doesn't have basic interaction skills, he thought, as though she's spent the last hundred years in complete isolation. Randall wasn't a psychologist, not nearly qualified to assess someone, but it didn't take a psychiatrist to see she was missing numerous social cues and lacking in her range of responsiveness.

"You think I'm dumb, don't you?"

He spluttered and stammered and coughed and denied it outright. "Look, my apologies, but there's something amiss here. You breathe water, don't know your name, walk around naked in the body of a goddess without any reservations or even insight as to the kind of response that a man might have to that—and don't seem to be feeling the slightest bit of anxiety about any of it. What am I supposed to think?"

"You're supposed to think what you're thinking. How could you think anything else? Whether you want to admit it to me or not is your issue. If you'd like to have sex with me, just say so. I used to charge for it, but I don't think I'll be doing that anymore. In fact, I'd rather like to have sex just for the pleasure of it, even with you." Nonchalantly, she stepped out of the formalls.

Blood rushed into his face. He knew he was swollen, and had been since seeing her. "Sorry, I'm married." He couldn't disguise his desire—or keep his gaze on her face.

She just as nonchalantly put them back on. "Now, as to you're thinking I'm dumb. You're welcome to think what you like. It's not my affair, but let's be clear about one thing: You need my help. I do not need yours. I'm not the one in distress."

And that was more distressing than his having been kidnapped in the submersible. "Why aren't you distressed?!" He realized he was yelling. And all he saw on her face was a dream-like look.

"I don't know. I'm just not." She shrugged.

Randall couldn't figure out why that set his soul on edge. "I have to get out of here. Computer, facility map, please." On his corn appeared a three-dimensional map, his position highlighted very near the bottom. "Map route to surface." A line appeared, and he headed for the door, striding around the upper tier. At the end was a pressure door, a wheel mounted in the middle. He turned the wheel and tugged.

Nothing.

The wheel seemed to be working properly. He turned it to its limits either way a couple of times, then turned it to open and pulled hard.

Nothing.

He examined the seam. If I could just pry it open. He looked around for something. Desks, headsets, an empty coffee mug, anything. Nothing.

Making sure it was in the open position, he put his foot on the jamb and pulled on the wheel with all his strength.

Nothing.

"I guess you're not supposed to leave." She stood in the same place, watching him placidly.

Her utter lack of concern was disconcerting.

"All right, so I guess I need your help. How do you propose we get out of here?"

"Find out why you're supposed to stay."

He didn't know whether to cry or scream. He snorted, shaking his head. "How am I supposed to know that?"

"Ask your computer."

"Computer, why am I here?" He hadn't used his trake and the soft contralto voice from the nearby desk startled him.

"I don't have that information available."

"Open the door for me."

"At this time, I have been instructed not to, Mr. Simmons."

"So I'm supposed to starve?"

"Adequate substance is available through the doorway on tier three to the right. To the left are elimination facilities, and straight ahead is a place for repose, relaxation, recreation, and procreation."

Shannon giggled.

Randall scowled at her, then turned back to the desk.

Below, in the cavern, the blue glowing columns seemed brighter than they had been.

"Computer, are those people in those tubes down there?"

"Yes, Mr. Simmons."

He sat, the blood leaving his face. No wonder no bodies have ever been found! he thought. Sparkle crept into his peripheral vision. "What's being done with them?"

"They're being kept alive, Mr. Simmons."

"For what purpose?" A hiss grew louder in his ears. Somewhere, a pounding began.

"To preserve their lives. Pardon, Mr. Simmons, but my sensors indicate a high degree of physical distress. Are you well?"

Randall saw the hands being retracted from his bare chest, the soft blue glow on the ceiling above Shannon looking familiar for some reason. He knew time had passed, but he didn't remember how he'd arrived on the floor, face up, nor how his enviroshell had been opened.

"What happened?" His voice was a bare whisper.

"You had a heart attack."

He felt his chest with his hands, as though a surface-exam might yield information. "My chest doesn't hurt. Shouldn't it hurt?"

"I repaired the damage."

He brought her face into focus.

She looked as puzzled as he felt. "You … almost drowned, earlier. I helped you then, too."

"I know." Carefully, he sat up, saw the blue columns on the cavern floor, remembered the reason for his distress. "Didn't you hear?"

"To preserve their lives," she repeated.

"Help me up." Standing unsteadily, Randall looked again across the cavern, trying to reconcile the fact that these were people. "Who are they?"

"Please clarify request, Mr. Simmons."

Randall wanted to smash the soft contralto voice into oblivion.

"Physical distress again detected. Are you well, Mr. Simmons?"

He soothed himself, breathing deeply. "Is a list of names available?"

To one side of the control theater, a screen appeared, on it three columns of names.

Randall recognized some of them. He'd responded with the EMT crew to the places where the seaweed had dragged them underwater. He saw one: "Angus McKutcheon." He remembered Ruth McKutcheon saying her husband had been diagnosed with leukemia one week before the seaweed had snatched him from the dock. "Detail, McKutcheon, Angus."

Beside a still image, demographic information spilled down the screen. Under medical issues, "Leukemia, inoperable," blinked in red.

"Next profile, alphabetical." He didn't recognize the name, but the blinking red letters highlighted the terminal illness.

He cycled through several, seeing some with incurable or inoperable conditions whose etiology ended in death. Sighing, Randall ran his fingers across his chest where Shannon had placed her hand. He looked down at his chest and raised his gaze to her face. "Can you cure them?"

* * *

"Who was she?"

Brian snorted. "You idiots don't give up, do you? How many times do I have to tell you? Some cheap whore I met on Bora Bora. Name was Honeydew Diamond. With a name like that, what else could she be?"

"She followed you from Bora Bora?"

"Yeah, maybe thought I'd be her Star Man, you know?"

"Don't get coy, Mr. Franks. Why's she got half-a-dozen suits in here?" The detective was glancing through the closet.

"'Cause I bought 'em for her, that's why. You know those are Humani? Cheap whore like her would never be able to afford a Humani. Never!"

"Most cheap whores have an arrest record. She doesn't. None here, none on Sydney, Bora Bora, or Brisbane. Nothing this sector. She wasn't cheap, in other words."

"How do you know? Maybe I was her first job. Bit amateurish, if you ask me."

"Save the rocket exhaust, Mr. Franks. No cheap whore is going to land a job like you on her first time out. She was what, thirty-eight years old?"

"Forty-four," Brian said automatically, then wished he hadn't.

"Forty-four and calluses on her back thicker than trawler-crew hands. Come on, Mr. Franks, out with it. Why'd you bring her here? Who was she, really?"

Brian was tiring of the charade, knowing if he'd told the truth and all the truth, they'd likely ship him off to the head shrink shop for some chemical rebalancing. "You aren't getting any more information from me, because I don't know any more than that. Now, unless you're charging me with a crime, I'd like to go."

"You've been in our sights for years now, Mr. Franks. Suspicious, how quickly you rose from trawler brat at age forty on Pago Pago to CEO at sixty without a lick of schooling and no family connections whatever. I've been waiting to nail you with something for ten years. If I get a hint you lifted an eyebrow in that woman's death, I'll tack your foreskin to the decks with a plasma gun so fast, you'll wish you'd had your dick discounted at birth."

Empty threats, Brian thought, watching them leave.

As soon as the door had closed behind them, Brian raised Sandusky on a secured com channel. "Where's that Xenobiologist, Sandusky?"

"Uh, I don't know, Mr. Franks."

"What do you mean, you don't know?"

Sandusky, a beefy man with thighs thicker than Brian's waist, quailed under his glare.

"I told you to put her under surveillance! I told you to put a mic on her! I told you to know her exact location every minute of the day!"

They both knew the last was untrue but the tiniest peep of protest would draw only further ire and perhaps a shuttle ride groundward without the shuttle.

"Well?!" Brian screamed at the visual.

Sandusky's face was bright red, and sweat glistened on his brow. "Last spotted running from the crowd in front of her hotel, Sir."

Brian remembered encountering the crowd as he and Honeydew had gone to the quay to look over the recovered trawler. "Running from them?"

"They were pretty angry, Sir, expecting the Xenobiologist to keep the weed from attacking our ships. She hasn't returned for that equipment she ordered."

Brian raised an eyebrow. "Equipment?"

"Yes, Sir, a research bot of some kind. To replace the one destroyed in their crash."

"Where is it?"

"Hotel has it, Sir, awaiting her return."

"Get someone on it, put in a tracer, have them contact her by optimitter and have 'em deliver it."

"Yes, Sir, right away, Sir."

The com went dead.

Brian swore at the blank screen.

Honeydew having sacrificed herself so the ferry might be spared, she had done more to stop the tide of seaweed attacks than this supposed alien expert.

Frustrated with the numerous government agencies, the stockbrokers, the board of directors, the distributors, the suppliers, and the shippers, Brian swore again.

"Sir?" Steve asked.

Brian looked over at his attaché. "Yes?"

"Vice President Burlinson, secure channel."

He waved and nodded. "Burl, you tame those regulators, yet?"

"Worse, Brian. We've been slapped with a subpoena by the Water Quality Board to produce waste records for the last five years."

"Tell 'em to get in line." His corn blinked. Another incoming. "Better yet, Burl, tell them we've already submitted all required information to the appropriate agencies, and if they want it, they'll have to get it from their own bureaucracy."

"Yes, Sir."

Brian saw that the incoming com was from legal. "Stay on the line, Burl. Stew, how are you?"

"I'm well, Brian." The face of Stewart Katz appeared on his corn. "Bad news—"

"Well, I'm not having it. Listen, I want a restraint of trade lawsuit against every bureau, board, council, or agency that's decided now's a good time to go after AI. Now that I have you on the line, let's get Gale on, too. I need to consult with you both on a buyback."

The com beeped twice while a channel opened to Gale Florina, the Chief Financial Officer.

"Gale here, hello, Brian, Stew, Burl. I'm sure you've seen the stock price, Brian. Never been so low."

"Exactly my point. How much do I have in seafood futures?"

Stew gasped. "You aren't considering ..."

"I'm doing exactly that. It's a perfect time to take Aquafoods private. Gale, projections on my desk in four hours. I know our cash reserves are low, but I'm prepared to swap out my futures for AI stock."

"Then you'll want a private equity group to shill for you," Stew said. "If the regulators see the sale of futures linked with the buyback, they'll construe it as proof of market manipulation."

"Set it up, Stew. Gale, you know my portfolio; at a glance, do you think we'll land in the black?"

"At a glance, yes, Brian, but there's not much room if the stock drops again."

"If the stock drops again, we'll be delisted, and then we might as well fold. I've got everything riding on this, which is why I'm here on Nartressa. Get me those projections, Gale, and have Cindy link in. Stay with me, Stew, as I think for this next piece, I'll need privilege."

Privilege meant privacy. When a lawyer was present, the conversation was considered privileged, and no amount of legal chicanery could force the participants to disclose the content.

"Brian, Stew, last time I talked on a secured com channel with both of you, I was charged with fraud. What am I looking at this time, ten to life? Or is just a million galacti fine?" Cynthia Moynihan was a blazing Irish redhead with an attitude to match.

Brian chuckled. "Cindy, I've got a circumstance here on Nartressa that requires some special contracting."

"Just weapons, or personnel and transport too?"

"All three. Yields are down a third, and I'm not about to let a weed do that to our volume."

"How many trawlers are there? A few thousand, last I checked. Escorts for them all, or just for the suborbitals?"

"Given the scale, let's start with the suborbitals, but your contractors need to ramp up and quickly."

"Brian," Stew said, "you'll have every advocacy group denouncing AI, every environmental group, every—"

"Get media relations off their fat asses! Cindy, how long before we've got some firepower?"

"Two days minimum, and a week at least until we've got all the suborbitals covered. The trawlers will take a month."

"Tell them five days. Offer bonuses of ten million galacti for every day they're under the deadline."

"What about our profit margins, Brian?"

He looked at Stew's image. "The profits from one container of Nartressan fish will fund ten small suborbital fighters. And if this weed is as smart as everyone tells me, it'll learn its lessons fast."

* * *

Honeydew withdrew her hands from the chest, seeing at the cellular level how the bone marrow continued to produce warped and misshapen cells.

Angus McKutcheon's leukemia was incurable.

"It's not working," she told Randall, sighing.

"You cured me," he said, on his face a frown.

"I know, but ..." She knew why she couldn't cure the old man on the table, but didn't have the words to articulate. "Yours was damage to the heart muscle from lack of air. This ..." She shook her head. "I don't know how to say it.

The seaweed does something inside the cells so his bone marrow makes better blood cells. That's the best way I know how to explain it."

Randall nodded. "Here, help me get him back in."

The two of them maneuvered the limp form back into the fitted tube. When closed, it held the body upright. Randall used the extensible suspended from the ceiling to return the tube to its cradle, a foot-wide socket on a pedestal.

The tube flickered, then came on, emitting the same soft blue light that all two hundred or so body-filled pillars emitted. A bundle of tendrils descended from the ceiling and attached themselves to the body.

Honeydew retreated from the cavern, plodded up the stairs to the first observation tier, disappointed. She felt conflicted, unable to explain why people were being kept inert and lifeless.

"Why aren't they allowed to die?" Randall had shouted earlier, after discovering that each person entombed in the cavern suffered from a fatal malady. "This isn't living! How long will they be kept mummified? What purpose does it serve to keep them here, suspended, alive but unliving, frozen for eternity? What gives the seaweed the right to take away the little that remained of their shortened lives and to imprison them deep underground in some tube?"

The computer had warned him again of unstable vitals, and Randall had distracted himself.

Honeydew looked at the display to the left of the cavern, where details of McKutcheon, including his picture, were still on display. The still of the older gentleman, his shoulders hunched, his black hair thinning, his brow thick and jaw strong, looked to Honeydew as though it were moving.

She pointed it out to Randall, who'd stopped beside her.

"You're right," he said. "The lips are moving. Computer, play speech."

"Playing," the soft contralto voice said.

"My name is Angus McKutcheon," the still said. "I was taken from the dock near my home on Shoalhaven in October, 2486. I have been diagnosed with a rare form of leukemia, which is fatal without extreme medical intervention, treatments that will likely leave me in constant pain, wheelchair-bound, and requiring weekly treatments to keep the disease arrested. Not a fate I'd wish on anyone, and not a future I'd want to inflict on my family." The figure was crying softly. "When offered the opportunity to have my body suspended and my disease arrested, and to have the knowledge gained from my treatment added to the body of research being gathered here, I chose to make this small contribution. My hope eventually is to be cured, of course, and I am not concerned how long that might take."

"You'd remain entombed forever?" Randall yelled at the image.

"Yes, if need be," Angus replied, "but I have also been given the choice. If a time comes when I think I no longer have anything to contribute, or I simply tire of this existence, I need only ask, and my body will stop functioning."

Honeydew and Randall exchanged a glance. "You can hear us?"

"Why, yes. And yes, I'm interacting with you. I see you don't believe that. Do you think I'm some manufactured automaton that this underground computer has assembled just to entertain you?"

Honeydew could see by Randall's expression that he'd been thinking exactly that. "Are you happy?" she asked.

The image smiled. "A somewhat ambiguous question. I'm ambivalent. I wish dearly that I could be with my wife. I wish my eldest son were alive, and I wish I were with all my family at Shoalhaven, free of disease and pursuing my interests as it pleased me once to do. Yes, I wish all of those things. Right now, I'm free of pain and discomfort. I do have the company, albeit a discorporated kind of company, of the other individuals in this cavern, who endure similar circumstances, and I look forward to a long if limited existence. Am I happy? No, I'm not. Content might better describe it, and pleased that I have been given some choice over my fate, living a better existence than I'd have done if I had sought conventional treatment for my leukemia."

Honeydew frowned. "Thank you, Angus."

"You're welcome." And the display collapsed.

She looked over the softly glowing tubes in the cavern, wondering what entity had conceived the idea, and what its ultimate purpose was.

"Playing god," Randall muttered, his brow furrowed.

Chapter 12

Janine sighed and pushed away from the desk, blinking fatigue from her eyes.

She'd been at it for hours, searching through the partially-recovered archives to discover why the Nartressa Research Station had been abruptly shut down. Had they not removed the last two years of archives, Janine might have discovered the reason for the station's abandonment.

Clearly they hadn't anticipated someone trying to reconstruct the archives.

She retreated to the rest station behind the control room. A bunk, shower, and toilet occupied a small room down a short corridor from a functional refectory. Janine wasn't surprised that all the equipment worked, reasoning that forty-four years of disuse wasn't likely to damage equipment designed to withstand an equal amount of misuse.

The bunk looked inviting. I need to get out of here, she thought, wondering why she was being imprisoned. What or who had instructed the central processor not to let her out?

The research station had been experimenting on a protein processor constructed from the six Nartressan nucleotides, four of which were shared with the Terran evolution, and two entirely new proteins. A triple helix, as Janine now thought through the idea, would seem stronger and more resilient to genetic breakdown than a double helix, as a triploid would carry three copies of the same gene and would be less subject to heterozygous variation, chromosomal abnormality, and therefore malignancy.

What does mitosis look like? Janine wondered.

Haploid-division mitosis was the double-helix method of cell division, the DNA strands separating along all twenty-three pairs. How would triple-helix mitosis look? she wondered. Three daughter cells each containing a haploid? Or two cells, one with a double helix and one with a single helix?

And how does the Nartressan environment isolate free radicals? The two new nucleotides, epsidine and zetasine, were chemically unstable and oxidized instantly. Somehow inside the cell, they remained isolated from free radicals.

Oddly, a similar instability in the human genome had been the focus of work in the early genetic experiments of the twentieth century. People had consumed mouthfuls of antioxidants daily, hoping to stave off exposure to free radicals, which were thought to degrade the genome and introduce heterozygous variations, mutations that might lead to cancers. Such experimentation had continued until it had been proven that antioxidants were no more likely to bind with free radicals than the body's own chemical manufacturing processes.

Janine realized she'd stood staring at the bunk for nearly ten minutes, twisting the triple-helix permutations in her head in a way reminiscent of her doctoral studies at Brisbane, a time when ribbons of nucleotides had danced like sugar-plum fairies through her dreams.

If I were designing a computer with a six-nucleotide, triple-helix genome, I'd want it to be self-programming.

She found herself back at the terminal, reviewing snippets from the last days before the shutdown.

"Did you see this algorithm?" One woman said to another, a brightly-colored column in front of her. "The enzymatic sequence matches itself to the aggregate data stream. It's remembering, duplicating, then resuming its original structure."

The vid disintegrated, and Janine chose another.

"What do you suppose Doctor Ericson wants with this embryo? Never tried to put an alien genome inside a Terran nucleus. What's the point? The cell membrane remains pervious to oxyradicalization. The osmality alone will cause the nucleotides to oxyphiliate. What's he thinking?"

The vid switched to a cell, which promptly exploded.

"See?" the voice continued, "Told you!"

Janine switched to another segment.

"The haploid triplets have heterozygous variations that appear to be adaptive, Doctor Ericson."

"Functional variations?" The black-haired biologist said, his eyebrows crawling up his forehead.

"Precisely, Doctor."

"You mean, we're seeing it evolve in front of us?"

"I think so ..."

Lines wiped out the vid and a screech replaced the audio.

Janine switched to another, this segment very near the shutdown.

"Doctor Ericson!" A frantic voice said, sweat dripping down the young man's face. "Containment breach! The protein processor has become cross-contaminated! We've lost integrity!" Behind the sweaty face, red flashing lights reflected off the wall of a rock cavern. Warning buzzers and emergency messages repeated in the un-alarming central voice added to the chaos.

"What happened?" Doctor Ericson's face looked grim.

"Not sure, Sir! Initially we thought a seaweed root had burrowed close to the perimeter, but an external scan indicates that the breach originated from within the vessel."

"Within? But that would mean—"

"Afraid so, Doctor. Our baby brain is trying to get—"

The vid collapsed, and Janine stared at the dead corn image.

The protein processor had attempted to breach its own confines. Had it chosen to do so? she wondered, or had it simply grown so large that the pressure of its growth had breached the containment wall?

Battling her fatigue, Janine searched for other vid sequences near the same time. She yawned, finding momentary fragments, half-completed reports, corrupted sensor streams, distorted audio excerpts.

The triangular blue tubing sprawled across the sea floor, shooting tendrils outward and downward, a thick layer of interwoven tendrils soon carpeting the thick accretion of sediment that had lain undisturbed for centuries on the sea floor, an occasional seaweed plant penetrating into the crust and sending its long stalk winding upward toward the light, billions of tentacles sprouting from the sides of larger plants.

The thick mat of interwoven tendrils climbed the sides of the ancient seaweed stalks, clinging to the sides like ivy to an oak, semi-parasitic. The blue tendrils at first were rejected by the greenish brown seaweed stalk, but the paraphilic structure of the tendrils was similar enough to the dominant indigenous Nartressan flora that it quickly adapted itself to the plant.

Taught to self-program, where before the ancient wisdom embodied in each of the singular stalks of seaweed was isolated to that majestic plant, the blue tendrils replicated and integrated knowledge that had heretofore remained un-exchanged.

Janine woke with a start, gulping for breath, her heart beating rapidly and the chill of sweat beading on her brow.

I have to get out of here, she thought.

"Monkey, let's go," she said, and she forced herself to her feet despite her fatigue.

* * *

"I can't go with you."

Randall stopped on the threshold and looked back.

She stood framed by the lift, the light behind her filtering through her for-malls and silhouetting her voluptuous figure.

"What did you say?"

"I can't go with you, Randall."

A few feet away was freedom. The two of them had rested for a few hours in that cavern, the cryomedic tubes nearby glowing softly blue.

Laying there, on a bunk, listening to her soft breathing a few feet away, Ran-dall had stared at the ceiling.

They had both showered, Randall trying in that confined space not to notice how alluring she was, trying to distract himself from just how much the back of his knees ached with desire. Randall had traded the stuffy enviroshell for a pair of formalls, which disguised his erection even less.

Somehow, his desire unabated and his flagpole flying full colors, Randall had slept, and of course he had dreamt. His dreams had been filled with his wildest fantasies, their joining taking him to a culmination beyond anything he might have imagined, and when he'd awakened, her soft snore from one bunk over, her position unchanged from when he'd fallen asleep, he'd sighed and won-dered if it had all been a dream.

Then they'd risen, retrieved food from the synthesizers, and had left the cav-ern to make their way toward the surface.

She had led the way, opening doors that were blocked to him, finding vents and access culverts that eluded him, guiding them surely toward the upper reaches of the underground facility.

"Why is it that you seem to know your way?" he'd asked her.

She had shaken her head, looking as mystified as he.

And then they'd arrived at the lift which he and Janine had used to descend from the building basement.

Randall stood at the edge of the lift. "You can't stay down here forever."

Standing back and shaking her head, the woman who didn't know her name had a distant look in her eyes. "Soon enough I'll emerge, but I'm not ready yet. For now, I'll stay."

"I still don't know your name."

"There's a reason I can't tell you, and I think it's because my name is changing. I don't know my name because I don't know who I am yet." Then she smiled. "But I will soon."

Randall shook his head, bewildered. "All right, mystery woman. Thank you for helping me get out of there." He stepped backward off the lift.

The cage door closed, and through the grid, he watched the lift descent until she was out of sight.

What a bizarre experience, he thought, making his way through the building basement. Something to tell the grandkids after I retire? he wondered. Something to bury in his subconscious, never to see the light of day again!

Reaching the sidewalk, he looked around to get his bearings.

Mid-morning pedestrians ignored him studiously, the sun slanting between buildings, the wind off the bay cutting through the seams of his formals.

A few blocks away, towering over the surrounding buildings was the Rockdale Hilton.

The street in front of the hotel was absent the crowd he and Janine had encountered. Trawler crew had seemed to be awaiting Janine's return the last time the two of them had tried to enter the hotel.

He wondered at their absence, at what might've changed during his subterranean sojourn.

The lobby was mostly empty, the bellhop and concierge having a heated discussion over some hotel matter. A vid screen bantered banally to one side of the lobby.

Randall froze.

No! he thought, blinking at the vid. It can't be!

A woman stood on the dock of some ship, wrapping herself with a foot-thick tentacle of seaweed, a secret smile on her face, five other seaweed arms gripping the ship stern, a man standing nearby. The tentacle lifted her bodily and took her underwater, all the tentacles letting go of the ship. The smile had not left the woman's face.

Her face! Randall thought.

The vid played over again, mesmerizing him.

"Sir, are you all right?"

He nodded to the concierge. "When did this happen?"

"Day before yesterday, in the morning, Sir. Sacrificed herself, she did, and saved the ferry and all the trawler crew. They're holding a service this afternoon. You act like you ain't seen this. It's been playing endlessly half across the quadrant since it happened. What cave have you been hiding in?"

"Who's that man?"

"Brian Franks, CEO of Aquafoods Interstellar. Saved his fleece-lined behind too, she did. He's staying in the penthouse here. He'll be saying a few words at the service this afternoon."

Randall headed to the lift, barely able to take his eyes off the screen.

In the lift, he activated his optimitter, putting the vid on his corn. Stepping off the lift, he realized he was on the wrong floor.

"Something I can help you with, Sir?" One of the two beefy suits said in the small foyer.

"Yes, there is. I have a message for Mr. Franks. My name is Randall Simmons, and I've seen her body." Not exactly a fabrication, Randall thought wryly.

"Huh? You some kind of mental patient?" The bulky guard stepped toward him.

He sat on the floor. "I'll wait here while you tell him."

The beef-brain towered over him and could have easily booted him right into the lift. "Look, I got a job to do. Make my life easy and leave on your own. Make your own life easy, too."

Randall just glowered at him.

"Hey, Robby," said the second suit nearer the door, "I'll get the boss. He'll know what to do."

A few minutes later, another suited man appeared, this one without a bulge under his jacket. "Mr. Simmons, my name is Steve. I'm Mr. Frank's personal attaché. Your message is rather disturbing, given recent events, and due to the sensitive nature of the issue, I'd like some clarification before I tell Mr. Franks. What do you mean, exactly?"

Randall stood to greet the man. He glanced at the two bodyguards.

"Sworn to secrecy," Steve said.

"Sorry." Randall shrugged. "I insist."

Steve sighed. "This way, please." He led him through the door and into the entryway of the penthouse.

Randall could see it was far plusher than any place he'd ever stayed. He and Steve were alone, Randall saw. "My apologies, Steve," he said. "That woman is alive."

Steve's face went white. "Where is she?"

"There's an underground research station underneath Rockdale, abandoned some forty years ago. Janine and I were exploring the place, and we got separated." Randall realized if he recounted everything, the other man would think he was a mental patient. "I almost drowned, and that woman saved me. She helped me escape the research station, said she couldn't come with me. Now, I know why. Everyone thinks she's dead, don't they?"

"How long were you down there?"

"Two and a half days." Randall looked as if he'd been down longer, his face stubbled, his eyes bleary and bloodshot, his formalls rumpled.

"Wait here." Steve walked farther into the suite.

Brian Franks looked to Randall to be in his sixties. His hair was jet-black, and his skin so pale it was almost translucent. He looks like a Nartressan native, Randall thought.

"Please, have a seat."

The sofa soaked him into it, the twenty-foot windows on three sides showing stupendous views of the bay and surrounding city.

"Coffee? Pastry? Some smoked salmon for your bagel? The finest Nartressan salmon, of course."

Randall prepared himself a few victuals, hungry.

Brian began to pace. "It's ten am, and I'll need to leave for the funeral in three hours. You'll need about an hour to prepare, if we're to get you fitted, of course. Tell me what happened."

Between bites, Randall told him. Slowly at first, Randall recounted his and Janine's discovery of the laboratory and submersibles.

Franks asked a few questions, his manner nonchalant.

Randall described what happened with the submersible, how the door had continued to leak after it had trapped him inside, how the submersible had taken him deeper, the air inside growing more stale, the water replacing the air, until just a narrow slice of air was all that he had to breathe. How the submersible had settled in the crotch of a large bulb where triangular blue tubes connected with it. Randall found the other man's interest in the tubes disconcerting.

"And then you found yourself looking up at her?"

Randall nodded. "She revived me." He went on to describe the cavern they'd found nearby, the slim upright tubes and their disturbing contents, their efforts to try to cure the old man with leukemia.

"And this whole time she couldn't tell you her name?"

Randall shook his head, described their journey from the depths, how she had somehow known the route to the very place where he and Janine had entered over forty-eight hours before.

Steve interrupted. "The tailor is here, Sir."

"Go prepare yourself, Mr. Simmons, and meet me back here in forty-five minutes. I'd like you to accompany me to her funeral."

"Forgive me, Mr. Franks, but …"

"She's not dead?"

Randall swallowed heavily. "No, Sir, she's not."

"Her words, as you recounted them, were, 'I think it's because my name is changing. I don't know my name because I don't know who I am yet.' I suspect, Mr. Simmons, that Honeydew Diamond is undergoing or has undergone a transformation that's quite beyond our ability to understand. The Honeydew Diamond who was taken off the ferry deck is dead, and we shall honor her sacrifice."

* * *

Brian Franks finished his speech and stepped to the coffin where it sat delicately balanced on a plank, a hinge attaching the plank to the gunwale. Both ferry deck and superstructure were packed with people, and three more ferries floated nearby, likewise packed.

Slowly, ceremoniously, Brian turned the crank that raised the back end, tilting the coffin to a seventy-five degree angle, the plank now pointing toward the water. A simple catch was all that kept the coffin from sliding into the Nartressan ocean.

Brian raised his right arm. And brought it down.

Guns thundered from all four ships, superstructures sprouting towers of smoke.

And the coffin slid off the plank and disappeared between the waves.

Aboard the hover back to the hotel, Brian absently watched news clips of the event. Opposite him, Steve and Randall looked absorbed in their own thoughts.

Brian might have called off the funeral service at hearing Randall's tale, if he hadn't been certain in his knowledge that Honeydew Diamond was no more.

His dreams had told him similar, dreams of tunnels that honeycombed the bedrock underneath Rockdale, the site of horrific events. Somehow, Honeydew was part of those events, and she, like him, had been summoned for the purpose of rectifying the wrongs wrought at the research station.

The first of several dreams on the night of Honeydew's snatching from the ferry deck was still vivid to him now, three days later. He was sure those dreams were reflected in his sunken, dark-rimmed eyes

Dreams in which Brian was standing nose to nose with a woman whose hair was bright red, her uniform somber. He'd been arguing with for her at least an hour.

A blurry holo in front of him seemed to accuse him of something inhumane and horrendous, and he stared at it helplessly, remiss now that he'd pursued this course, seeing its result in front of him. A vein pulsed at his temple.

"See?" the woman screamed at him, "What did I say? We have to shut it down!"

The pressure in his temple redoubled, and he turned to her. "You're right, we've failed." His vision sparkled from the pressure at his temple. He looked among the staff, two tiers above and two tiers below, their attention on him, and he gave the order for the research station to be shut down.

Brian had awakened in a sweat, had dismissed that first dream, then and fallen back asleep, only to dream about the same woman, a military commander of some sort, asking him, "But why this?" she gestured to a tank whose contents were obscured from him. "How does this lead to a greater understanding?"

And again he'd awakened, had lain wake for hours, had tried to dismiss feelings of impending doom, his heart racing, his thoughts ranging from problem to problem, and finally, unable to still his thoughts, he'd gotten a bottle of the local green brew, drank it down in one gulp, then had gone back to bed.

The third and fourth dreams had been similar, taking place in caverns and passageways of bare rock, the place clearly underground.

The next night had been plagued with similar dreams, and when Steve had come to tell him a stranger was outside saying only that he'd "seen her body," Brian had instinctively known that Honeydew wasn't dead, that his dreams weren't dreams, but some altered, twisted memory of something terrible.

Like the dreams of triangular blue tubing and viscous green liquid which he'd shared with Honeydew, these more recent dreams were coming to him for a reason.

An unknown reason.

Brian didn't like the unknown. But when confronted with it, he never shrank from the challenge. Instead, he pursued it with a vigor that belied his age. He pursued the unknown until he felt he knew it so thoroughly that he'd never be surprised or overtaken by it ever again.

The weed was an unknown. The research station was an unknown. The dreams were an unknown.

"Where's Doctor Meriwether now?" Brian asked, drilling Randall with his stare.

"I don't know, Mr. Franks. Based on the condition of the twelfth-floor suite we have, it looks as if she hasn't returned. I think she's still down there."

"Then that's where we'll go."

* * *

Janine whirled at the sound. "Where the quasars did you come from?"

The beautiful woman in the plain formalls frowned. "I didn't mean to startle you. My apologies."

"Stars above, I nearly wet myself! I'm Janine Meriwether." She stuck out her hand.

The other woman shook. "I'm ... Shannon."

Janine heard the hesitation, saw the beginnings of carrot-red at the roots of the jet-black hair. Needs to dye, she thought, wondering why a woman with bright red hair would dye it black to start with. "You're not from around here, are you?" Then she realized Shannon was blushing. "Neither am I. Sydney. The Alien Microbiology Institute brought me in to figure out why the seaweed is attacking people." Janine turned back to the portal. Beyond was a submersible, and it was the only way she could think to escape.

"What's that?" Shannon pointed at the spiderbot.

"That's Monkey, my biopsy acquisition and analysis unit. Monkey, say hello to Shannon."

"Hello, Shannon." The spiderbot emitted a trill and a whistle.

Janine pulled on the door, expecting and getting resistance just like the last two hundred doors she'd tried. "You know any way to get out of here? I've been trying for hours."

"Here, let me." The door opened for Shannon without apparent effort.

"But I just tried it!" Janine frowned. "How'd you get down here, anyway?"

"I was wondering when you'd ask. I've been here for a couple of days. I just haven't been ready to leave. But I think I am now. Can I go with you?"

"Of course. These submersibles can hold three at a time." They stepped through the next hatch, Janine's ears popping with the pressure changes. Why didn't she answer my question? she wondered.

"You're probably wondering why I didn't answer your question," Shannon said. "It's a rather long and remarkable story."

"I guess we'll have time. Do you mind if we explore a little before we surface? I've been trying to get a good look at the seaweed."

They climbed aboard, Janine looking around at the array of sensors and extensors. On her last try, she'd only been aboard a few minutes when she and Randall had been separated, Janine stranded underground and Randall carried off by the uncooperative submersible.

"Here, can I put Monkey on your lap?" Janine had operated similar submersibles on Sydney, but the controls were dissimilar enough that the spiderbot in her lap would be a distraction.

The submersible came to life under her hands. Remembering what had happened to Randall, Janine half-expected it to take over its own controls and send them plummeting to the ocean floor. Janine told Shannon what had happened.

"We'd better make sure he's alright," Shannon said.

"It was at least thirty-six hours ago." Janine let the rest go unsaid, not wanting to think about it. Casualties occurred all too frequently, a hazard of operating on alien worlds. Janine was no stranger to loss, but she'd never had a fellow mission member die. "I'm sure he's fine."

"What was he wearing?"

Janine told her.

"Black hair, strong features, 'Randall' you said? Oh, he is fine. I met him wandering around below, couldn't find his own way out. Together, we found him an exit."

Janine felt odd, as though something were awry. "You didn't go with him?"

Shannon smiled. "I wasn't ready to leave."

Maneuvering the submersible from its dock, water gurgling around them, Janine mulled this over, concentration replacing concern. The rock-walled underwater cavern opened out onto a sheer cliff-face, the altimeter indicating a seafloor some six hundred feet below them, the surface a similar distance above.

Just visible ahead in the submersible floodlamps was a seaweed stalk.

As she watched, a school of green fish descended upon a red pistil, and the water clouded with particulate, obscuring what was going on. In a few minutes, the school of green fish dispersed, each one glistening with crystalline powder. The pistil they left behind looked significantly smaller and drooped as though wilting and flaccid.

While she examined the pistil, a single blue fish glistening with crystalline dust approached a nearby pod on the same red stalk—and appeared either to nudge it or nibble at it. The tip opened and the blue fish burrowed inside, turned around, and settled itself in the slender pod with just its head poking out past the gills. The pod began to contract, mildly at first, then more rapidly. It's going to crush the blue fish with its constrictions! Janine thought. With one great heave, the pod spat out the blue fish and closed up, while the blue fish sank like a stone, limp and lifeless.

Shannon giggled. "Reminiscent, don't you think?"

Of mating! Janine thought, laughing and blushing.

And then she realized. "That's it! The breeding cycle!" Excited, she summoned a sketch pad on the submersible computer. "Look, the green fish swarmed around the pistil, which was covered with a crystalline powder, coated themselves with it, then a single blue fish coated with that some powder burrows into a red pod, which then scrapes the powder off the fish and ejects it."

Shannon looked puzzled. "Why didn't the green fish go and fertilize that green pod from the other stalk? It was right there."

Janine shook her head. "I don't know." She looked around, seeing various types of fish, but only in those three colors—red, green, and blue. It's like some childhood rhyme book, she thought. She swung the submersible around, going deeper into the seaweed forest, until they encountered a blue-pistiled flower.

Janine noted a slight blue tint to the plant itself, which she'd not seen in any of the washed-up seaweed onshore. She tried to recall the live seaweed she'd seen. Each occasion had been during a trawler or suborbital attack, and she hadn't really noted coloration.

The blue-tinted seaweed looked no different in configuration, having the same two extrusions: pod and pistil.

She watched, fascinated, as a school of red fish descended upon the blue-pistiled flower, leaving behind crystal-clouded water and a limp blue pistil. Hovering near the seaweed, a slim pod nearby, she saw what she was waiting for: a green fish glistening with crystalline powder nuzzled the end of the red pod and burrow inside. The pod began to constrict with a rhythmic motion, and soon ejected the green fish, which then sank out of sight.

She and Shannon exchanged a glance. "Let's find a green flower."

Janine maneuvered the submersible down through the murky waters, alongside the green seaweed. "I'd better get some samples," she said, activating one of the extensibles. The manual control arm dropped from the ceiling, its motions mirrored outside the submersible by an arm that extended from the brim. She brought the submersible close to the green flower, the long green pistil looking full and engorged. She extended the extensible toward it, hoping to scrape off a sample of the crystalline powder.

She didn't need to.

A school of blue fish roiled around the green phallus, the powder clouding the water. She drew up a tube full of cloudy water and brought in the extensible. As it folded itself back into the submersible brim, the sample tube was thrust into the cabin right above Janine.

"Here you go, Monkey." She slipped the tube into one of the spiderbot sockets.

The bot beeped. "Sample obtained," it said, flashing a red light on Janine's corn.

"I want to get a sample from each flower," she said. "Maybe they're different enough that it'll provide us some insight into this odd breeding cycle, which looks like might be three-part."

"What do you mean, three-part?" Shannon looked puzzled.

"The three colors of fish, the three colors of flower, and I'm willing to bet that the different color pods are part of the cycle. It's as though there are three sexes of fish, three sexes of plant."

Shannon's brows drew further together. "Now, I'm confused."

"So am I," Janine admitted. "It's like no other life form we've seen, and I'm guessing there's a piece missing. I'm not sure where, but three sexes of plant, three sexes of fish—something isn't adding up. And the fish—they're like bees, carrying pollen from one plant to another—they take that crystalline powder from pistil to pod. Fascinating."

"What are the pods for?"

Janine's brows rose. She turned the submersible, looking among the pods sprouting from the trunk of the green-flowered seaweed. "Let's find out."

There! Above them, a turgid pod protruded from the trunk, so taut its flesh was nearly translucent. Janine found the floodlamp extensible and pushed the armature out toward the turgid pod and around to the far side, lighting it from behind.

They both gasped. Silhouetted, hundreds of tiny fish darted around inside the uterine-shaped pod, each trailing a small sac.

Janine was tempted to extract one for examination, the submersible equipped with multiple extensibles capable of doing exactly that kind of surgery. "I have a feeling the seaweed would take us apart if I cut open the pod."

Shannon nodded. "I wonder when they're going to hatch."

"They'll have to hatch soon, look at the size of those trailing sacs. Almost gone. Like the sacs inside a bird egg—once the sac is absorbed, the chick is mature and ready to break out of the egg." Janine retracted the floodlamp. "That explains the fish—which aren't really fish, of course. That's just what we call them. They're more like matured, mobile reproductive vectors. I wonder what happens once they've fertilized a pod. Remember that first blue fish that we saw, which dropped after the pod ejected it?"

"I wonder what happened to it."

They exchanged a glance, and Janine maneuvered the extensible toward a slim pod, one that looked unfertilized. The tip of the pod looked slightly brighter green than the dull brown-green of the main plant.

Soon, a single crystal-covered red fish nuzzled the brighter green pod tip.

"Computer, track red fish," Janine said.

The red fish appeared on a monitor as it burrowed into the pod, turned around and settled in complacently, its head poking out just past the gills.

The pod began to contract, its side undulating rhythmically. Soon the pod was pulsating with paroxysms and with one great heave, spat out the red fish, which arced, lifeless, toward the depths, plummeting like a stone.

"Track with remote," Janine said.

The submersible ejected a remote, and the image appeared on the inside of the submersible glasma as it might appear on her corn, the remote device propelling itself after the sinking, lifeless red fish.

Janine maneuvered the submersible down, following at a more leisurely pace, shining the floodlamps toward the thick stalk of the seaweed plant.

"Look at those blue tendrils on the trunk," Shannon said. "What do you suppose those are?"

Tiny blue strands wound up the side of the trunk, each emitting a slight glow. As they descended in the submersible, the tiny blue tendrils grew more dense.

"Have you seen stills of old Earth?" Janine asked. "Those great trees covered with ivy, sometimes so thick it would kill the tree? I wonder if it's some type of parasitic plant. It looks very different from the seaweed."

As they descended, the trunk grew thicker and the tentacles, pods and flowers grew sparser. The clinging blue tendrils grew thicker, however.

The trunk as it approached the ocean floor developed ridges from its mostly circular shape, as though spreading as it burrowed its roots into the thick muck. The blue glowing tendrils here were thicker as well, more intertwined, their weave almost matting the ocean floor.

The remote device had tracked the lifeless red fish to the ocean floor, where it lay between several strands of the glowing blue tendrils. Somehow, the dead fish had found a gap in the tendril mat.

Janine used the extensible to gather the dead red fish—confirming it was dead by prodding it—and brought it aboard in a medium-sized glass capsule. The sample too large for the spiderbot to analyze, she simply stowed it in a receptacle.

"Look at the other dead fish," Shannon said.

Several dead fish lay nearby, each of them having somehow found a gap in the matted blue tendril. As they watched, a dead fish dropped from above and settled to the bottom on the matting. The blue tendrils moved aside and created a gap.

"Did you see that?" Janine tried to understand what she had just seen. "What is this blue stuff?" One larger tendril appeared to get larger as it wound across the ocean floor toward Rockdale, up the underwater incline.

Tempted to follow it, Janine was distracted by a beep on her coke.

"Sample obtained," the spiderbot said, flashing a red light on Janine's corn.

Puzzled, she looked at the bot on Shannon's lap. Her corn told her that the spiderbot had two samples. But I've only given it one.

She raised her gaze to Shannon's face, seeing again the red roots of her jet-black hair. Why does she look familiar? Janine wondered. Her recall for faces was very good, which was how she'd recognized Randall after not having seen him for twenty years.

A seaweed tentacle smacked the glasma in front of her, cracks spiderwebbing across the viewport. Alarms sounded and lights flashed.

"Monkey, seal!" she managed to shout, and a second tentacle crossed the first, then the submersible electricity died and plunged them into darkness.

* * *

Randall stepped through the door of his suite at the Hilton and knew instantly that something was wrong. He held still, the door half-closed behind him, his skin crawling up and down his back.

He'd flown in aboard Frank's hover to the rooftop port at the Hilton, avoiding the gazes of the man beside him and the man across from him. It was the most uncomfortable flight he'd ever taken. The formal tuxedo hadn't helped, Randall having never worn one before, not even when he'd been married, and the absolute utter silence of the other two had been profoundly disconcerting.

While aboard the ferry, just before the ceremony, Randall had rubbed against something and had smudged the knee. During the whole ride back, he'd dreaded Brian Frank's seeing the smudge. He had these tailored for me, Randall thought, and he'd been sure Brian would explode at the perceived insult. How do people wear these things? he'd wondered.

Now, entering the Hilton suite he and Janine shared, Randall shivered.

"Come in and have a seat, Mr. Simmons."

Randall jumped at the sound of the voice.

A male voice. No motion, no sound.

His view of the suite limited, he knew he'd have to step farther in to the room to see the person. "Who are you?" He didn't move, his calves beginning to ache with his extended crouch.

"No need for all that anxiety, Mr. Simmons. My name is Shannon, and I need your help."

The voice was that of a person with all the power, the speech even and unhurried, mellifluous and casually inflected, its tones soothing and soft.

Another blasted Shannon! Randall thought, wondering if he were crazy. "Why should I trust you?" He tried to bend his line of sight around the corner, dreading what he might find.

"Because we have a shared objective. Please, Mr. Simmons, come forward. I'm here to help you as well."

Randall straightened and peered around the corner.

A man in a business suit sat in a chair facing the window, one eyebrow raised, his gaze upon Randall, a beneficent smile on his face. At his feet blinked a small machine. "It's a field-interference generator and emulator. It intercepts—and copies—electronic signal within its given range. All the surveillance devices in here are now broadcasting the same signals they emitted before I arrived. Quite the number I've found as well."

Randall glanced at the door to Janine's room.

"She hasn't been back, unfortunately." Shannon's manner was as nonchalant as a beach bum on meal break.

He almost looks bored, Randall thought. "What do you want?"

"Franks. Brian Franks. We suspect him of having murdered that young woman you two buried at sea today. We think you can help us to imprison him for the rest of his life. His other crimes are far more heinous, but evidence is difficult to obtain."

"Who are 'we'?" Randall hadn't moved into the room, stood tensely where he might still get out the door if "Shannon" were to apprehend him.

"Bureau of Investigation—interstellar crimes branch. It was a bit puzzling that he took you with him to the funeral. Why was that?"

Randall didn't know whether to lie or how much to trust this man. "You won't believe me, and you won't like it."

"What's there not to believe? What could you tell me that I won't believe? That she's alive and well somewhere? Now that would be unbelievable."

Randall looked away, wondering if the man were reading his thoughts.

"She is alive, isn't she?"

Randall confirmed it with his silence. He didn't say a word; nor did he motion in any way.

"And he planned all that, didn't he?"

Randall just blinked at the man.

"How'd he get the seaweed to do that? Amazing, just amazing. Blows our case out of the water, so to speak, but that happens. Listen, Mr. Simmons. You get any whiff of anything illegal, just give us a call." He stood and handed Randall a com chip. "Nasty smudge on your knee. Cost you as much to get it cleaned as to get new slacks. Too bad. Hope to hear from you soon, Mr. Simmons." And the man was gone before he replied.

What the weed was that all about? Randall wondered.

* * *

"Where the weed is he?" Brian wondered aloud.

"What was that, Sir?"

He looked around, realizing he wasn't alone. "I was just wondering where Simmons was. Should've been back by now."

"Uh, odd readings on the monitors. Sir. He's in the bathroom changing, but I didn't see him go in."

"Attention, Steve, attention. Let it waver for a moment, and they'll get past you."

"Yes, Sir. Here he comes now, Sir."

Brian stood just inside the door to the hoverpad, dressed in unmarked formalls, an enviroshell in his backpack. He felt about as uncomfortable in the formalls as Randall had looked in the tuxedo. How do people wear these things? he wondered.

Randall came in, dressed similarly, exchanged a greeting.

He looks lost, Brian thought. "Nervous? No need for it." He pulled back the left formall shoulder to show him the plasma blaster under his arm. "You want one, too? Steve, get him the spare." Brian waved away the man's protest. "You'll be protecting me as well, having one."

"But I'm assigned to escort Doctor Merriweather …"

For a moment, Brian was puzzled. "Oh, the Xenobiologist. Gone how long now? What were they paying you? I'll double it, pay you twenty-four-seven back to this morning, and release you back to your assignment the moment she turns up." Brian spread his hands toward the EMT. "Agreed?"

The other man nodded without much enthusiasm.

We'll be alone down there, Brian told himself. Anything can happen. "Let's go."

They took the lift to the basement and slipped out the service entrance, walking purposively, Randall leading the way.

The building they entered looked to be apartments. Brian noted the lack of passkeys, Nartressa having too few people to have a lot of crime. Randall led the way to the second floor elevator. The fifth floor where they got out was quiet, the hallway deserted, just the one elevator. Randall then led him down a floor.

"Two elevators?" Brian said.

Randall shrugged. "Not sure why," he said, stepping inside and pressed the "B" button.

"The other lift doesn't go to the basement, does it?"

Randall shook his head.

In the basement, a long, dark corridor led to a cage lift, whose only direction was downward. The air coming through the metal grate floor swirled around him, moist and smelling faintly of ... apples? Brian wondered.

After dropping a fair distance in black-walled shaft, the lift passed two, three, four doors, then abruptly jerked to a halt between the fourth and fifth.

Randall pressed buttons to no effect.

The fourth floor at chest height, Brian pulled, trying to pry the doors apart. Randall grabbed one door, Brian the other, and they were just able to get the doors open wide enough for a person to climb through.

Brian climbed up and helped Randall.

"You seem to be in pretty good shape," he said.

"I'm a young seventy-five," Brian said. "Where to from here?"

Randall shrugged. "Down I guess. When we were here the first time, we engaged the microfusion core. Some of the equipment should work."

"Shouldn't we try to find another way out? That lift isn't working, after all." He flicked on a belt light, as did Randall.

"Your call, Mr. Franks."

"Let's go up first, see if we can find another exit."

The rotunda where they stood had four corridors leading away from it. "This way," Brian said, sensing it was east. He activated his subdural, wondering whether the optimitter would receive a signal through a hundred feet of rock.

To his surprise, his corn lit up. "Map, please," he said on his trake. A map illustrated where they were, the catacombs around them highlighted like some alien ant farm.

They ascended to the first level underground, which was still a hundred feet below the surface. The map seemed to indicate an egress some distance along a bare corridor. The rough-surfaced walls, poor lighting, and inadequate circulation indicated a cavern rarely used—or not meant for frequent use.

"An escape route," Randall said, as though reading Brian's thoughts.

He's trained in rescue, Brian told himself, walking carefully across the uneven floor, trying to dispel the suspicious feeling he had.

The passageway seemed to go on forever, the walls hewn from naked rock.

His lamp picked up debris strewn across the floor ahead.

A section of wall had been blown inward.

Beyond was a ten foot shaft, and at the end, twenty feet below, at the bottom, some sort of rack or brace.

He detached the light from his belt and shined it upward.

A smooth bore, straight up, some sort of mechanism at the top.

"That's about surface level, wouldn't you say?"

Randall nodded. "Doesn't show up on the map."

Brian hadn't realized Randall had also tapped into the local optimitter. "Odd that it doesn't." He retreated to the passageway, walked forty feet farther, and saw what looked like a smoother patch of rock, shaped about the size of the blown section of wall forty feet back.

"Look," Randall said, "Microcharges."

Two miscolored lumps on each side and one above, and connected by a wire glued to the rock, the five charges looked placed in such a way as to open a passage into whatever lay beyond.

"The rack in that last shaft, a mount of some sort—like a launcher."

They looked at each other. "Escape pods," they both said.

And Randall added, "Probably with enough power to get someone into orbit."

"Someone used one," Brian said.

They counted another eight such escape pods before reaching the end of the corridor, where they found a sealed hatch, its wheel unyielding.

Their maps indicated that beyond the door lay a cavern.

"Let me try," Randall said. "Central, unlock port."

A "snick" came from the door, and it turned easily.

Beyond was a cavern, the floor littered with the detritus of many years, the air dank and stale.

"Why did it obey you, but wouldn't open for me?"

"Did something similar with me and Honeydew," Randall said. "Opened doors for her that I couldn't budge."

"She had that talent, didn't she? Opened doors with just a smile." Brian noted the past tense in his own words. Do I think she's gone? he wondered. Or perhaps transmogrified?

The underside of the ceiling was ribbed with girder, Brian saw, noting hefty crossbeams on what looked like tracks to either side of the cavern.

In the center were eight hovers. The far hover beckoned, its door cracked open, a quadcart nearby. By mutual agreement, they approached the hover, the rearmost in the cavern.

Across the floor of the hover lay a long, gray metal cartridge, six inches by four inches by four feet. Etched in one end was an inscription. "January 2441—"

Brian looked at Randall. "What do you make of that?"

Randall shrugged and looked around, then up.

"Someone tried to escape with it, looks like." Brian stepped away, toward the hefty crossbeams. He saw they weren't even attached to each other. Inspecting the tracks they were on, he saw a series of chains inside the track, their links six inches thick. Looking at where the diagonal beams attached to the underside of the ceiling, Brian concluded—

"Mechanical roof," Randall said, stepping up beside him. "The girders counter-weighted inside the walls. One switch and they'll fling open."

Brian looked around.

No egress. One entrance, which they'd come through. Solid if rough cavern walls. Brian traced a few potential climbs, but there appeared to be no break in the ceiling. He checked the time of day. Broad daylight on the planet surface.

"Douse your light," he said, shutting off his own.

Pitch black. No leakage.

Brian thought about it. If he were designing an escape dock, he'd want it completely sealed from the environment. He turned his lamp back on. "No way out." He shook his head and headed for the hatch.

In the passageway beyond, he heard the door snick shut, as though the underground computer were tracking them.

"Well, we know where to come if we need to get off-planet in a hurry," Randall remarked as they passed the blown-in passageway wall.

"Think it all works after . . . " He did the math in his head ". . . forty-five years?"

"Janine said these places are intended to hold up for five hundred plus years. The microfusion core is supposed to last that long without maintenance."

They made their way back to the malfunctioned lift, then mapped out a route downward to the command theater where Randall had gone with Janine.

They were mostly silent, the cold dank stairwells imposing a silence like a tomb.

The level where they emerged two-thirds of the way down was a rotunda. In the center, the lift shaft was empty of lift.

The shape and feel sent a shiver down Brian's spine, the structure sparking the memory of a dream, as though a dream within a dream, a red-framed face thrusting into his, "We have to shut it down!"

Brian snapped back to the present. A vein pulsed at his temple.

"Around here was the laboratory," Randall said.

As in a dream, Brian watched him try a door to no avail.

"And over here was the command theater."

That door opened for Randall, and Brian felt himself being propelled toward it, as though a giant hand pushed him.

The quarter-circle command theater was five levels deep, all the levels pointed toward a grid of at least fifty displays, each now showing a different vid sequence, each audio stream at normal volume, the combination a cacophony. Among the faces, a red-framed face thrusting into the vid.

"I've got the worst headache I've ever had," Brian said. He didn't need to hear what the red-haired woman was saying on screen. He read her lips with dread, knowing his dream wasn't a dream.

His temple throbbed and bright spots of light occluded the sight in one eye.

Randall thrust his face into his vision. "Are you all—"

His vision went dark.

* * *

Knowing now that it wasn't her name, Honeydew put her hands to the cracked submersible glasma and shouted in her mind, "No!"

The tentacles froze.

"Away," she said, feeling the presence now around them.

The tentacles slid away, all but one, which pushed the ship along. Another tentacle whipped toward them out of the darkness and herded the submersible farther along while the first tentacle slid away. They were pushed past the thick trunk of a giant plant, its surface covered with blue, glowing tendrils. The surface under them, like the trunk, was covered with a matting of blue tendrils, the gentle incline distorted occasionally by a protruding rock.

Another tentacle emerged from the darkness ahead, the previous one retracting.

"Where are they taking us?"

Honeydew shook her head. She sensed it was someplace safe. Her initial contact when the seaweed was about to crush them had left her with the impression of a large group of individuals.

A group sensing its own community, a group sensing a threat to its existence. A group trying to formulate a response to a threat.

She looked a Janine. "Our understanding of this planet is lacking. The seaweed takes us to a place of greater understanding."

The other woman looked puzzled. "They're acting in unison?"

Honeydew nodded.

"How do you know that?"

She shook her head, feeling the burn of the other woman's stare. Honeydew glanced at her, then returned her gaze to the tentacles moving the submersible along. "You're a scientist. You want answers. And what's happening here doesn't fit our existing frames of reference. We'll need to discard our fundamental belief systems to understand. All that I'm sure of is that I don't understand."

Scanning the ocean floor with her gaze, Honeydew saw a pattern in the integration between the seaweed stalks and the matting of thin, blue tendril, a translation between systems, and an emergence derived from the confluence of multiple experiences.

"Do you know what they did here forty-four years ago?"

Honeydew wasn't expecting the question—but neither was it unexpected, as events on Nartressa were beginning to impinge upon her consciousness without her having to seek the knowledge. "I know that they thought it had gone awry, and that they tried to stop their own creation." She turned to look at the Xenobiologist. "They weren't successful."

"The blue tendrils," Janine said, gesturing beyond the cracked glasma, "their experiment. It continued to grow, and that's what's bringing all these seaweed attacks, isn't it?"

When confronted with that information, Honeydew could not deny it. As much as their tentacles and leaves might intertwine with each other, the seaweed plants could not communicate.

Except through the blue tendrils.

"They tried to fashion a protein computer using the six Nartressan nucleotides, and it got out of control."

"Yes," Honeydew said, certain now that that's what had happened. "It escaped its containment vessel and has grown ever since." In the silence that followed, Honeydew wondered what the other woman was thinking.

Below them, the gently-rising ocean floor and its blue-tendril matting had begun to change. A ridge had formed, and it appeared they were being pushed along it. The ridge was overlaid with the same blue tendril matting, but Honeydew detected a change in its quality. The blue glow, she realized, was coming from the ridge itself.

"The tendrils!" Janine said. "They're growing from the ridge!"

Honeydew nodded, seeing where they joined the spine, or peak. The ridge meandered between stalks, never coming very close, as though it had chosen to remain a certain distance from the seaweed. From the gentle curvature at the peak, Honeydew saw that the ridge was shaped like—

"The triangular blue tubes!" Janine shouted.

"You've seen them before … dreamt about them, haven't you?"

Janine's face changed expressions three times, finally settling on what appeared to be bemused wonder. "When were you on Nartressa?"

Honeydew smiled. "Several years ago, perhaps ten. I was brought here by a client for the weed that could be found on the beaches. Instead, the seaweed found me, and the next thing I remember, I was on an interstellar flight back to Sydney."

The other woman searched her face. "Any medical issues?"

Honeydew hadn't expected this question. "I don't remember, no, wait, yes, yes, now that you mention it. I'd had a malignant pap spear just the month before. I remember because—"

"The next one was completely normal," Janine interrupted.

How did she know? Honeydew wondered.

"And no abnormal ones since."

She raised an eyebrow at her.

"Anyone ever tell you that you look young for your age?"

"It's the seaweed, isn't it?" Honeydew said finally, knowing it was.

Janine nodded at her, looked out through the glass at the tentacle guiding them slowly along.

Honeydew followed the woman's gaze, saw on her face the cascade of thought.

"Gene repair is finally within our grasp," Janine said. "Why didn't they realize it? That's what the research stations are for—to discover new technologies and explore biodiversities. Why did they abandon it? What forced them to evacuate?"

Honeydew and Janine exchanged a glance.

* * *

Colonel Karen Delaney thrust her face into his. "We have to shut it down!"

Samuel Ericson, Chief Civilian Research Director, Nartressa Station, felt the vein pulse at his temple. "You're right," he said, dropping his gaze. "We've failed." He looked around command central. "Everyone, your attention, please. All stations, begin emergency disconnection protocol, then evacuate immediately. Archive control team, please remove the memory core containing last two years and secure it in hover bay twelve aboard shuttle gamma."

His coke beeped and corn flashed as he received acknowledgements. Then without a word he turned for the door.

"What about that other monster, Doctor?" the woman called after him.

But he was already in the quadcart and requesting that the biomainframe plot out a secured route. The quadcart took off under him, and he clutched the controls to keep from falling out. The quadcart plunged down a ramp headlong, its horn blaring, the biomainframe clearing traffic from the route.

Twenty minutes to microfusion core removal! he thought, knowing he had just enough time to stop at his private laboratory below before he ascended to hover bay twelve. He'd be among the last to be airlifted to safety before the containment bulkheads moved permanently into place over every egress, the black operation having triple redundant termination protocols, the last being the ultimate termination device: microfusion core overload.

The quadcart swerved to avoid a pedestrian then spun around a corner into the corridor leading to his personal laboratory.

The door snicked aside just ahead of the quadcart, and then closed behind it as it lurched to a stop.

"Doctor Ericson!" His young lab-tech, not fifteen years old and apprenticed to him for a year, looked white as a sheet. "We're really going black!?" In both arms, he cradled a bundle.

"Get in the back! Get down inside and hold on for life! Now, boy, move it!" Samuel grabbed a blaster from the small-arms arsenal near the door, then climbed back in.

The boy got in, clutching the bundle, and Ericson signaled on his trake. "Let's go!"

Chapter 13

The adaptive potential of this genome! Janine was thinking. What Shannon went through confirms what I've been wondering all along. Somehow, the seaweed detects people's medical conditions and cures them! Either the seaweed manufactures the chemical antagonist or repairs the diseased tissue itself.

Bacterial and viral antigens were relatively simple to reverse engineer, but the difficult task was always the administration. How did the seaweed get the antigen where it was needed without destroying the surrounding healthy tissue or introducing noxious waste products?

Janine could come up with a few hypotheses as to how the seaweed provided the cure, but what baffled her completely was how the seaweed knew that people were sick.

As the seaweed forest handed off their disabled submersible from tree to tree, all the while following the glowing blue ridge, Janine watched in fascination as the ridge grew in girth and height. The spine where the blue tendrils attached pulsated, as though shunting a fluid.

Soon a smaller ridge joined the larger, and the combined ridge stood us tall as she.

The triangular blue tube from her dream, she knew.

What else have I dreamt that'll turn out to be not a dream at all? she wondered.

"Up ahead is our destination."

Janine looked at the other woman. Shannon appeared to be about thirty years old, was startling in her attractiveness, her shapely body invoking an envy that Janine found disquieting. Shannon's otherworldly expression, her ethereal look of having a direct com channel to God, caused Janine nothing short of awe.

"What did you do before coming to Nartressa?"

"I was a prostitute."

Revulsion and fascination pulled Janine in equally opposite directions. She would have been shocked had the answer been less than forthright. In Shannon, Janine saw no hesitation, no internalized opprobrium, not a hint of shame. "Travel and independence," she remarked.

"Boring interactions with shame-filled men who swear they've never done that before and always ask to see you again."

Janine laughed. "Sounds like some of the men I've dated."

The other woman laughed as well. "Is your spiderbot waterproof?"

That disquieting abrupt change of thinking. Janine nodded, puzzled, sensing again that Shannon possessed knowledge beyond what their immediate environment indicated. "Why?"

Ahead, a bulbous nodule emerged through the viscous liquid, easily large enough to house the submersible.

Funny, I don't ever think of seawater as thick, Janine thought.

"Because we swim from here to there," Shannon said.

"But ..."

"Trust me," the woman told her, a dead certainly in her gaze that would not be denied. "We'll swim up underneath."

But Janine was just as certain it would kill her. The poisoned Nartressa oceans were deadly within minutes.

"What's that?"

Just off starboard, in the notch where two triangular blue tubes joined the module, just visible through the murky waters, was a submersible identical to theirs.

"That's Randall's! Where is he? Is he all right?"

"I took him back to the surface a day ago."

Relieved, Janine traced the route. No matter how quick the swimmer, it still meant at least a few minutes fully exposed to the poison water. "How do I know you're telling the truth?"

Shannon smiled and shrugged.

The submersible began to tilt, and Janine kept her feet by climbing over equipment, Monkey in hand.

She ended up standing on the portal. "Now what?"

The other woman released the catch.

"What are you doing? The water pressure at this depth will kill us!"

Shannon smiled and shook her head. "Watch. It's a short swim." Warning buzzers went off as she pushed open the hatch. And she plunged feet first into the water.

Janine watched through the glasma as Shannon swam lazily, almost casually, toward the bottom side of the bulbous nodule, looking back occasionally to see if Janine would follow.

Why isn't she gasping for breath? Janine wondered, realizing Shannon had stopped just under the bulb.

On closer examination, Janine realized she was seeing the expansion and contraction in Shannon's rib cage.

It looks like she's breathing the water! Janine thought, stunned. The prion! Janine realized, the prion isolates free radicals!

So deadly to humans, the microscopic, virus-like organism called a prion found in every drop of Nartressan ocean water had to be the agent that removed free oxygen from that same water, thereby keeping the two Nartressan nucleotides from oxidizing. The prion that monopolized all available oxygen in the human body when a person was submerged for more than a few minutes, resulting in a swift death, was not harming Shannon in any way.

"How did you adapt to the prion?" Janine yelled.

And she realized the only way for her to find out was to follow.

Holding monkey tight, she plunged into the poison Nartressan ocean.

* * *

Randall recognized instantly what was happening to Brian.

After he'd followed the older man into the command theater, its screens ablaze with scenes from the past, Randall had watched in prurient curiosity as Brian's face had gone from astonishment to horror to revulsion, his temple twitching ominously. Then his face had twisted and he'd fallen to the floor, spasms wracking his body. The beet-red face, the sweat, the involuntary twitching, all indicated a major cardiovascular event, probably an aneurysm.

Randall leaped for the med-surge extensible on the wall. He ripped it out of its casing and dropped it beside Brian's head, then plunged his arms into the arm-length interfaces.

The med-surge extensible replaced his senses with its own, taking full control of his coke, corn, trake, and subdural.

Randall saw instantly this was not the extensible he'd used in trade school. Instead of fine-tuned mechanical pincers, scalpels, clamps, endoscopes, and arthroscopes, this extensible had blue tendrils which slid right under Brian's skin without apparent need for incision.

The tendrils helped him locate the problem immediately: massive aneurysm to the right parietal lobe. Brian had blown a blood vessel.

Using the four types of tendrils—visual, tactile, injectory, and extractory—Randall stabilized the heart rate by injecting a beta-blocker, constricted the vessel upstream of the aneurysm to stanch the flow, sewed the rupture closed, vacuumed up wayward blood, then reopened the constricted vessel to let the blood through again. He withdrew the visual tendrils just far enough to examine his work, and quickly saw that the repairs would hold.

Then he realized that the blood vessel showed evidence of a prior rupture, scars farther down the same vessel, the surrounding tissues evidencing necrotic shrinkage.

He's had an aneurysm before, Randall thought, withdrawing the tendrils completely.

He pulled his arms from the interface, realizing as he closed up the med-surge extensible that he'd just performed emergency brain surgery.

"What happened?" Brian asked, his voice weak.

"Aneurysm," Randall replied, standing with an effort, feeling as though he'd just run a race, his legs weak and sweat pouring off him. He replaced the extensible in its receptacle, the machine beeping and humming as it sterilized itself. It appeared to be a modified version of the same extensible he'd trained on. But modified by whom? he wondered, the blue tendrils piquing his interest.

"Aren't those usually fatal?"

Randall nodded, told him what he'd done, still not sure how he'd done it. "Let me see your head." He examined the other man's scalp through thick black hair. No evidence of incision, puncture or break. As though the tendrils had been part of the man's flesh.

"Am I bleeding?"

"No, you're not. In fact, the incision sites are already healed. Whoever modified that med-surge extensible really knew what they were doing."

"You saved my life," Brian said, probing his head with his fingers.

Randall nodded, glancing at the screens. "Pretty upsetting?"

"Must have ... not sure ..."

The EMT decided to probe further. "What's today's date?"

"August second."

"Day of the week?"

"Sunday."

"Year?"

"2443."

"Current location?"

"Nartressa, underground research facility."

"Name?"

"Sa ... Brian Franks, CEO Aquafoods Interstellar."

"What's the year?"

"You already asked me that."

"Tell me again."

"2443. Why? What's wrong?"

Randall looked at the older man calmly. "Because, Mr. Franks, it's 2487, and that face—" He pointed at one of the screens—"that face is your face."

* * *

"That's ridiculous. I've never been here before!" Why did I think my name was something else? Brian wondered, staring at the EMT.

"Really? Why was it such a shock to come in here, then?" Randall asked him. "Something caused you to have an aneurysm."

"That med-surge—you shouldn't have been able to do that. You said it's been modified?"

The younger man nodded. "Blue tendrils, the same blue tendrils we found at the cavern, keeping those people alive. We should get Janine to look at a med-surge. I'm thinking they're some smaller version of those triangular blue tubes."

"You dreamt of those, too?"

"Dreamt? I was in one, with ... her."

"Wasn't a dream, eh?" Brian got unsteadily to his feet, waving off the other man's help. How much else have I dreamt that wasn't a dream? he wondered.

Scenes from the past continued to play on the many screens in the command theater. Brian remembered the dream he'd had as the blood vessel was bursting in his brain. A red-haired woman shouting, his looking around the room and ordering the closure of the research station, his going to his personal ...

"This way," Brian said, stepping toward the door. On his trake, he ordered a quadcart to take him to Doctor Ericson's laboratory.

"Where're we going?" Randall asked.

A quadcart appeared, intact but for dust. Brian settled into a seat, annoyed at having to get his formalls dirty. "Get in. You'll see."

The quadcart took them downward, the vehicle moving through a series of caverns, dark dank corridors, steep ramps both up and down. Brian reflected on how much space appeared to be wasted, as little of the traverse passed what looked to be occupied space. What other secrets do these rock walls hide? he wondered.

The quadcart stopped in a small cavern with four doors.

Brian knew exactly which door to try. "This one," he said.

"How do you know?"

Brian ignored him and stepped toward it. The panel slid aside.

"It knows," Randall said. "Janine and I were shown a pair of rooms somewhere down here. We could only open our own rooms, but neither of us could open the other's."

"They tried to shut it down."

The young man's head spun around. "What'd you say?"

"Doctor Ericson gave the order to shut down the research station just before he came down here to his laboratory. Let's go see what was so important that he had to retrieve it before they evacuated." Brian gestured at the open laboratory door.

The lights went on as they entered.

The walls held the usual equipment: coolers and fume hoods, flasks of compounds, extensible mounts. The ceiling was festooned with machinery, hundreds of mechanical arms, from delicate spidery arms to beefy gargantuan arms. On the far wall was an enclosure whose prominence announced its importance. Elevated a few steps on a round platform, the glasma-enclosed bladder looked immediately familiar.

"It looks like a womb," Randall said.

* * *

Honeydew removed her hands from the young woman's chest.

She coughed and sputtered, rolled to one side and wretched, then shook her head. "I don't believe I did that." She looked at Honeydew. "Why didn't it kill me?"

"Because it doesn't want you to die." Honeydew smiled and helped her up. "You're important, and you'll be protected." She saw the younger woman looking around.

"The triangular blue tube! Just like in my dream. What else have I dreamt that wasn't a dream?"

Honeydew smiled and gestured the other woman to follow. She stepped into the triangular blue tube that curved down and to the right, the rubbery surface under the soles of her formalls giving slightly with each step.

Honeydew knew for certain now that that wasn't her name, that she had been brought here for an urgent purpose, one whose directive could not be deterred from fulfillment. I don't know yet why I'm here, but I know it's important, and I know each step that I have to take as I take it, even if I don't know the eventual goal.

She led Janine down and around to a hatch where the tube burrowed into rock.

Janine examined the place where the tube joined the hatch. "The tube looks grown, but the hatch was built."

"A curious blend of biology and mechanics." Honeydew opened the hatch and led the way through. The rock-walled passageway led into a cavern.

Twisted bundles of blue tendrils dropped from the ceiling, each bundle plunging into a columnar tube. Hundreds of tubes marched away in rows in two directions.

Inside each pillar was a body.

Janine gasped beside her. "Who are they?"

On the rock wall beside the hatch, a display lit up. A seaweed attack on a trawler played out on the screen. The camera zoomed in on a crew member, her thick rubber envirosuit draped shapelessly around her. Behind the glasma faceplate, her eyes were wide with terror. A tentacle smashed the gunwale beside her, then wrapped around her midriff and pulled her under, on her face, an eerily silent scream. The tentacle pulled her deep as far as it could go, passed her body to the next tentacle, deeper and deeper, one tentacle to the next, until she reached the sea floor. There, a tentacle pushed the body into an opening on a triangular blue tube, and the body was propelled through the tube, length after length, the tube penetrating rock, and into the column she now occupied, set up on a pedestal. A twisted bundle of blue tendrils dropped from the ceiling. The tendrils slipped under the skin and found their way to the major organs and revived the woman, albeit keeping her in an unconscious state.

Honeydew knew of this already, but the vid had not played for her benefit.

"All the trawler crew who've died in the seaweed attacks," Janine said. "They're not dead—not a single one! They're all down here, aren't they?"

Honeydew nodded.

Janine's eyes traveled across the ceiling. "Where do those tendrils all go?"

"This way." Honeydew walked down an aisle between two banks of columns, the widths varying slightly with the size of the person, their naked forms relaxed and at peace. She sensed how the blue tendrils monitored all the biologic functions for each person, introducing nutrients, extracting wastes, and massaging muscles to maintain tone, all the stimuli needed for long-term, nearly-cryogenic storage.

"They need to be returned to their families," Janine said. "Why aren't they being released? What gives the planet the right to hold these people captive like this?"

Honeydew had also wondered about the ethics of keeping them here, knowing Janine was right, to some degree. "Randall asked the same question." She told Janine about the people with incurable illnesses.

"That's different!" Janine insisted. "These people aren't responsible for sending the trawlers out."

"You're right. They aren't individually responsible, but ultimately, collectively, we all are."

"What?" Janine looked at her, her brows drawn together.

"Everyone who's eaten Nartressan seafood is responsible. When we consume like gluttons without regard for consequence, we're surprised when natural systems attempt to rectify our excess."

Janine blinked at her and then looked at the columns they passed.

They reached the other end of the cavern, where Honeydew looked back. "The consequences could have been worse. The seaweed wasn't obligated to save them. Its only obligation is to save itself." Honeydew sensed the younger woman's disquietude as she led her through narrow corridors, across caverns, up and down ramps, and to a hatch wide enough for five people abreast, the largest hatch they'd seen.

On her trake, Honeydew said, "Open hatch, please."

Somewhere motors whined, and the inches-thick metal door retracted slowly into the ceiling. Beyond was a cavern dominated by a bubbling pool of glowing blue water. The surface churning with underwater currents, and diaphanous mists obscured the opposite wall. A low balustrade separated the deep blue pool from a walkway against the cavern wall.

Honeydew and Janine strode along the walkway, fascinated by the roiling blue liquid, surrounded by the smell of apple cider.

Visible under the surface was what looked like coral, but like only one kind of coral Honeydew had ever seen.

"Brain coral," Janine said.

They passed a portal leading out of the cavern, then another, the coral growing to the edge of the pool walls, but not touching it.

"I wonder if one of those portals leads downward to where we can see the brain stem," Janine said.

They came upon five platforms extending over the roiling blue liquid, each about two feet wide, six feet long, separated by two feet, breaks in the low balustrade at the foot of each platform.

"Looks like just enough space for a person to lie down," Janine said.

"Why are there five of them?" Honeydew asked.

"Why would someone want to lie down on one?" Janine smirked.

The walkway ahead was fissured, its edges jagged. The pool surface was particularly turbulent, sounds of gurgling clearly audible. The fissure was three feet wide, a stream of water pouring into the pool. Within, visible under the flow of water, was a three-foot thick bundle of blue tendrils.

"They tried to shut it down after it broke out of its containment vessel," Janine said.

"They shut down the research station, but they couldn't stop their experiment." Honeydew wasn't sure how she knew.

They leaped the three-foot fissure, and the path curved around to follow the cavern wall. Ahead a glasma pane replaced the wall, and beyond it they saw a tiered control room, three semi-circular platforms, all the desks empty, looking as forlorn as the other empty control rooms she'd seen. Honeydew tried to imagine the place crowded with people, observing their experiment through the glasma containment wall, their sensors alight with readings.

Arms reached into the incubator and lifted her from her cocoon, pulled her from its warmth into the cold laboratory beyond. She wailed at the cold air washing over her and—

"Come on, Shannon," a voice called.

Honeydew snapped back into the present and saw Janine gesturing from an open doorway. She looked down; a single blue tendril retracted itself from her ankle and slid back into the pool.

She followed Janine into the control room, noting the med-surge extensible near the door. If Randall hadn't pointed them out to her in the other cavern, she might not have known what they were. She followed down the steps to the orchestral pit, the glasma wall towering above them. Beyond it, coral blossomed like cauliflower gone wild.

"This was where they lost control of their experiment," Janine said. "They were alerted to a containment-wall breach, but then that too went silent. I'm guessing that their artificial protein brain had already infiltrated their sensor network, and that they lost control of their experiment months before they shut down the research station."

"It began to control the information they received."

Janine looked at her strangely. "How do we know it isn't doing so now?"

"We had better assume it's been doing so all along."

The other woman looked pale. "You don't seem disturbed by that."

Honeydew smiled. "I'm not. In fact, it's somewhat a comfort. You look puzzled. I've been baffled by event after event since I arrived on Nartressa, and I suspect it's all been the doing of this same brain. The comforting thing for me is that all actions were taken with the singleness of purpose, and weren't random acts of chaos." Honeydew looked at the other woman, seeing the same fascinated revulsion that she'd seen when she'd told her she'd been a prostitute.

"You told me you've loved alien species all your life. Here, we have an alien species born of human experimentation, and you shrink in horror. How is it any different?" She turned to regard the gargantuan brain just beyond the glasma, thick blue fluid shot through with bubbles surging around it. How strange we act when we encounter something far more powerful than anything we've ever had to reckon with.

"I shrink because I don't know its overriding directive."

Honeydew considered that. How many thousands of science fiction vids had been premised on technology come to life, on experiments that achieved sentience, on monsters become self-aware? In each was the premise that self-awareness meant self-preservation, and in self-preservation was the underlying assumption that self must be preserved at the cost of sacrificing other, even if that meant destroying one's own creator.

Especially when it meant destroying one's own creator.

And how often in those tales did the monster, in seeing the destruction it had wrought, then turn and cast itself into oblivion, its life truncated before it had achieved any semblance of maturity?

"How will you discover its overriding directive?" she asked the Xenobiologist. "How will you know you've discovered it, without being deceived by the information that it's allowing you to receive?"

The brows came together, dark hair on white skin, lupine singularity in focus. Then Janine smiled. "I think I know. Come on."

Chapter 14

Janine stared at the remains of an exploded cavern wall. From her experiences at the Sydney Research Station, she knew exactly what had happened.

"Someone escaped." She gestured Shannon to follow her into the short, jagged passageway, picking her way carefully through rubble. "All the research stations have emergency escape pods, carefully sealed and obscured. In the event of enemy attack, natural disaster, or contaminant outbreak, these pods are here for those who know about them. Research Station personnel are briefed on them, and emergency evacuation drills mention them as alternatives to the usual exit routes. I've never seen one used."

She shined her light upward to the underside of a retractable roof, then down to a metal bracing scorched with burn marks. Sniffing, she smelled only dank cavern walls. No explosive or propulsive residue from the escape pod launch.

"A long time ago," Shannon said, nostrils flaring.

Janine nodded and retreated to the passageway. The two women had been walking for hours, ascending endless flights of stairs, traversing long sinuous tunnels and large caverns. Janine knew where she was going but had only a rudimentary understanding of the station's layout. She had reasoned that a research station built to study the aquatic life would have its hover bays inland in order to disturb the life it studied the least.

Their discovering the exploded passageway wall and the empty escape pod chamber told her they were close to their destination. The fact that an emergency escape pod had been utilized alerted Janine to the possibility that—

"Do you think the evacuation went awry?" Shannon asked.

"That's exactly what I'm thinking. Let's go see." Janine smiled and gestured along the tunnel, glancing back the way they'd come. I'm glad Shannon found me, she was thinking, the prospect of traversing this catacomb alone was enough to send chills down her back.

"How many people would typically work in a research station like this?"

Janine glanced at her, her attention on the rough rock wall as they strode along the wide tunnel. "Difficult to say. The one on Sydney housed at least twelve hundred, but that wasn't a dark op. This one, which was a secret operation, probably a lot fewer, maybe six hundred at most. Three hundred or so is more likely."

The rough rock wall here looked different somehow.

"What's this wire?" Shannon said.

Janine traced the wire up, over, and down, seeing blobs of what looked like clay that the wire went through. "Hard-wired explosive for the emergency escape pod. I'll bet we find more."

She counted eight total before they reached a pressurized hatch where the tunnel ended, the smooth floor clearly designed to accommodate wheeled vehicles. On the hatch was a large "12." The hatch was purely mechanical, the center wheel spinning easily to the touch, the equipment designed to last.

Beyond the hatch was a hangar, the ceiling crisscrossed with beams. Hovers stood in rows on the hangar floor, two rows of four each, the last and farthest from the door had a quadcart beside it.

"Look—footprints."

Four pairs of footprints were clear in the half-inch thick dust. Two pairs clearly led directly to the last hover, and two others led back.

"They look recent."

The two women exchanged a glance. "If we're careful, we can use those same footprints."

Janine traced the steps carefully, but when looking back, she could clearly see her own smaller footprints inside the larger. "Maybe no one will notice the double set. They'd have to examine the footprints pretty closely."

The clear trail disintegrated at the quadcart and hover, and it wasn't possible any longer to obscure their footprints.

The rear hover door was open slightly, the footprints under it numerous.

Janine pulled open the door.

Across the floor of the hover lay a long, gray-metal cartridge, six inches by four inches by four feet. Etched in the endplate was the inscription "January 2441—"

Janine gasped. The archive control team had been ordered to evacuate with the module containing the last two years of the research station's record, a record that Janine had tried to reconstruct using the parity files. "This is it!" she said, excited. "Here, help me with this." She and Shannon wrestled the heavy cartridge onto the quadcart. "They were evacuating with this archive module. I'm guessing they didn't make it." None of the hovers looked as if they'd moved in hundreds of years, and the only signs of disturbance had been the quadcart near the last of eight hovers, and that hover's open door.

"What are we going to do with this?"

"Find out where they took it from, plug it in, and try to figure out what went wrong here on Nartressa. Then we'll know what we're dealing with and why the seaweed is attacking people. Let's see if this quadcart still works."

* * *

Doctor Samuel Ericson felt the quadcart under him fail, the motor losing power, the controls going flaccid under his hands, the control panel shutting off.

"What's going on? Why are we stopping?"

"Hush!" he hissed at the boy huddled in the small, rear compartment, a bundle tucked in his arms. Ericson punched buttons to no avail, the quadcart rolling to a stop. He could feel that he still had manual control, but either the optimitter link to the central computer had failed, or the computer itself had shut down.

"Central, what the hells' going on?" he asked on his trake.

No response. Dead air.

He pressed the "manual override" button.

The quadcart did not respond.

The corridor where they'd stopped was empty, but intersections ahead and behind bustled with evacuees, their quadcarts working just fine.

We're still a mile below ground, Ericson estimated. Too far to walk, he decided, and he ripped open the quadcart maintenance panel. No schematic, but he didn't need one, having a doctorate in chemical and electrical engineering. There! He ripped out a wire and jimmied open the underside of the manual override, connected the wire, and the quadcart roared to life.

"Stay down," he told the boy, and stomped on the accelerator.

The quadcart launched itself down into the turn, another quadcart beeping in alarm at the narrow miss, the wind whipping through his thick dark hair.

The ceiling lights passed overhead like strobes as they gained speed. He slowed for a ramp, ascended, spun at the top, people scattering, disgruntled voices reaching him long after he'd plowed past their owners. Up another ramp, through a cavern, around a rotunda, up another ramp. Then the lights flickered overhead.

Still five minutes to shutdown, Doctor Ericson thought, wondering what caused the power fluctuations.

A hatch slammed shut in front of him, and he slammed on the brakes, turning to the right and throwing himself that way.

The quadcart smashed into the door.

He crawled from the smoking wreckage, an electrical short buzzing intermittently. "Steve! Are you all right?" His temple began to pulsate. He pulled himself up the side.

The wide eyes of his lab-tech stared at him, then blinked.

He took the bundle from the boy. Inside, the infant girl gurgled placidly. Relieved, he helped the boy out of the cart.

"What happened?" the boy asked.

"Not sure," Dr. Ericson said, "but let's go." Fifteen feet back along the corridor was a hatch marked "emergency exit."

The hatch wouldn't budge.

"Stand back," he said, handing the infant to the boy. He whipped out his blaster and blew the lock off the door.

The stairwell inside was empty. Five levels up, Ericson estimated. They went up and around, both of them taking the stairs two a time. The girl began to cry out at the jostling. They reached the fifth level and stopped. He took the girl from the young man to try to comfort her. He was murmuring to her when the lights died.

Ericson flipped on a pocket lamp. "Here." He handed the infant back to the boy, knowing he wouldn't be able to open the door. "I suspect our little experiment has taken over the research station entirely." He tried the door anyway.

Locked, of course.

"How'll we get out?" The boy's eyes were wide with fright.

Dr. Ericson smiled. "The hover bay has a manual overhead door. We'll try the hover bay first. Step back. I'll have to blow open this door, too." The vein throbbed mightily at his temple. He had the worst headache he'd ever had.

The door exploded outward. The short narrow corridor intersected a wide, smooth-floored tunnel, wide enough for two quadcarts abreast.

The lights flickered on for a moment. In the distance stood a wide hatch, slightly ajar. On the hatch, a large "12."

He'd chosen hover bay twelve for its distance from the main research station. The other eleven hover bays were likely bedlam, clogged with quadcarts full of people seeking an escape route. No evacuation in his experience had ever been orderly.

"Doctor Ericson!" Colonel Karen Delaney came running up behind him. "I thought I'd find you up here." She looked over his shoulder toward his lab-tech, Steve. Her eyes alighted on the bundle in his arms. "How dare you bring it! That monster will escape your control, too!" She loped toward the hover bay door and pulled it open.

A blue fog poured from the hover bay, and she collapsed instantly.

"Colonel Delaney!" the boy said, lunging that direction. "Karen!"

Doctor Ericson stopped him, his temple numb and the vision gone from his right eye. "Too late," he said, shining his light on the wall, looking for the tell-tale wire.

The blue fog crept down the corridor toward them.

"Steve, stand back!" He pulled the boy against the wall and down, telling him to crouch, located the trigger and turned his back, using his body to shield both boy and infant girl.

The explosion nearly knocked him over anyway.

His ears ringing, rock dust causing him to cough, his right eye blind and a hammer smashing his temple repeatedly, Doctor Ericson guided the boy with the bundle into the escape pod, the red cross of a med-surge extensible right beside the door.

Doctor Ericson collapsed into a chair, the hammer at his temple turning into a jackhammer. He cried out as his sight went black.

* * *

Riding in the passenger seat, Randall looked over at Brian.

The older man braked and stopped the quadcart.

Randall saw that his eyelids were at half-mast. "You all right?" He felt the rising adrenalin of an incipient medical emergency.

"Fine ... just tired," the other man said, "You take the wheel."

Randall stepped around the vehicle, the other man dragging himself across the seat. "You sure you're all right?" Randall waited, the quadcart eager to take off.

"I'm seventy-five blasted years old and just suffered an aneurysm, of course I'm not all right! Step on it anyway, man! That memory core is the only thing that can tell us what happened down here."

Randall stepped on it. The quadcart took off, quickly picking up speed. The man in the seat beside him seemed able to take the first few turns in spite of what looked like severe fatigue. Without restraints, he was worried that Brian would fall out. Soon, Randall focused only on driving, the narrow tunnels and exposed ramps dangerous at high speeds.

Why is he so focused on what happened here? Randall wondered. It seemed a question more likely to come from Janine the Xenobiologist than from Brian the Seafood Mogul. What could have possibly happened forty years ago that would impact the fish harvest?

He kept glancing at the drowsy man beside him, the oldster having far more pluck and venom than most people half his age. And this was the guy whom the other woman followed to Nartressa? Randall had ceased wondering why people sought the company of others whom they had nothing in common with. They'd never ceased to amaze him, his job taking him into homes and lives that most people would never see.

Randall hoped Janine was all right. The fact that he'd heard nothing from her for days was worrisome. He didn't know if she'd even escaped the research station, remembering his own difficulties finding an exit. Then he snorted to himself—as if she'd want to escape!

He headed in the general direction of hover bay twelve; the map on his corn indicated a somewhat remote spot beyond the eastern edge of the subterranean facility.

And the woman who hadn't known her name, her breathtaking beauty only enhanced by her mysterious manner. Randall wondered how she'd even found her way into the research station. Saving his life in that blue bulbous...plant, the triangular blue tube from his dream. What was going on down here? Who was she, and why did she seem so at home in such a forbidding place? And those tubes with all those ill people in them. What sort of being would keep them in perpetual suspension like that, their minds active but their bodies imprisoned?

Randall hunched over the quadcart controls, Brian slumped drowsily toward him, his eyes barely open. Worried that the old man might be failing ill again, he stopped the cart.

"What are you doing?"

"Making sure you're all right." He inspected the man's color.

Skin slightly ashen but still within normal limits. Temperature thirty seven degrees, slightly above normal, slightly moist skin, pupils normal and reactive.

"Light hurts," Brian mumbled.

"That's a good thing." He checked the other pupil. Equal size, also reactive.

Pulse a hundred, slightly elevated. The wrist cuff gave him a blood pressure of one-forty over ninety, also slightly elevated.

The altered mental status worried Randall. "We should get you to a hospital, do a full cranial exam."

"Blast it, that'll take days," Brian growled. "My head felt better when you had that med-surge thing on me. Why not use that again? That way we won't have to wait. We can go to the hospital after we recover that memory core."

Randall sighed, reluctant. He looked around, this corridor mostly featureless, but for two doors on one side. "Let me see if I can find one."

The first door slid aside as he stepped in front of it. The personal quarters beyond lit up.

A two-bedroom, one-bath unit, decorated in aboriginal fashion, a didgeridoo and dingo depicted in dyed-and-dried Kangaroo grasses on one wall, and laid out in wood-stained eucalyptus, the piquant aroma still evident.

Beside the door was a med-surg extensible.

He pulled it from its holder, wondering at how many there were. Probably didn't have much more than a small infirmary down here, he thought, doubting they would access the full-sized hospital in Rockdale hundreds of feet above them. You don't run an underground dark op by interacting a lot with the above-ground population, he thought.

In the corridor, he set it to automatic and positioned it behind Brian. A small bundle of blue tendrils extruded, crawled up his neck and slid under the skin.

Randall shuddered, the idea of the quasi-alien tendril inside his brain making him queasy. He secured the med-surge to Brian's shoulders. "I don't want it to get dislodged."

Back at the controls, comforted that Brian looked immediately better, Randall guided the quadcart swiftly through tunnels that might have otherwise proved too narrow.

Then the right half of the tunnel fell away, and Randall slowed.

The cavern was large, and they sat on a ledge fifty feet above the surface of an azure pool. Whips of mist floated above it, as though the water were steamy. The water surface looked bubbly, as though some chemical engine generated gasses deep below the surface. The smell reminded Randall of apple cider.

The shelf where they sat reached out over the pool surface, and he couldn't tell from this vantage what was directly below them. Across the cavern, a similar pathway wound its way along the cavern wall, thirty feet below theirs. In the middle was a treacherous turn.

"You'd think they'd have railings or something," Brian said.

Nodding, Randall accelerated, the map on his corn indicating some obstruction ahead. The path wasn't clear, anyway. He wasn't surprised that the map appeared incomplete, as though multiple parts of the research station weren't documented. He suspected large portions required secure access and clearances for them even to appear.

The tunnel twisted and dropped, spiraled once downward, turned a few more times.

"Come on, why so cautious?" Brian muttered. "We haven't got all day!"

Miffed, as he'd been going as fast as he'd thought safe, Randall sped up, and the tunnel wall fell away on their right again.

The fog was thicker here and Randall began to slow.

"Come on! What are you afraid of, boy!?"

Randall threw an annoyed glance at the old man.

"Watch out!"

He yanked the wheel left and stomped the brake, sending the quad into a skid. He leaned into it, his head nearly horizontal, tires screeching, the quad shuddering to a stop.

"That was clo—"

He heard a distant splash.

The seat beside him was empty.

Horror coursed through him. He peered over the edge.

Large ripples radiated from a bubbly froth, the blue liquid having swallowed Brian whole.

Randall got out, looked over the edge.

Twenty feet below, the ripples dissipated, wisps of steam snaking lazily up from the surface.

The edge of the pool was sheer rock wall. Even if he jumped in after the old man, he'd have no way of pulling him out. Randall sat on the ledge and wept for yet another victim of the voracious monster.

* * *

Janine took the first turn she found, betting that it would take her downward. The rudimentary map of the research station on her corn appeared to have large portions missing. Even within a dark op, security clearances would restrict access only to those with a need to know.

The ramp spiraled downward.

"Where are we taking this?" Shannon asked, gesturing at their cargo.

"We're going to reinstall the memory core and find out what happened down here."

They dropped into a cavern glowing with blue light.

Janine braked, smelling apples, and looked around. "What happened here?"

The ramp curled around the wall, and at the base, the rock had fissured, the fissure running vertically up the cavern wall. Inside the fissure was a foot-thick bundle of blue tendrils.

Janine carefully guided the quadcart across the fissure. At the base, three passageways lead away, one each to the north, south, and west. She guessed they were at the eastern edge of the complex, only the remote hover bay to the east of their location.

"I want to look at that fissure," Shannon said.

Janine watched the other woman over her shoulder, her foot on the quadcart brake.

Shannon stepped to the fissure and straddled it, threw her head back to peer upward. "Looks like it goes straight up. I wonder where it leads."

"Probably infiltrates the ground-level communication network," Janine said, smirking. "It's what I'd do if I were an alien brain down—"

A bright blue gas hissed from the bundle and enveloped Shannon, who crumpled.

"Shannon!" Janine went to climb out of the quadcart but the gas spilled to the cavern floor and surged toward her. She stomped on the accelerator, and the quadcart shot into a tunnel. In the next cavern, she stopped. What the galaxy was that? she wondered, watching the tunnel behind her for approaching blue gas.

Is Shannon alright? she wondered, debating whether to return to retrieve the other woman's body, not knowing whether she was unconscious or worse. With enough warning, I can get away from the gas. And if I don't get too close to the blue tendrils, it shouldn't be able to get me with the gas as it did Shannon.

She spun the quadcart around and drove slowly back toward the other cavern, the headlights picking out the passageway detail. Seeing no gas, and smelling only the mild scent of apples, Janine crept along, ready to throw the quadcart into reverse.

The blue-lit cavern visible ahead, she saw no gas.

At the tunnel entrance, she stopped.

Near the base of the ramp, where the fissure intersected the cavern floor, where Shannon had fallen when enveloped by the glowing gas, was now only bare rock.

The bundle of blue tendrils glowed contentedly inside the fissure but the cavern was empty.

Janine backed the quadcart along the tunnel, panic rising inside her. What had the alien protein brain done with Shannon?

* * *

Brian opened his eyes, a blue fog swirling above him.

He sat up, startled. He knew he'd slept—or had been put to sleep—but he didn't know how long.

All he remembered was his rising panic after he'd been pitched from the skidding quadcart into the pool twenty feet below, the warm blue liquid closing around him like embalming fluid. He hadn't been able to breath, and he'd thrashed around until his lungs couldn't take it anymore, and he didn't know which way was up or which way to swim, and the bulky med surge strapped to his shoulders kept him from propelling himself, and his head was thundering, and his lungs were on the verge of exploding, and the screaming of his own voice in his own mind was nearly deafening. Then his lungs gave out, and he expelled the stale air from them, and the viscous blue liquid flowed into them, and he knew he was dead.

Sitting on the ledge, he felt his heart pounding at the memory.

The placid blue pool stared back at him from just a foot below the ledge. Somehow, he hadn't drowned.

Brian shook his head, wondering how he'd survived.

He inspected the med-surg on ledge beside him. It looked intact.

He checked the blaster at his belt. It too looked functional, a full charge showing on the indicator. Gingerly, so as not so fall in again, he lay chest down on the ledge, his right arm above the pool, and he lowered the blaster into the blue liquid.

He felt the moisture around his hand up to his wrist, the temperature the same as his skin. He estimated he might be able to see three feet through the semi-transparent liquid. He inspected the weapon in his hand, both immersed now.

The readout looked normal. The liquid was non-conductive!

He aimed it away from the wall and pulled the trigger.

A six-foot tongue of flame leapt briefly from the barrel, and the blue liquid boiled and grew bright, then the brighter liquid mixed in with the surrounding darker liquid and dissipated.

After a few minutes, only a lighter nimbus marked the place where he'd fired the blaster. When he pulled his hand out, it wasn't wet.

What is this stuff? he wondered, sitting up. Brian wasn't an expert in fluids or fluid mechanics, but he'd worked on enough ocean-going trawlers to know that the blue liquid wasn't behaving like water, or any other liquid he'd seen.

He'd have to ask that Xenobiologist, if he ever met her, what it might be. If I don't shoot her first, the meddling bitch.

He looked around, knowing he needed to get out of here. By himself, he was vulnerable. Where'd that EMT go, anyway? Brian wondered, not knowing if he too had been dumped into the pool. And if I didn't drown, he probably didn't either.

To his left was an exit from the cavern, but the mist was so thick he might have missed it. The far side was obscured, so vague he wasn't really sure how far away it was. The ceiling might have been sky and he wouldn't have known it.

The tunnel he entered was mostly featureless, the dim light at his belt reaching not twenty feet ahead. He passed a few doorways before he recognized that he'd done so. Choosing one at random, he did what he'd seen Randall do: stood still in a doorway.

The door slid aside, and the light went on.

Bamboo and mahogany seemed to be the theme. Brian rolled his eyes at the utterly pedestrian decor. A two-bedroom, one-bath suite, a holo display in the corner, a kitchenette too cramped for one person, a living area not big enough to die in.

The mealmaker still worked, and he ordered a steak on his trake. He felt oddly unhungry, as though he'd eaten recently. He knew he hadn't. He ate doggedly, just for the sensation of food in his mouth.

He didn't feel replete after eating, which he thought odd. What'd somebody do, turn off my hunger reflex? He considered a second steak but decided not to. As he stepped to the door, a clean-bot scurried out to tidy up after him.

The corridor led to a rotunda, a lift sitting in the middle. Calling up a map on his corn, he ordered the lift to take him east.

The lift came to life, going up a level before taking off laterally toward hover bay twelve, where he and Randall had been heading before he took a dive into the blue goo. As it slowed, Brian prepared to step off.

End of the line, he saw.

Instead of a shaft to take him upward, there was a spiral ramp that disappeared into the ceiling.

What was that? he wondered, thinking he'd heard something. When the sound didn't repeat, he set off, climbing the steep ramp with the energy of someone thirty years younger.

Within minutes he was breathing heavily, but his lungs seemed remarkably clear and he didn't get winded at all, in spite of his seventy-five years. I should take a bath in that stuff more often, he thought.

A tire squealed, and he flattened himself to the inside curve as a quadcart barreled past him, the driver's eyes almost as bright with fright as the headlights. Sparks flew as axle ground against rock, the woman swerving to avoid him. She wrestled the quadcart to a stop a half a turn below him.

"Who the hell are you?"

"Who the hell are you?"

* * *

After leaving the cavern where Brian had been pitched into the pool, med-surg and all, Randall had driven blindly through tunnel and cavern, disgusted that he hadn't tried to rescue the other man, remonstrating himself for going too fast in the quadcart, feeling guilty that he'd glanced away from the path to throw an annoyed look at the old man when he should have been paying attention to the narrow path in front of him.

Finally, Randall had stopped, forlorn and weary, realizing he hadn't slept in who knew how long, and he'd tried a random doorway looking for the nearest bed to lay his head.

And the door slid aside... Randall stared at the figure enclosed in a blue tube, a thick bundle of tendril entwined into the figure's hair, neck, and back.

It's like some bizarre neural interface, he thought, the bundle pulsating softly in time with the woman's breathing.

Or what appeared to be breathing. Immersed in the viscous blue liquid, she looked to be breathing, her chest rising and falling, but no air issued from her mouth.

Her face a foot above his, the tube sitting on a short pedestal, Randall stepped close enough for his breath to fog the glasma. Tiny bubbles in the gel swirled in the currents near her mouth.

She was breathing the liquid!

Her eyes snapped open, and he started, leaping backward two feet, his heart thundering in his chest.

The expression blank, the eyes followed him.

He couldn't be sure, but he thought it was Honeydew.

The hair was redder than he remembered, but the face and body were just as mesmerizing. He wondered how she'd ended up here.

When his heart settled down, he inspected the blue columnar tube, wondering how to get her out of there. At the base, he felt no seam to indicate where glasma began and rock base ended. He walked around it once, feeling the glasma for a seam with a finger.

And admiring the view. She was difficult not to admire.

He looked at the top, which was open. Standing on tiptoe, he managed to slip his fingers over the lip. Through the glasma, he saw that his fingertips were in the liquid, but they didn't feel wet. Try as he might, he couldn't tell by feel when his fingers were immersed. When he removed them and brought his fingers down to his face, they were completely dry, as though the liquid didn't stick to anything. He tried splashing some out. When the drops hit the floor, they disappeared instantly, either evaporated or absorbed into the rock.

What is the stuff? he wondered.

He pushed on the tube to see if it would budge. There! He thought he felt some give. Would it break when it fell over and maybe injure her? If it were the same glasma widely used throughout the galaxy, it wouldn't. Randall doubted it was, however, as he suspected it was manufactured here, the cavern he'd seen with hundreds of such tubes indicating a local source. Who would ship them here from off-planet for this ... He looked up at the bundle of blue tentacles.

I can't just leave her in there, Randall thought.

Planting his feet, he leaned against the tube. The rubberized soles of his formalls gripped the stone well, and he pushed.

Oddly, the base slid off the rock stump and thumped on the floor, the tube teetering. The tendrils began retracting, and Randall leaped to catch the unbalanced tube before it fell.

Inside, Honeydew smiled at him.

He eased the tube to the floor, the blue liquid pouring out and seeping into the floor instantly. He helped her out and to her feet.

"Thank you," she whispered, looking dry already, the last of the liquid sliding off her.

"You're welcome." Embarrassed at her nudity, he said, "I wish I had some clothing to offer you ... "

"Where are we?"

He shook his head, realizing he didn't know either. In his driving frenzy after Brian had been pitched into the pool, Randall hadn't really paid attention to where he was going. On his corn map, he saw they were at the southern edge of the underground research station, under thousands of feet of water.

"Let's find you some clothes." He stepped out into the corridor and saw three or four other doors, the quadcart where he had left it.

The first door he tried was some sort of dispensary, racks of bottles behind a counter. The second door was a laboratory supply closet.

"We must be in a non-residential part of the complex." He gestured to the quadcart, and she joined him, barely room for two on the seat.

Randall was glad to have the controls to hold onto. The woman beside him so alluring, he felt intoxicated. He drove them through several caverns and up one level, liking the feel of her against him.

"Let's try one of these."

He stopped the cart and stepped from it, unable to disguise his ...

She giggled.

Behind the first door they tried was a three-bedroom suite, the kitchen large and accommodating, the living room quite plush.

Where he sat.

She returned with formalls in hand and stopped in front of him.

She let them fall to the floor.

Chapter 15

Janine could see enough of his face. "You!"

"You," he replied, laughing. He pulled out his blaster and aimed it at her.

"Shoot me, you bastard. The galaxy will know soon enough about your horrific experiments down here!"

The soft chuckle wasn't what she expected. "I don't know what you're talking about. And if the galaxy will hear anything, it'll be news of a meddling Xenobiologist's death." Again the soft chuckle.

"What happened to your oath, Dr. Ericson? You swore above all to do no harm!" Janine looked around frantically, half twisted in the quadcart's front seat, the memory core in the cargo container behind her, the cart wedged against the spiral ramp wall where it had ground to a halt. She'd swerved to avoid him and had nearly wrecked doing so. I should have just run him down, she thought.

"I'm no more Doctor Ericson than you're Honeydew Diamond!"

"Who?" He's just not right in his head, Janine thought, wondering if he'd been smoking the weed.

"That woman wandering around down here, the one Randall tells me is down here somewhere."

"Why would Randall tell you anything?"

"Because he's a fool, just like you. Now tell me, fool, what do I do about the seaweed? How do I stop it from attacking my ships?"

"What ships?"

"My trawlers and suborbitals. What other ships would I be asking about?"

Now she was confused. "You aren't Dr. Samuel Ericson?"

"No, of course not! Unlikely look-alike ... No relation. I'm Brian Franks, CEO of Aquafoods Interstellar, and I want to know how to stop the seaweed from attacking my ships!"

The blaster barrel hadn't wavered. He wants something from me, so he won't kill me. "You're over-fishing the planet." She lacked any faith that he'd heed her advice.

"Nothing to do with the seaweed! Why the hell should it mind if my trawlers take a couple of tons off planet every year?"

"The seaweed has a three-stage gestation cycle and a three-species breeding pattern. The fish are the second stage of the gestation cycle. The seaweed gives birth to the fish, the fish fertilize other seaweed pods, and the pods drop to the ocean floor as seaweed seeds. Your trawlers are taking a link from the reproductive chain. The three-species breeding pattern requires a blue fish born of a green stalk to inseminate a red pod, a green fish born of a red stalk to inseminate a blue stalk, and a red fish born of a blue stalk to inseminate a green stalk."

"Red fish, blue fish, all just nursery rhymes! What are you talking about?"

She knew he wouldn't understand. "Look, what's important is that the reproductive cycle is threatened by the amount of fish that you're harvesting. And so is the six-nucleotide genome! Two of those nucleotides oxidize rapidly, and some agent removes the oxygen from the Nartressan oceans, giving rise to the anaerobic prions that are to deadly to humans."

"What the hell does any of that have to do with me?"

Cantankerous old man! Janine thought. "Everything! Doctor Ericson harnessed enough of the genome to adapt it to these med-surg extensibles. And he built a brain out of the proteins, but it escaped his control and now links the seaweed into a community, allowing them to communicate. The seaweed can now detect when someone is ill. And cure them. And what makes you think the seaweed is killing the trawler and suborbital crews anyway? Somewhere below us, there's a cavern filled with blue tubes, hundreds of them, and in each tube is a living, breathing human being—every single one of them an employee of yours."

"I don't believe you."

"Hop in and I'll show you." Janine patted the seat beside her. "Come on, old man, what are you waiting for?" She saw his gaze drop to the object in the cargo bed.

"What are you doing with that?"

She decided to appeal to his cupidity. "That holds all the secrets. What happened here in the last two years, the formulas, the schematics, the progressions—once we have access to that information, we'll make money faster than they can print it."

"Is that all you can think about is money?"

"That's a trawler calling an orbital a barnacle-encrusted scow!" she shot back, disgusted.

He threw his head back and laughed, then climbed in. "Let's go."

Janine smiled and stomped on the accelerator before he changed his mind.

* * *

Brian gawked at the hundreds of tubes filling the cavern.

"It's not the cavern I saw earlier," the young Xenobiologist was saying. "These are people clothed, and the others weren't."

They'd driven downward and to the west, encountering numerous doors that wouldn't open. "I'd swear we're being herded," she'd said.

Then they'd shot through a tunnel with a dogleg left at the end. Beyond had been the cavern, its ceiling thick with pulsating blue tendrils, and thick bundles dropping into each tube, rows upon rows of tubes, in each tube a human being.

Every ten rows was a gap wide enough for the quadcart, which made counting easy. Four sets of a hundred tubes stood in the cavern, and Brian walked among them, staring up into the faces.

I know these people, he thought. Reading the names embroidered into each left breast.

And yet he didn't know them. Their faces looked familiar, but he couldn't pair the names to the faces. Nor could he say when he might have met them or where. He felt as though some of them might have been childhood friends whom he'd not seen since, as though the echo of memory reverberated against a thickly-padded wall, absorbed and silenced.

One item he began to notice—they were all facing the same direction.

"Interesting," Janine said. "I've seen some of these names before."

Brian walked in the direction they faced.

"I was searching for research station personnel who'd disappeared—and I think these names were among them."

Brian reached a corner, where one tube stood empty, the corner that all the bodies faced, as though everyone stood behind this one empty tube.

Or the person who should have been in the tube.

Four rows back was another empty tube. "It's almost as though the empty ones are intended for specific people," Janine said.

Brian looked at the short stone pedestal on which the tube rested. Unremarkable, as was the upper edge.

He looked into the face of the person in the next tube.

A red-haired woman in a uniform bedecked with medals stared back at him.

"But what about that other monster?"

"What monster?" Brian asked.

"Who are you talking to?"

He whipped around. "Huh?" He saw her gaze go to the woman's face.

"Colonel Karen Delaney! It's her! That's the military commander of the research station. She's—what's wrong?"

Brian remembered the face from his dreams. At the left breast, just below the elaborate medals, was the tag "Delaney."

He knew this person. They had been lovers, and they had intended to marry once their assignments on Nartressa had been completed.

"Why are you crying?"

He hadn't been aware that he was. His fingers came away wet from his cheek. He looked up again into the face, a proud face, a haughty face but a face in whom he'd instilled joy and devotion, a face that had looked at him with admiration, a face that he'd hoped to grow old with and to cherish to the end of their days together.

But that day had come too soon, for there was no recognition in the eyes now. Only the blank stare of someone who was hypnotized or comatose.

Brian looked among the other faces behind the empty tube in front of him. Now, he knew who this empty tube was for, and he wept anew, for a past that that not happened.

The tube had been meant for him.

And he wept that he had not spent the last forty years beside his one true love.

* * *

Randall shook his head and turned the quadcart onto a ramp, the mysterious woman asleep in the seat beside him. He still didn't know her name.

His corn map indicated he'd reached the top level, the hover bay at the end of a sinuous half-mile tunnel. The walls here were rough, as though unfinished, but the floor was smooth as though designed for wheeled traffic. The dim lights of the quadcart picked out not more than forty feet of the tunnel.

He slowed when he saw the rubble on the tunnel floor, the left wall having crumbled or blown inward, leaving a cavity tall enough and wide enough for two people to get through.

As he came abreast, he stopped the quadcart, realizing that this was the place where they'd found what appeared to be the empty berth of a launched escape pod.

The whine of a motor and headlights approached from behind.

He jostled the woman awake.

The other quadcart slid to a stop behind them.

"Janine!"

"Randall!"

"Brian!"

"Honeydew!"

* * *

Brian looked over the other three as a proud father might his brood. "We're a fine bunch, aren't we?"

The chatter went silent, and then they all burst into laughter.

Somehow, Brian knew that they weren't laughing at him. They were laughing at themselves. He joined in the laughter, having not laughed in what seemed like decades.

Brian was particularly surprised by Honeydew's seeming ease with everyone. He shouldn't have been surprised, beginning to see she was in her element, or as close to it as she could get. The Xenobiologist had appeared to be the most uncomfortable, her eyes searching his face, her manner wary.

She represented the opposition, he realized. Those who would halt the harvest on Nartressa if given the chance.

Over the course of the past few days, Brian's reason for being on Nartressa had changed. Now he was driven by something more primal, something deep, dark, and internal. Yes, the seaweed's disruption of the harvest and attacks on his ships and personnel were certainly concerns, but the mysteries made manifest in this abandoned research station had grown paramount. Somewhere inside, Brian intuited that at the heart of the station's hidden past lay the reason for the seaweed attacks. The hidden past contained in the memory core, which they'd left in the quadcart near the research station exit.

"I dreamt ..." He looked among the other three. "I dreamt that I ordered the memory core removed to hover bay twelve. But it wasn't me!" he protested.

"Why do you look like him?" Randall asked.

"I don't know." Brian looked among them. "Something happened down here, and all we know is that they had to take this dark site black." He heard Janine gasp. "I'm no scientist, and I'm certainly not Doctor Samuel Ericson. I don't know why the resemblance. It's as disturbing to me as it is to you. Somehow we've got to find out what's on that memory core, figure out what happened here, and do our best to discover what's driving the seaweed."

* * *

Honeydew looked around the penthouse, painfully aware of the terror that had possessed her the last time she was here. And feeling fascinated at the absence of terror now.

The curtains wide, the floor-to-ceiling windows looked out over the city of Rockdale and the ocean surrounding the isthmus on three sides. Honeydew knew only joy and wonder now.

Unconsciously, she strode out on the balcony, facing west, and stepped to the balustrade. The perpetually chilly wind buffeted her, her formalls no match for the deep, penetrating bite of the Nartressan breeze.

She needed no protection.

She felt the others behind her, watching her warily. On the way up to Brian's penthouse suite, they'd recounted some of their adventures. They'd discussed inconsequentials thus far, separating briefly to attend to their hygiene.

"I haven't had a hot shower in days!" Janine had said.

Brian had looked closely at Honeydew when they'd been riding up in the hotel lift. "You've changed," he'd said.

She'd nodded and smiled. "I'm not Honeydew anymore."

"And your hair." He brought a lock around for her to see.

Deep dark copper.

"I swear I don't dye it."

And they'd all laughed.

The others behind her, Honeydew stood at the balustrade and spread her arms to the wind. From her perch at the outermost edge of the Australian constellation, Honeydew looked toward what she'd always thought her home, the planet Sydney, and now she knew Nartressa was her home. Here, she had been born. Here, she was one with the environment, the waters, the seaweed, the wind, and the planet entire. Perhaps she'd been raised in a brothel on Sydney, but that had been an adoptive home at best, torn prematurely from the place she'd been born.

She lowered her arms and turned. "I was born here on Nartressa forty-five years ago."

Janine gasped.

"Yes, Janine, shortly before the research station went black." Honeydew looked at Brian, at Randall. "I know truths you're not ready to hear. Horribly beautiful events occurred here on Nartressa, the culmination of years of experiments, but the final form is just now emerging, incubating under the seas, spreading its tendrils around the planet and intertwining itself with its genetic cousin, the seaweed."

"The blue tendrils," Janine said. "Those are neurons, aren't they?"

"They could be considered the equivalent of neurons, yes," Honeydew said. "A better analogy would be some combination of optical fiber and wire, capable of transmitting both signal and power, but they also have the ability to conduct fluid."

"There isn't a species like it anywhere," Janine interjected.

"You said 'genetic cousin'," Randall said. "How is it related?"

Janine answered. "The research station built an experimental protein brain assembled from the four Terran nucleotides and two unique Nartressan nucleotides drawn from the seaweed genome. They were far more successful than they intended."

"The brain grew these last forty four years," Honeydew continued. "When it achieved sentience, we're not sure, perhaps when people first started disappearing. At some point, it recognized that the trawler harvest was causing a die-back in the seaweed forest, and it began to fight back." Honeydew told Brian and Randall about the hundreds of trawler crew who were now held suspended in blue columns in a cavern deep beneath Rockdale.

"Brian and I saw something similar—one whole cavern with hundreds of columns, and in one column I saw that red-haired woman in uniform we kept seeing in those vids." Janine glanced at Randall.

"Colonel Karen Delaney," Brian said. "The military commander of the dark site."

Honeydew felt something shift inside her, new knowledge that opened catacombs of implication. "Let's go inside."

Tea awaited them inside, Steve waiting patiently to do his master's bidding.

"Thank you, Steve," Brian said, easing himself carefully into a chair.

Honeydew looked upon him and knew. "The silent, knowing member of our group."

Steve's eyes went wide.

Honeydew stepped toward him. "How long have you been with Brian?"

His gaze darted over her shoulder at his patron. "I'm here to serve. How long I've done so isn't important."

"Forty-six years. More than half his life, nearly all of yours." Honeydew looked at the rest of them. "Steve Gallegos was apprenticed as a laboratory assistant at the age of fourteen. Special dispensation had to be obtained due to his minor status, and when the research station went black, he disappeared. Now, he calls himself an attaché, the personal secretary of CEO Brian Franks." She turned back to him. "How did you manage all those years, in the beginning, especially?"

The manservant shrank from her, kept glancing between the floor and his master. "Please, Mr. Franks, make her stop!"

"No, Steve. We have to hear it. Tell us what happened." Brian's voice was tired, his shoulder slumped, his face resigned. "You're the only one who knows what happened at the end. The memory core won't tell us everything. We need you to tell us."

Steve looked at each one of them, as though seeking an ally. Sweat rolled into an eye, and he wiped it away, blinking. He brought his gaze up to Honeydew's. "I saved you. I saved you both. The escape pod was sealed once I got the door closed, but you—" He looked at Brian "—Doctor Ericson, you collapsed on the floor, and you just lay there twitching. I knew you were dying. There was a med-surge extensible, one of the modified ones ..." Steve bit off a sob. "I did the best I could, Doctor, I swear! I knew if I didn't launch the pod, it would get us, just as it had everyone else in the research station. I know I should have used the med-surge first, but by the time I got to you, Dr. Ericson, there was a lot of damage." Now, Steve was weeping openly, and his words were nearly unintelligible. "When you woke up, you didn't remember who you were!"

Honeydew led him over to a chair, and Brian comforted him while he wept.

"Saved you both?" Janine asked. Randall looked equally puzzled.

Honeydew nodded. "I was less than a year old. Just after Doctor Ericson ordered the research station to go black, Steve pulled me from my crib and huddled with me in his arms in the back of the quadcart while Doctor Ericson—Brian—drove toward shuttle bay twelve. The memory is as clear as if it happened yesterday." She looked toward the manservant. "Throughout my infancy, Steve held me as though I was his very own, doting over me at all hours, changing me, feeding me, comforting me. The father any kid could want, and most can only dream of."

Steve looked at her. "I couldn't do it anymore. I couldn't care for you both. I had to choose. I had to—" And he began to weep anew.

"You had to place me in the care of the madam. You had to. At first, Brian couldn't do anything for himself. He was like an infant all over again, except twenty times heavier. Of course there wasn't a way for you to care for us both. You kept trying with Brian, using the modified extensible to rebuild what you could of Brian's brain. The extensible seemed to know what to do, and within two years, you were able to bring him back to a certain level of functioning, an almost full physical recovery."

Steve nodded, wiping away a tear and sniffling. "But he never recovered his memory." He looked at Brian. "You didn't know who you were. We'd take walks on the quay, and the only thing that caught your interest were the trawlers we saw offshore."

Brian nodded, his gaze vacant. "I'm lucky to be alive."

"So am I," Honeydew said. "Without your help, Steve, we'd both be dead or suspended indefinitely in some blue tube somewhere below."

Steve nodded, his gaze in his lap.

"You did the best you could." Honeydew sighed.

Chapter 16

Janine chewed on the inside of her cheek, bothered by something she couldn't quite name. She watched Honeydew draw out the attaché Steve like the finest of interrogators, making a painful process seem like a relief.

But there are huge gaping holes you could fly a starliner through! she thought. "We've been through that facility a dozen times, and we still don't really know what we're dealing with down there!"

The other woman nodded. "You're terrified."

"Of course I'm terrified!" Janine realized she was yelling, and put a hand over her mouth. "Sorry. Look, this isn't just some alien species that's decided it doesn't like its human cohabitants anymore. It's an intelligent entity with a far greater understanding of this planet than we'll ever have."

Janine turned to the Aquafoods CEO. "Whatever else is at stake, we may have to abandon this planet as they did the research station forty-four years ago. Those blue tendrils are spread across the sea floor. They grow up the stalks of the seaweed like ivy on a tree. I'm willing to bet that we'll find blue tendrils on the other side of the planet, just as thick there as they are here. And if I were a protein brain, I wouldn't want all my thinking power concentrated in one containment pool deep beneath Rockdale. I'd have at least six neural clusters with equivalent processing power distributed around the planet. If the seaweed genome has the sort of explosive adaptive potential that I think it does, then a protein brain made of the same nucleotides is sure to have applied that same potential to itself."

Janine looked around at everyone, seeing that they were rapt. "I'm willing to speculate that the central computer that ran the research station was infiltrated and taken over by the protein brain long before the research station was abandoned."

"For all we know," Randall said, "it could be listening to us right now. Every bit of information that we receive on our subdural optimitters could be contaminated."

"Count on it," Honeydew said.

"Which brings us back to our main question: what are we dealing with down there?" Janine looked among them, knowing her face had to be white. She knew she should have long ago contacted the Chief Xenobiologist at the Institute of Alien Microbiology on Sydney. As Associate Chief of the New Species Research Division, she spearheaded all the investigations of potentially new forms of life across the galaxy, and the only reason she'd been tasked with the Nartressan assignment was her specialization in genome evolution. The seaweed attacks had looked too much like an adaptive response to human intrusion to leave the investigation to someone with less expertise.

Janine knew now that she was over her head and had been since day one, when she'd been pushed—

She gasped. "That bastard!" Now, she was furious.

"What? Who?"

"Doctor Thomas Carson, Chief Biologist at the Marine Institute. On the day I arrived, he found me on the dock at Randwick, getting a seawater sample. At first I thought it was a dream, but it wasn't! It wasn't a dream! That bastard pushed me off the dock into the water. Pushed me!

"And then the seaweed dragged me under, and I lost consciousness. I woke up on the dock again, and he was standing over me, just like before! He must be working with the seaweed, or under the brain's control. Why would anyone do that?" She looked around, furious.

Honeydew was staring at her. "You were ill."

Janine gasped, remembering now that she'd been diagnosed with uterine cancer a year before her arrival, and that when she'd gone back for further testing a month before, they'd told her it had metastasized.

"Uh, they didn't find it at the hospital," Randall said, frowning. He told the others about their odd hover crash on a sandbar. "After we crashed, they said we not only suffered no injuries, but that we looked healthier than anyone could reasonable expect at our ages."

"Your formall was burned right off you!" Janine reminded him.

"Did either of you lose consciousness?" Honeydew asked.

Janine looked at Randall. "We both did."

Randall nodded, looked at Honeydew. "Why are you asking?"

"The seaweed," she said.

"It saved us?" Janine could tell that Honeydew was certain of it. "How do you know? In fact, you seem to know a lot more than you should. And how do you remember being less than a year old? Our brains don't have the neural assemblies necessary to make memories at that age. The human brain doesn't assemble the physical capacity for memory until one year!"

All eyes focused on Honeydew. "And yet I do remember." Her voice was as light as a feather. She wore a calf-length formal that clung to her beautiful curves.

Janine was perturbed. "If I didn't know better, I'd say you're another Nartres-san experiment." Janine covered her mouth and stared wide-eyed at Honeydew, knowing she was right, not sure how she knew, but knowing nonetheless. "And Colonel Karen—"

"Was my mother," Honeydew said, her voice a whisper.

"And I'm your father," Steve said.

Janine's eyes grew larger. "But you were—"

"Sixteen." His elbows propped on his knees. Steve dropped his head between his shoulders, his gaze on the floor. "She seduced me. Wasn't difficult, I guess. She and Doctor Ericson—" He glanced at Brian, dropped his gaze back to the floor—"discussed it for weeks. She was reluctant. I heard them arguing, often in the evening, trying to keep their voices low, trying to keep me from overhearing. A year before the research station went black, she began to invite me to her quarters. At first, it was a project she wanted my opinion about, and then it was dinner, a game of chess. She seemed to like my company. I was flattered." He hung his head, his voice almost inaudible. "I guess I knew what she was doing, but ... but ..."

"She seduced you, not you her," Janine said. "She raped you, Steve. It wasn't your fault."

"But I enjoyed it, several times!" he protested.

"You were a boy! And she was twice as old as you. It was wrong. It was rape." Janine stood and sat next to him and comforted him while he wept, feeling Brian's stare, wanting to remonstrate him for his opprobrious deeds, wanting to vilify Brian Franks for something that Doctor Samuel Ericson had done. Her fury remained unexpressed. I can't blame Brian, she thought. He's not the same person. He lives in the same body, but wasn't the person who initiated this travesty.

Janine looked across at Honeydew, knowing the zygote had been removed from Colonel's womb. "We have to find out what Doctor Ericson did. Unless you can tell us, Honeydew."

"As much as I wish I could tell you," the other woman said, "I can't. Pre-birth, preconception, I don't know it."

Janine nodded. "That memory core. We have to find out. We have to reinstall the core." She looked among the four others, one by one.

"We have to go back down there."

* * *

"Halt!"

Brian winced, looking around, the order on his coke so loud that it hurt. The other four, their hands to their ears, had heard it too. They'd just left the Hilton and had been headed to the apartment building that contained the Byzantine entrance to the research station when the order had come. Where did it come from? he wondered.

A hover came out of the sun, its hum echoing off the surrounding buildings.

Four of them stopped but Janine hissed, "Run! Come on!"

But none of them did. Brian felt rooted to the street.

Four other hovers converged on all sides, military markings emblazoned on their flanks. Two hovers landed, and a bald-headed, gristle-faced officer stepped off the smaller one. "Admiral Jackson Lockhart, Commander of the Sixth Fleet." He looked at each one of them in turn. "Brian Franks? Janine Meriwether? Randall Simmons? Stephen Gallegos?" Then he turned to Honeydew. "And the supposedly deceased Honeydew Diamond." Lockhart looked among them again. "Where to in such a hurry?"

Brian exchanged glances with Janine. "What do you want, Admiral? You've no jurisdiction here. Unless you're going to arrest us for piracy. Any of you commit piracy in the last couple of months?" he said to the others, feigning a laugh. Brian stood poised to walk off, the galactic navy having no business interfering with a private citizen ground-side.

"Cork it, Franks. You're all charged with trespass on galactic property. The government is willing to overlook those offenses, however. An evacuation of Rockdale will commence in an hour, and the Prime Minister has requested that I personally escort you five off-planet—to insure your safety, of course."

To insure we don't interfere with your plans, Brian thought. "Evacuation?"

Janine looked furious. "Why evacuate Rockdale? What are you planning?"

"Why should the government overlook any offense, anyway?" Randall said, looking equally furious.

"All in good time. That hover will take you to a suborbital just north of Rockdale. You're the first to be evacuated. Consider it an honor."

Guards herded them into the larger hover, an eight-seater, its passenger compartment a glasma dome. Brian sat near the front, a burly guard with a mean face sitting backward in the chair, his blaster held at ready. As the hover lifted, Brian glanced through the glasma at the Admiral still standing on the Rockdale street.

What the hell's going on? he wondered.

"They're going to blow the research station out of the ground." Janine looked at Brian. "Can't you stop them?"

He knew she was right the moment she said it. "Secure com to Sandusky," he said on his trake. Static responded. "They've cut off our optimitters," he told her. "They've probably appropriated all channels to notify people of the evacuation."

"We can't just let them blow it up," Randall said.

Brian looked at Honeydew.

She glanced at him, on her face a dreamy look.

Brian turned toward the pilot. "It'll be faster to take us out over the bay. Besides, I want to glance at that trawler they dredged up the other day."

Between two guards, the pilot looked back over his shoulder, then returned his attention to the controls.

"These bastards are going to blow the protein brain into the next century," Janine snarled, "and you want to look at a dredged-up trawler?"

Randall glanced at Brian with a "what are you thinking?" look but Steve smiled slyly.

The hover shot from between two buildings and banked out over the bay. Visible was the drydock where the trawler sat, the glistening bay under them.

The water exploded, and seaweed tentacles yanked the hover into the bay.

* * *

Randall loaded the memory core into the quadcart, his arms bulging with strain.

"Impressive," Janine said under her breath.

"A little oil, a few more reps, then it's Mister Galaxy." He shot her a glance and caught a smile.

After their hover had splashed into the bay, seaweed tentacles had taken the hover apart, immobilizing the guards. Other tentacles wrapped in blue tendrils had grasped each of them and had pulled them under. At first, Randall had struggled, terrified he was being dragged to a watery death, but soon a dreamy lassitude had settled upon him. Trying to scratch an itch on his forearm, he realized it was where a tendril had slipped under the skin. It's sedating me, Randall thought, losing consciousness.

He'd awakened inside a triangular blue tube, a hatch leading into the research station nearby, his four companions beside him just getting to their feet. They'd made their way to the place they'd left the memory core, the two quadcarts nearby.

They climbed into the two-seater, while the others were in a quadcart behind them. Steve was squatting in the back, using an empty box of ammo for an improvised seat.

Randall couldn't believe they were going back down. This place is a nightmare freakshow, he thought. The ramps, tunnels, tubes, and tendrils looked like a giant chemistry experiment gone awry. I can't believe I let them talk me into this!

When Janine had said they had to reenter the abandoned research station, Randall had leaped to his feet. "Absolutely not!"

Three people had instantly shouted him down.

Then a quiet voice had said, "We must." Brian, his face long, his expression bleak, had looked at all of them. "I did terrible things as Doctor Ericson. Going back is something I have to do. It's the only way I know to right the wrongs done to all of you."

It would have been easy, Randall thought, clutching the quadcart controls, to have pounced on the frail old man and pummeled him into oblivion. Randall had been horrified that the thought had crossed his mind. He, EMT extraordinaire, compassionate beyond all expectation with victims and families alike, to have such a thought!

But he knew its source, and he knew why he was angry. He knew the destruction that had been wrought by a seaweed awakened to the human threat by a mutant brain. That brain had escaped its masters and its creator, the biologist Doctor Samuel Ericson. The very same person who had sat there blathering about "the only way I know to right the wrongs."

Randall had flown to fifteen rescue sites in the last two years, only to encounter the same thing: a bereaved and disconsolate family member wailing loudly at the disappearance of loved one from a dock or a beach or a boat, never to be found again, snatched by the weed to a watery death.

And though he'd seen with his own two eyes the blue vertical tubes in a cavern, row upon row, likely all people who'd been pulled under the waves, Randall knew they were not really alive. They were sustained above the threshold of death by a bundle of pulsating tendrils, the purpose unknown. Those suspended in timelessness were deprived of their families and loved ones as surely as if they were dead.

"Randall, slow down," Janine said, leaning into a nasty turn.

He didn't know he'd been going so fast. "Sorry." The map on his corn guided them relentlessly downward, toward the main breaker room where he, Janine, and Shannon had reactivated the microfusion core, the map indicating a central processor two levels under that.

The trip took forever, and Randall couldn't get there fast enough. After hearing what Janine had found, the EMT wanted only to get himself and his wife off the planet as soon as possible.

Oddly, the hatches opened en route as they should have. An optimitter on the quadcart signaled their approach, and doors slid aside with a whoosh just ahead of them.

Doesn't seem as if the beast wants to stop us, he thought.

"I hope this memory core is still viable after all these years." Janine said.

"Huh?" He realized he was staring at her and almost hit a pillar. "What are you talking about?"

"The central processor is protein, as are all its memory cores. They have to be either kept connected to an infuser or at least inserted periodically. Even idle, they require at least intermittent rejuvenation. Unless it has a built-in infuser."

Now she tells us, Randall thought. He drove the quadcart toward a last door. Beyond, a ramp would take them to the next level below and into the central processor.

The door slid aside, and a wave of heat washed over them, the walls, ceiling and floors matted with thick layers of interwoven blue tendrils.

The ramp too, and Randall braked. The quadcart shuddered down the ramp, stopping at the bottom. The smell of apples was thick.

The quadcart behind them had managed to stop at the top.

"Come on," Janine said, leaping from the cart. "Over there." She pointed toward the bank of memory cores, and the gaping hole where theirs had been removed more than forty years before.

Randall couldn't bring himself to step onto the tendrils.

Under Janine's feet, the tendrils had darkened. He saw the imprints of where she had stepped, the older footprints brightening toward their usual glow.

"Randall!" Janine put her hands on her hips.

"I'll get it," Steve said, walking down the ramp gingerly, Honeydew and Brian right behind him.

Randall forced himself out of the quadcart, suppressing his disgust. The matted tendrils were rubbery and gave slightly under his weight. Feeling sick, he helped Steve lift out the heavy core, and they carried it over to the slot.

Bright blue tendrils clogged the slot.

Randall realized that the memory assembly was shot through with tendrils. The entire bank had been infiltrated by the alien protein brain. "Now what?"

"Just get it in," Janine said. "I'm guessing it'll go right in."

They lifted and aligned it with the slot and then slid it home.

It snicked into place and lit up.

"Central," Janine said, "Test core integrity."

"Testing," Randall heard on his coke. He looked toward Honeydew, standing between Brian and Janine and looking resplendent. He'd barely been able to take his eyes off her since he'd found her suspended in a blue tube.

He glanced down and gasped.

Blue tendrils were creeping over her feet and up her shins, right up to the calf-length formalls.

"Oh, not to worry," she said, giggling and lifting a foot. The tendrils fell away easily. "They seem awful curious about me."

"Memory core compromised," Randall heard on his coke. "Attempt repair?"

"Attempt repair and use existing parities to reconstruct," Janine instructed. "Well, let's see what happens."

"Janine," Randall said, pointing to Honeydew's legs. "What does that mean? Why are those things doing that?" He could barely suppress his revulsion.

"I don't know," Janine said. "Honeydew, I suspect that your zygote was either made from Nartressan nucleotides or was grown in a solution of them. That's what I'm hoping this memory core will be able to tell us."

"Probably both, would be my guess," Brian said.

The old man looks proud of himself, Randall thought. He stepped up to him, looked him straight in the face. "Out with it, Franks, you remember ever last bit of the atrocities you committed down here, don't you? Every bit! Admit it!"

Hands dragged him away and Randall realized he'd been screaming and that he'd brought his hands up and had tried to choke the older, smaller man.

Honeydew hurled him against a wall with a force that emptied his lungs.

Gasping, her face inches from his, he realized that a dim blue glow emitted from her skin.

The glow faded as she released him. "Sorry, I couldn't let you hurt him."

Recovering his breath, Randall glared over at Janine. He saw in her eyes that she'd seen what he had.

Janine stepped to the woman's side. "Hold still." She brushed Honeydew's check with the tips of two fingers. Where fingertip touched check, a dim blue glow emerged. "Come here," and she gestured at the quadcart. "Lift this."

"I couldn't possibly lift that." At Janine's gesture, Honeydew tried anyway.

Two wheels came off the floor easily.

Honeydew covered her mouth.

"Monster!" Randall screamed, startled to hear the words coming from his mouth. "Abomination!" Then his cheek stung, his ears rang, and his head spun.

"Randall!" Janine shook her hand and winced, sucking on a knuckle.

What's happening to me? Randall wondered, touching his check where she'd slapped him.

Janine grabbed his lapels. "We're all scared, blast you! And we don't need you to make it worse! Get control of yourself or we'll do it for you!"

A sob escaped his lips. He couldn't believe he'd done that. "I'm sorry," he managed to say, folding his arms to keep from coming apart completely.

"Repair attempted," he heard on his coke, "Partially successful. Parities corrupted, but partly implemented. Sixty percent memory reconstruction achieved."

"Good. Let's get to the command theater, where we can all see what we're facing. Randall, you with us?" Janine looked at him, her manner all business.

Randall looked among them, seeing his own fear reflected, and seeing forgiveness. Even from Honeydew.

"We're all scared, Randall," Honeydew said. "We all are."

He realized that she had far more to fear that any of them.

Randall took a deep breath. "Yeah, I'm with you."

Chapter 17

Janine's hands flew across the tactile interface, as familiar with the controls as she was with her own body. She'd spent years on Sydney operating identical equipment. Her corn, coke, and trake were alive with activity, her subdural linked directly with the brain through a bundle of blue tendrils.

"Come on!" Steve said. "They'll have Rockport evacuated within a couple hours."

The screens in command central were alive with the past, showing the torrid love affair between Delaney and Ericson, his personal laboratory the site of their frequent amorous liaisons.

"Better than studio porn," Randall muttered. Then he glanced around uncomfortably.

Brian looked equally embarrassed.

Janine skipped through those scenes at fast forward.

They reviewed the initial planning session from some fifty year before. The initial intent appeared to have been to develop a protein brain. Nothing elaborate or specialized, simply a standard-size zetabyte, zetahertz computational processor using six nucleotides, instead of the usual four. On the screen were projections of the estimated capabilities, charts comparing a four-nucleotide brain with a six-nucleotide brain, manufactured with the two additional Nartressan nucleotides, epsidine and zetasine.

The protein processor had come alive at first try, and its self-programming algorithms had taken a quarter of the time to develop. Further, the brain operated a hundred times faster than anticipated, and its memory capacity grew to about a thousand times larger—with the same number of nucleotide pairs.

"This brain has properties we can't even imagine," Janine said. She looked over her shoulder at the other four, realizing belatedly that the analysis wasn't as easily understood by others.

"I'm no neurologist," Honeydew said, the images on screen coloring her face, "but it looks sophisticated."

Then the researchers had noted the tendrils sprouting spontaneously from the brainstem, and had transferred the brain from its laboratory incubator to a rock-lined pool deep inside the research station. There, the brain had grown at an astounding pace.

About the time that it had filled the pool with convoluted gray matter, Doctor Ericson and Colonel Delaney conceived the idea of pairing the Nartressan nucleotides with a human zygote.

At first, their discussion appeared to be purely clinical, an abstraction, centered around the best time to introduce the Nartressan nucleotides. Doctor Ericson appeared to be advocating for sooner—doing codonic level surgery, introducing proteins directly into an ovum or sperm prior to fertilization. More complex than a re-allelolectomy, the removal of a human allele and the insertion of a seaweed allele, codonic surgery was also more likely to succeed in producing a viable gamete. Finally they settled on a fertilized egg—a zygote—placed in a solution rich in Nartressan nucleotides, the same solution used in marinating the protein brain to life.

These discussions had taken place across weeks, the two of them interspersing their discussions with amorous flirtations. Then one evening, Doctor Ericson turned to Colonel Delaney and said, "We need a donor."

"You're not serious, are you?" She looked flabbergasted.

He insisted he was. "Why not you? You're thirty-five, excellent genetic history, smart as that brain we made and far more beautiful ..."

"Thanks," she said, sardonic.

And then he'd spent another month convincing her to make a donation.

"And who'd you have in mind for the father?"

"I think we've seen enough," Brian said, looking ashamed.

Janine stopped the recording.

Beside Brian, Steve looked at the floor, his face a deep red.

"Let's at least see what happened to the brain," Randall said.

"And how the zygote was brought to viability," Honeydew said.

Six months after the zygote was placed in an artificial womb, and immersed in the protein rich solution, the protein brain sent a tendril through the containment wall, setting off alarms. Those same alarms shut off moments later, to everyone's bewilderment, and no actual breach was found.

"That's probably when the brain took over the central computer," Janine said.

A week later, three months premature, the baby was "born," but came squawling into the world as though fully developed, exhibiting no ill effects of an early birth. Prenatal scans had indicated an accelerated development, but neither Doctor nor Colonel had expected early viability.

"Baby pictures," Brian snarled.

"You're practically the father," Janine said.

Brian and Honeydew exchanged an uncomfortable glance. The woman shifted slightly, moving away from the older man. Steve put his arm around her upper back, and she relaxed somewhat in his fatherly embrace.

One month passed, and an earthquake shuddered through the complex, tripping warning sensors throughout.

A visual inspection revealed the source: the brain had extruded a ten-foot wide bundle of tendrils through the base of its containment pool and had sent tendrils into every major facility control point. The containment pool break had caused a fault-line shift.

"I wonder why it let anyone escape," Randall said.

"All behavior's purposive," Brian said.

"Do you suppose it let the three of us go?" Steve asked, a nod to indicate Honeydew.

"Hey, Janine, what about those med-surg extensibles? How'd they adapt the blue tendrils to those?"

Janine plugged in the search, and four vids popped up.

In transferring the protein brain from its original smaller container to the large containment pool at the lowest level, a technician had lifted the gray hemisphere with gloved hands, and a blue tendril, one of twenty dangling from the brain stem, had slipped down the labcoat sleeve without anyone's noticing, then had torn free from the brain stem and remained embedded in the technician's arm.

Hours later, the horrified tech had commed Dr. Ericson, frantic at this tendril protruding from his wrist.

Rushing to his side, Dr Ericson pulled the tendril slowly and harmlessly from the arm, leaving no trace of any damage at the entry point. The tendril survived another five hours on the laboratory table, wriggling every few moments, probing from side to side as though seeking a host.

Such autonomic neural responses were normal in nature, but unheard of in a laboratory-grown offshoot. Doctor Ericson quickly realized its value after the technician reported a complete relief of pain and restoration of motion in an arm that had suffered a multiple compound fracture one-and-a-half years before. Bioscans of the arm detected no remaining trace of fracture or tendon damage, despite the orthopedic surgery that had been required to rebuild the arm.

Doctor Ericson quickly devised a miniature protein regeneration unit, scaled down from those used for protein brains, and he then attached a small group of tendrils to a med-surg extensible, replacing the robotic endoscopes and other surgical tools with tendrils.

It worked so well, he deployed a crew to manufacture the units and replace the med-surg kits throughout the facility. They had just completed the conversion when the earthquake struck.

The 8.6 temblor had caused massive destruction topside, nearly leveling Rockdale, but much of the underground facility survived unscathed. The ten-foot crack nearly five thousand feet underwater and the tendrils already spreading at a rapid clip across the ocean floor and having already infiltrated all the information systems, along with the power distribution circuits and environmental controls throughout the facility, had brought home to Doctor Samuel Ericson and Colonel Karen Delaney the cold hard fact that they'd lost control of their creation.

And that their only recourse was to escape.

Janine shut off the vids and pushed away from the interface with a sigh. "Only three people made it out," she said, looking amongst Steve, Honeydew, and Brian.

"Odd that it didn't start attacking trawlers until recently," Randall said.

"What do you suppose it wants?" Steve asked.

"Whatever it wants," Janine replied, "it appears to have orchestrated our being here now, in this room." She saw Honeydew cover her mouth. "What is it?"

"A man..." She glanced at Brian "...came to me, asked me to spy on Aquafoods. Shannon, he called him—"

"What?" Randall said. "Gray-haired, bearded, spoke with one side of his mouth—"

"He was waiting in my apartment on Sydney as though he owned the place."

"He was waiting in a bar in suburban Rockdale as though expecting me."

Janine looked between them. "Intended." She glanced at Brian. "When I first arrived, I thought I dreamt that Doctor Carson had pushed me off the dock at Wainsport. We've all dreamt a watery death on the end of a seaweed tentacle, haven't we?" Janine didn't need to look for nods. "And we've all known things that we have no way of knowing. And we've all been pushed here today, to this cavern, for a purpose we've yet to discover. And I think it's clear that the seaweed or the brain could have killed us long ago. It's clear it could have wiped out the human settlers long ago as well. Instead, it's chosen to take a few people—people with illnesses, often incurable illnesses—and preserve their lives in a semiconscious or comatose state. It's destroyed several trawlers and a few suborbitals, but has chosen to save the lives of their crew, albeit in that same semi-conscious state. Further, the research station personnel were similarly captured when the site went black. And instead of killing all these people, the seaweed-brain instead preserved them."

"Why are you calling it that?"

She looked hard at Brian. "The Nartressan genome shows an adaptability not seen anywhere in the Milky Way. How could a dedicated scientist, inculcated in the ancient ethics of informed consent, and a Colonel, with deeply held convictions about following protocol, even begin to imagine these atrocities that they committed together down here. My theory is that they couldn't."

Steve gasped, and Brian and Honeydew exchanged a disturbed glance. Randall's brows had drawn together.

"How could the seaweed influence them like that?" Brian asked.

"Wouldn't that require some sort of infectious or invasive pathogen?" Steve asked.

Randall was shaking his head. "The more important question is why. Janine, that young man on Shoalhaven, what did he say?"

Janine struggled to remember. She had been so startled by its clarity. "The triple helix is exponentially more complex, the nucleotide pairings more numerous to the power of six, the heretofore ionic imbalances offset by the two nucleotides endogenous to the Nartressan evolution." She looked among the others for the impact.

"Uh, English, please?"

"Oh, sorry. The six-nucleotide, triple-helix structure allows the Nartressan gene far greater flexibility than the four-nucleotide, double-helix structure does our own gene. It's far more adaptable."

"Even to the extent of wearing through people's moral bedrock?"

"Look what happens when people smoke the seaweed leaves."

Glances exchanged all around them, then to the floor and walls of the command theater.

"Of course we're being influenced right now," Janine said, articulating everyone's greatest fear. "Do any of us sound grandiose or psychotic? As much as we might dislike being influenced, particularly against our will or at least without our permission, what's clear now is that none of us is engaging in egregious or opprobrious acts that we ..."

Janine noticed none of them looking at her, each concentrated on some inanimate object. Randall and Honeydew, in particular, didn't look at each other. "Never mind." She sighed. "Randall's question is far more important, however."

"Why? Why would the seaweed influence the Doctor and the Colonel to build a brain so powerful that they were sure to lose control of it?"

"And why," Honeydew said, "would they experiment on human life itself and create a hybrid, a monster, a freak?"

Janine regarded the older woman, their appearances chronologically equivalent. "That's not who you are."

Honeydew stood a bit taller. "It's not. And it's not how I feel."

Janine smiled, liking her.

Randall snorted, "So can we get to the question, Doctor Xenobiologist?"

"The sarcasm is unnecessary," Honeydew told him.

"Listen—"

"Stop it, both of you," Brian said.

They both mumbled an apology.

"Go on, Janine," Brian said.

She nodded, feeling the tension between them all. Randall's behavior earlier—lunging for Brian and yelling epithets at Honeydew—had been a small preview of the volatility now brewing among them.

"First, as Brian reminded us earlier, all behavior is purposive. Built into the seaweed, as in all life, is the will to survive. The seas of Nartressa have been trawled for fish for nearly three hundred years without apparent impact on biodiversity.

"Apparent. No one ever studied the biosphere thoroughly enough to know. My thought is that the seaweed began to decline because of the overfishing—keep in mind that the fish are integral to its reproductive cycle. When it realized it was beginning to suffer, the seaweed sought some way to communicate with its human cohabitants, so it arranged for a dark-site research station to be built—"

Nearly everyone chimed in at the impossibility, but Janine shouted them down. "Hear me out, blast you!" And she realized she wasn't immune to the stress that they all were under.

"Sorry, I didn't know I could yell like that." She sighed and continued, the others watching her with wide, startled eyes. "And for the chief Biologist Samuel Ericson to experiment on a brain. Further, the seaweed—or seaweed brain, since it was functioning by then—sought to find a way to communicate with humans. Now, why it chose the method that it did is still obscure to me, because the amount of time that it took to develop this means of communication would at first glance seem to be prohibitive. All I can logically conclude is that the seaweed-brain needed to make itself manifest in a form that human beings could understand. So they would know just who and what the seaweed is." She looked among them. "I can see I've lost you." Janine stood and stepped to Honeydew's side, turned them both to face the other three.

"Everyone, I could like to introduce to you Nartressa's personal envoy, Honeydew Shannon Diamond."

* * *

"Attention Randall Simmons," a familiar voice said on his coke, the gristled face and bald head intruding on his corn.

Randall looked at the others, saw from their expression that they too were receiving similar messages on their subdural optimitters.

"This is Admiral Jackson Lockhart, Commander of the Sixth Fleet. Nartressa is surrounded, and Rockdale has been ninety percent evacuated. Your subdural positioning beacon indicates that you have trespassed again upon the shuttered dark site, the former Nartressan Research Station. Once the evacuation of Rockdale is complete, the research station will be demolished, minus one hour and counting. You are ordered to proceed immediately to hover bay twelve to remand yourself to the custody of Naval Marshalls. You are under arrest."

"They can't do that," Janine said.

Randall shook his head, knowing they couldn't be stopped. "We knew the government was completely aware of what was happening down here." He sighed, dejected. "Let's go. They're as likely to blow us up along with the research station as to come and get us."

"You're just going to give up?" Brian asked.

"Yeah, and maybe once this weed-brain is dead, it'll stop attacking people, and I can go back to living a normal life." Randall knew that that was what he'd wanted all along. He looked directly at Brian. "Whatever sick, twisted fantasy you've brought upon us is yours to deal with, Doctor, and no amount of subdural hematoma or brain surgery is going to cure you, because what you need is moral surgery." He looked at them all. "Anyone else coming with me?" He turned and strode toward the door, not caring if anyone did.

He stopped short, pushing against what seemed like a stone wall. Looking back over his shoulder, he saw Honeydew, a hand out toward him, a vacant look in her eyes.

Blue tendrils had snaked up through the floor and were entwined around her leg.

"Randall," a voice said on his coke. It was Honeydew's voice, but it was the voice of several hundred beings. On his corn appeared a cavern filled with blue glowing tubes. In each tube was a body, their faces upturned, their eyes searching his.

The voice of everyone, he realized, entombed by the seaweed brain.

"They come to destroy us. We who were rescued or saved by Nartressa and brought to these caverns to be healed of our grievous wounds or illnesses, we do not matter to this Admiral. He seeks only to erase all trace of what he sees as his own government's malfeasance.

"We are here by virtue of our having been preserved and nurtured by the seaweed, and yet they would destroy us all to get at the being who has kept us alive. You suffer because you are committed to helping and have been prevented from doing so by the swiftness of the seaweed. And thus you reject the seaweed as the source of your suffering, and you disregard the fact that it has saved you, not once but three times.

"We need your help. Condemn us if you will to being obliterated when they destroy the brain. We would ask otherwise. We would ask that you help to save us. You alone must make your own decision."

His coke went silent, and his corn went blank.

Randall looked at his companions, saw they were committed. I can walk out the door and return to being an EMT, he thought.

Or I can choose a future whose experiences will take me to realms I can't even imagine.

The comfort of certainty or the terror of the unknown?

"I know what you're thinking," Janine said, her face inches from his.

Randall hadn't seen her approach.

"You can't go back, however much you'd like to. Galactic charges of trespass, a wife who knows you haven't been faithful, a boss likely to fire you for abandoning your position and exceeding your authority. The only thing certain you can look forward to is more uncertainty, and your self-condemnation that you abandoned these people down here. That you abandoned us, your friends."

Randall looked into Janine's eyes and saw in her the qualities he'd always wanted for himself—the courage of conviction and the singular will to pursue that conviction. "Will you teach me how you do that?"

Her brows narrowed. "Do what?"

"How you instantly know what to do?"

"I can try."

Randall nodded. "All right." He looked at the others. "I'm committed to making Nartressa a safe place to live, and to helping the people trapped in those caverns. Beyond that, it's up to the weed-brain and the extent to which it shares my goals."

Honeydew nodded. "I think you'll find that it shares them fully. Come with me. We don't have much time."

Janine took his hand as they turned to follow Honeydew.

Holding her hand, Randall found comfort.

* * *

"You want us to lay down on those?" Brian looked at Honeydew with disbelief.

"Like this." And she stepped halfway out onto the two-foot wide, six-foot long stone tongue, turned to face them and sat, then lowered herself to the stone, laying face up, the top of her head even with the end of the stone. Below her bubbled the thick blue soup, the coral-like brain surface just visible beneath the protein brew.

Shuddering, Brian looked among the other three.

Randall stepped onto the stone tongue beside hers, sweat beading on his brow, his breath rough and audible over the bubbling soup. He lay down, extended his arm toward Honeydew, who smiled and took his hand.

Janine and Steve quickly followed suit, taking the two farthest from Honeydew and Randall, leaving the center slab empty.

Brian knew what was going to happen. A day ago, when he'd looked up into the vaguely familiar face of the buxom female who resembled Honeydew, the name tag at the left breast above the resplendent set of medals declaring "Delaney," Brian had known instantly what had happened to her, the dream of his escape from Nartressa still vivid from some forty-four years before, a dream that had been no dream, the aneurysm quickly filling his brain with blood, occluding his sight and only moments away from killing him, Steve dragging him and an infant child toward an escape pod, the blue fog behind Colonel Karen Delaney enveloping her down the corridor from them and rendering her unconscious as then-Doctor Ericson watched.

She wants me to lay down on the stone slab so the seaweed brain can insert its tendrils into me, just as it did into Karen some forty-four years ago, Brian thought.

And he found himself rooted to the stone, unable to move, his terror clutching at his heart, which throbbed like a snare drum being beaten relentlessly by a vindictive child, arrhythmic and stuttering and ...

"Brian!"

The voice was distant and the face in his vision was that of Randall, who brought a fist around over his head and into Brian's sternum like a sledgehammer.

The shock did not seem to reach him, and Brian vaguely felt the jostling as the cavern overhead changed orientation. A glimpse of others wrestling his body into position struck him as ludicrous, but a hand found each of his hands on either side and warm scents of apple reached his nostrils.

The soft tips of blue tendrils massaged his scalp as his world went gray.

* * *

The world went gray as Honeydew looked up into the Nartressan sky, the wind coming off the bay as invigorating as it was cold.

Although she seemed to be alone on the promontory, a mound of rock that sufficed for a hill on Nartressa, she felt the presence of her other four companions as though they stood beside her, as though their arms were linked with hers, their minds linked with hers.

She felt Brian's terror recede instantly, saw the blue tendrils surrounding his heart and repairing the tissue damaged by the heart attack, slowing the ventricular fibrillation and recalibrating the atrial-ventricular timing, his heart now beating in long slow rhythms.

Her mind linked up with the four companions who'd shared her journey and with the nearly thousand people sustained on thick bundles of blue tendrils. Honeydew felt a sense of community that she'd never known before, a sense of other but also of being with an other, a sense of community heretofore known only by enlightened spiritual beings, people who'd shed the restrictions of the flesh and freed their minds to join the cosmos.

And now she knew why the people who'd been captured by the seaweed and were sustained in blue tubes by a bundle of tendrils did not object to the restrictions of a body held in indefinite suspension. Their minds had been freed.

Honeydew looked up into the Nartressan sky and rejoiced.

The contrail of a missile entering the atmosphere evaporated her joy.

The missile, launched at Admiral Lockhart's order, carried in its belly a microfusion bomb calibrated to yield a sphere of destruction a few hundred feet larger than the known size of the research station. Capping the missile was a tunneler, whose engines were designed to bore through earth, rock, and metal to deliver the microfusion bomb to the predetermined location at the center of the research station.

Admiral Lockhart had dined on Nartressan fish the night before, and the residual protein from his meal swam through his bloodstream and refracted his thoughts. The proteins sent a coded signal from his subdural to the planet surface. The coded signal contained knowledge of the missile, what its target was, what its payload was, and what ciphers were needed to abort the missile strike.

Honeydew intercepted the ciphers with her awareness and beamed them at the missile using the infiltrated facilities in Rockdale, where blue tendrils intertwined with nearly every electrical device on the planet.

The missile diverted itself into the ocean to the west of Rockdale, where seaweed tentacles quickly dismantled it moments after it sank below the waves.

A hubbub of radio traffic followed, most of it containing a frantic dismay.

Honeydew smiled and flooded the radio spectrum with her voice. "I am Nartressa," she said.

She sent the same message through residual proteins ingested by people across the galaxy, and everywhere that the fish had reached, to everyone who'd supped on the succulent catch from the world of Nartressa. They all felt the presence.

"The galactic government sends its navies to destroy our planet, fearing what it cannot comprehend. These navies will be thwarted by any means necessary. The destruction of Nartressa is unnecessary. We are not your enemy.

"Three hundred years ago, your species discovered the abundant aquatic life thriving on Nartressa, and you tasted the fish and found it delicious. Your harvest began and your trawlers have plied these waters ever since, seemingly without impact on the abundance.

"But we began to die back, the fish necessary to our reproductive cycle. And so we sought a way to communicate with you. The research station built what we needed—a brain to unite us all and a child to represent us.

"The child escaped and our plan went awry. Our seaweed stalks continued to perish. Thus we sought another way to get the human attention.

"Yes, we wrecked your trawlers and took the lives of their crew. Even now, these crew may be found on the beaches of Gosford, Randwick, Wainsport, and Rockdale. They are alive but unconscious, and may be easily aroused.

"We also captured the research station personnel, hoping to contain the secret of our creation. But three people escaped us, among them Doctor Samuel Ericson, who suffered an aneurysm in his escape, and now does not remember having been the director of the research station. We were able to secure his return to Nartressa by making him the CEO of Aquafoods Interstellar and causing a situation here that required his personal attention.

"We also took people off beaches, docks, and boats. Sometimes publicly. People who were ill and in need of medical treatment. Those whom we could cure and return, we took with stealth, and left them where we had found them.

Those whom we could not cure, whose diseases were so severe that they had to be sustained artificially, we took publicly, causing their friends and family untold grief. We took them publicly for a purpose, to bring to Nartressa the individuals who might understand our delicate reproductive cycle and the impact that the trawler harvest is having on our ability to sustain our species.

"We are remorseful for the grief we have caused your species. Now that you know the grief you have caused ours, our hope is that the harvest will stop, that the assault will stop.

"We are not your enemy, and we hope one day we may even call you friend."

* * *

Janine pinched herself to make sure she was wake.

The Galactic Nobel Peace Prize ceremony was about to begin, the famed Sydney Opera House filled to capacity, and trillions more people watching via subdural optimitter. Janine sat on the stage, beside the podium.

In the front row were Randall, Brian, Honeydew, and Steve.

The Chair of the Nobel Society rose to stand at the podium. "For her accomplishments in Xenogenetics, Human Health, and Alien Diplomacy—by far the most varied combination of disciplines recognized by the Nobel Society in a single individual—the Society presents to you, Doctor Janine Meriwether, the winner of the five hundred and ninetieth Nobel Peace Prize."

The lights blazed and vids flashed, and somehow Janine remembered to smile and found her way to the podium, and there she waited for the roar to die down, and when it increased instead, she waved and smiled, not knowing what else to do, and soon she saw they were on their feet, and she didn't understand, and she realized she didn't have to.

Brian in the front row wore a blue, glowing collar, a medi-collar, developed by Aquahealth Interstellar from the Nartressan nucleotides. The collar kept him alive, his health now in steep decline.

Two years ago, the five of them had discovered the proliferating protein brain of Nartressa, its memory banks filled with startling advances in the three fields for which Janine was being honored tonight.

In the audience, Janine saw a sprinkling of similar medi-collars, obtainable only at exorbitant cost, Aquahealth factories manufacturing them as fast as they possibly could. The need far outstripped their ability to supply them.

The roar died down, and Janine realized how unbecoming such behavior was of this staid, reserved audience, the Nobel Society among the ancient institutions still in existence after humanity had spread across the galaxy from its Earthly home.

"Thank you, Members, your greeting says it all. Honored Chair, I am so proud to have been a member of the team who serendipitously delved into the Nartressan biosphere and decoded the message written so delicately in the genes of the seaweed.

"The metamessage we may derive from the six-nucleotide genome is the same message humanity has received since the beginning of time in symbols laid before us on planet Earth—alien abductions, the Stonehenge, Easter Island Monoliths, crop circles, the pyramids—that we occupy a universe alongside other beings, other races, and other forms of life, that intelligence abounds around us, if we but have the senses to see it and the imagination to embrace it.

"And embrace it we must, for in welcoming the other—that horrible frightening unknown other, whose difference from us sets our souls on edge and causes us to fear for our very existence, the other who is simply another manifestation of our selves—in welcoming the other, we welcome the lost and rejected parts of ourselves.

"Humans all—you, me, and the person beside you—humans are and always have been that species whom we have feared that we would discover since time immemorial to be our nemesis.

"We are the neighbors we've always feared would move in next door.

"More succinctly, we have seen the enemy, and it is us."

Janine waited for the applause to die down. "Our genes are composed of four nucleotides, the Nartressan genome six. Four nucleotides in common, two that are not. How many other neighbors have already moved in next door whom we have yet to meet? For whom we don't possess the senses to see nor the imaginations to embrace?

"Look at the benefits we have already reaped in embracing our Nartressan neighbor! Those two extra nucleotides have allowed us to cure conditions that have plagued humanity since we learned to walk upright.

"When I first arrived on Nartressa, I was told, 'Don't drink the water.' Now, I say to all of you, 'Drink the water!' 'Jump in head-first!' 'Embrace all that is alien and unknown!'

"Because we are all the richer for it!"

About the Author

Scott Michael Decker, MSW, is an author by avocation and a social worker by trade. He is the author of twenty-plus novels in the Science Fiction and Fantasy genres, dabbling among the sub-genres of space opera, biopunk, spy-fi, and sword and sorcery. His biggest fantasy is wishing he were published. His fifteen years of experience working with high-risk populations is relieved only by his incisive humor. Formerly interested in engineering, he's now tilting at the windmills he once aspired to build. Asked about the MSW after his name, the author is adamant it stands for Masters in Social Work, and not "Municipal Solid Waste," which he spreads pretty thick as well. His favorite quote goes, "Scott is a social work novelist, who never had time for a life" (apologies to Billy Joel). He lives and dreams happily with his wife near Sacramento, California.

Where to Find/How to Contact the Author

Websites:
https://www.facebook.com/AuthorSmdMsw
https://twitter.com/smdmsw

Lightning Source UK Ltd.
Milton Keynes UK
UKHW040722130121
376872UK00021B/007/J